# ALWAYS IN MY HEART

# ALWAYS IN MY HEART

*by*

Kate Jackson

**Magna Large Print Books**
Long Preston, North Yorkshire,
BD23 4ND, England.

British Library Cataloguing in Publication Data.

Jackson, Kate
    Always in my heart.

    A catalogue record of this book is
    available from the British Library

    ISBN   978-0-7505-3921-0

10|14

First published in Great Britain in 2013 by D.C. Thomson & Co. Ltd.

Copyright © Kate Jackson, 2013

Cover illustration © Lee Avison by arrangement with
Arcangel Images

The moral right of the author has been asserted

Published in Large Print 2014 by arrangement with
Kate Jackson Bedford

Magna Large Print is an imprint of Library Magna Books Ltd.

Printed and bound in Great Britain by
T.J. (International) Ltd., Cornwall, PL28 8RW

## Grace's Daughter

Bessie Rushbrook pressed harder into the pedals. With a final effort she rode up and over the steep railway bridge, then swung her bicycle into the station yard. She braked and jumped off. With a practised heave she pulled her trade-bike on to its stand next to a neat row of tomato plants, growing where flowers had flourished before the days of Dig For Victory.

Catching her breath, Bessie smoothed down her silver-threaded hair, tucking away escaped strands from the roll at the nape of her neck, and checked her hat was straight.

'Evening, Bessie.'

The voice startled her. She turned and saw Tom Bussey, the stationmaster, standing in the booking hall doorway.

'Meeting the Norwich train, are you?'

'That's right, Tom. Is it running late?'

'Just a few minutes tonight, could be worse.' He pulled a watch out of his waistcoat pocket and checked the time. 'You here for your evacuee girl? Your boy, Peter, told me you were having one come.'

Bessie nodded.

'I expect she'll be worn out by the time she gets here.'

'That lot we had here last week were, poor little mites.'

'At least they're safer here.'

Bessie knew Tom would happily talk until the train arrived, but she didn't feel like chatting tonight; her mind was on other things.

'I'll go through and watch for the train, Tom.' With a quick smile at him she walked in through the booking hall doors, whose glass panes were criss-crossed with anti-blast paper, and stepped out on to the platform.

Pacing slowly up and down, Bessie thought about the letter which had started all this. Grace's letter. Its arrival had come as a shock after years of silence. They'd known nothing about her life in London, her marriage or her eight-year-old daughter, Marigold. Yet suddenly Grace was asking them if they would take in her child and give her a home away from the dangers of London!

Bessie and Harry didn't hesitate to say yes, and they'd agreed to honour Grace's other wish as well. Looking after Marigold was their chance to start closing the gap that had opened up between them and Grace. What did it matter that Marigold would not know who she and Harry really were? The important thing was to get the girl away from London and out of danger.

A regular, rhythmic noise carried across the still evening air and Bessie turned to see puffs of grey smoke in the distance. The train rounded the bend and slid in underneath the railway bridge, coming to a halt with a hissing squeal of brakes. Bessie watched, dry-mouthed, as carriage doors opened and a handful of passengers spilled out. There were several GIs returning to the nearby base, their exotic voices contrasting sharply with the murmur of the locals.

Bessie spotted a pair standing near an open carriage door at the far end of the train. A young woman and a small girl who looked so much like Grace that Bessie stared, unable to move for a few seconds. Then, blinking back tears, she waved, pasted a smile on her face and hurried along the length of the platform towards them.

'You must be Mrs Rushbrook? Bessie?' The young woman smiled and held out her hand as Bessie approached. 'I'm Helen MacDonald. I work with Grace.'

'Hello.' Bessie shook her hand.

'And this wee lass is Marigold.' Helen laid her hand on the girl's shoulder.

Bessie wanted to throw her arms around Marigold, hug her tightly and tell her who she was. To let her know she wasn't coming to strangers. But she couldn't. She'd promised Grace, and she would keep her word. Like she always had...

Bessie smiled instead and held out her hand.

'Hello, Marigold.'

The girl eyed her cautiously. Bessie noticed her eyes were a deep blue, exactly like Grace's.

'Hello.' Marigold spoke quietly as she briefly took Bessie's hand and gave it a soft shake.

'Grace?' Helen paused as the guard shouted for passengers to get on board. He started slamming carriage doors shut at the front end of the train, heading their way. 'We don't have long. Have you got all your things, Marigold? Case? Gas mask?'

Everything was there.

'Well, Marigold, I'm sure you'll be fine here with Bessie. It's much safer for you than in London.'

Helen smiled reassuringly and kissed Marigold's cheek before squeezing her in a quick hug.

'It was good of you to bring her,' Bessie said.

'It's no bother. I was pleased to help Grace.' Helen glanced at the guard who'd almost reached them. 'I'd best get in. It's nice to have met you, Bessie.'

Helen climbed up into the carriage, closed the door behind her and stuck her head out of the open window.

'Grace sends you her best wishes, Bessie. She said to tell you she knows Marigold will be safe with you.'

Bessie nodded.

'We'll take good care of her.'

'I'm sure you will.'

The guard raised his green flag and blew loudly on his whistle to signal to the driver.

'Goodbye!' Helen waved as the train jolted forward and began to slowly pull out of the station, the engine belching out great chuffs of smoke as it picked up speed.

Bessie waved back and watched until the train rounded the bend and was gone, leaving just a sooty taint in the air. Suddenly the platform seemed very empty. It was just her and Marigold now. Marigold was standing quite still, staring down the line where the train had disappeared. What must she be thinking and feeling? All she must know was she'd been left in a new place with a strange woman, miles from both her home and her mother.

A wave of protectiveness surged through Bessie, and she silently vowed she'd do all she could to make Marigold welcome and happy.

'You must be tired.' Bessie smiled at her. 'Let's get you home.' She picked up the suitcase and held out her hand.

Marigold looked at her, hesitated for a moment and then slipped her hand into Bessie's without saying a word.

'I've brought my bike to carry your case,' Bessie explained as she led Marigold out through the booking hall. 'It can go in the basket.'

With the case safely stowed in the big wicker basket on the front of her trade bicycle, Bessie pushed it along with one hand and held on to Marigold's hand with her other.

'Have you been to the countryside before?'

Marigold shook her head.

'It'll seem strange to begin with, and be a lot quieter for you, but I'm sure you'll soon get used to it. Did your mummy tell you much about us?'

Marigold shook her head again.

'We live at Orchard Farm. We've lots of animals, and a new calf born just last week! She's a real beauty.'

Marigold still didn't speak, but she seemed to be listening. If she didn't want to say anything at the moment, Bessie would carry on doing the talking for both of them. But at the pace they were going it was going to take a long time to get home. She glanced at Marigold and saw how pale she looked, dark smudges of tiredness under her eyes.

'How about a ride in the basket along with your case? It'll give your legs a rest.'

Marigold looked at the basket doubtfully.

'Come on, I'll lift you in.' She turned back to

11

pick Marigold up, but halted at the sight of the child standing with her arms held out ready. It seemed as if the years had suddenly peeled back and she was about to pick up a young Grace again. Only this wasn't Grace, Bessie reminded herself. This was Marigold, Grace's daughter. Swallowing down the tide of emotion threatening to overwhelm her, Bessie forced herself to smile as she scooped up Marigold and lifted her into the basket.

'There you are.'

Marigold gingerly settled herself down, sitting down on top of her case so only her head and shoulders could be seen sticking out of the top of the high-sided basket.

'Are you comfy?'

Marigold nodded, her hands gripping on tightly to the sides of the basket.

'Come on, then.' Bessie took care to keep the bike level and give Marigold a smooth safe ride.

'Look, there's Peter!'

The twelve-year-old was on top of the gate as they rounded the last bend in the lane leading to the farm. She'd told Marigold about him and everyone else who lived at the farm as she'd wheeled the girl along. Bessie didn't mind that Marigold still hadn't spoken. She knew she would talk when she was ready.

Peter waved, jumped off the gate and ran down the road to meet them, his pet jackdaw flying close behind him. He skidded to a halt beside the bike.

'Hello, Marigold. I'm Peter.' He smiled warmly at her.

12

Marigold shrank back into the basket, her eyes fixed on the jackdaw which had landed on Peter's shoulder and was gently rubbing its beak against his cheek.

'There's no need to be scared of Hana.' Peter whistled between his teeth and the jackdaw side-stepped down his arm and on to his hand. 'She won't hurt you. Hana's just nosy.' He stroked the bird's head. 'Look, she's very tame.'

Peter picked her up, wrapping his hands around Hana's wings so she couldn't flap.

'You can stroke her, if you like.'

Marigold looked up at Bessie, her eyes uncertain.

'Hana's very friendly.' Bessie stroked the bird's sooty feathers. 'See?'

Marigold reached out one finger and timidly touched the bird's back. Hana cocked her silvery head on one side and looked at Marigold. The girl froze for a few moments. Then, to Bessie's surprise, instead of drawing her finger away she began to gently stroke Hana's back.

Peter smiled.

'I think she likes you. She can ride back in the basket with you, if you want,' Peter suggested.

Marigold looked at Peter and nodded. He gently settled Hana on the rim of the basket, and Marigold continued stroking her as they walked the final few yards to Orchard Farm.

## Homesick

Marigold stared at the house, which was like none she'd ever seen before. It was nothing like her own home within a terraced house, one of a line of identical houses making up the street. She and her mother lived in the upstairs half, while Mrs Fox, their landlady, had the downstairs.

This house was low, with windows along the sides. It was painted a bottle-green colour.

'This way.'

Bessie climbed up a short flight of wooden steps and in through the front door from a small porch. Marigold followed, with Peter close behind carrying her case.

'Everyone's looking forward to meeting you.' Bessie opened an inner door and walked inside. 'Here we are, then.'

Marigold stepped inside behind Bessie, then halted as three strangers turned to look at her. She reached out and slipped her hand into Bessie's, who squeezed it gently back.

'This is my husband, Harry.' Bessie waved her other hand towards the man sitting in the armchair by the stove.

'Hello, Marigold.' He got up and limped across towards them, smiling so broadly the corners of his blue eyes crinkled up. 'Welcome to Orchard Farm.' He held out his hand to her.

'Hello,' Marigold whispered, shaking his hard,

rough hand which was huge compared with hers.

'And these are Dottie and Prune.' Peter pointed to the two young women who were washing up. 'Dottie's the small one, and Prune's the tall one. They're timberjills, and work up in the woods.'

'Hello!' they chorused and smiled warmly at her.

Marigold did her best to smile back.

'You sit down here' Bessie said, leading Marigold over to the table, 'and I'll get you something to eat. Peter, will you put Marigold's case in her room, please?'

Sitting at the table, Marigold watched as Bessie cut slices from a loaf of bread, buttered them and finally spread raspberry jam on top. Marigold hadn't seen so much butter being put on bread for a long time. At home they just had a scrape of margarine.

'Is there any spare for me?' Peter sat down at the table opposite Marigold. He smiled at Bessie, his grey eyes hopeful.

Bessie laughed.

'Of course!' She handed them each a plate of bread and jam and a cup of creamy milk. 'I knew you'd be hungry, too.'

Dottie dried her hands on a cloth and came over to the table.

'This boy...' she wrapped her arms around his shoulders and popped a kiss on his cheek '...is always hungry, Marigold. It's lucky for him he lives on a farm where food's not in such short supply, otherwise he'd eat a whole week's rations in one go!'

Peter smiled at Dottie and started to eat greedily.

15

Marigold stared down at her own slice of bread and jam. It was different from what she'd normally eat at home – richer and more colourful. She picked it up and, as she raised it to her mouth, the smell of rich, yeasty bread hit her and her mouth instantly watered. As she bit into it, the tang of sweet raspberries, combined with creamy butter, mingled on her tongue making her tastebuds tingle and fizz. She chewed slowly, savouring every delicious morsel.

'I'm going to check on the cows.' Harry lifted his cap from a peg by the door. 'You'll be able to meet them tomorrow, Marigold. You can even have a go at milking one, if you like.'

Marigold stopped chewing and stared at Harry in horror. Did they really expect her to milk a cow? Her insides twisted. She'd never seen a cow before today. They'd passed some on the train, and they looked huge beasts with sharp, pointy horns. She didn't want to go near one of them, let alone milk one!

'Have you ever milked a cow before?' Prune was asking.

Marigold shook her head.

Peter put down the cup he'd just drained.

'Don't worry about the cows, Marigold, they're lovely, and very gentle. They're beautiful Jerseys with big brown eyes and their coats are the colour of toffee.'

Marigold looked at Peter and tried to smile at his reassuring words, but her mouth didn't seem to work the way it should. Everything about today was odd. Leaving her home, coming out of London, this strange place and new people...

16

Bessie laid a gentle hand on Marigold's shoulder.

'Don't worry, it can all wait until tomorrow. You must be tired out, so eat up and then we'll get you to bed.'

Half an hour later Marigold lay snuggled up with Blue, her toy rabbit, hugged tightly in her arms, breathing in the faint smell of home from its soft fur. She closed her eyes and pretended she was back there, in her own bed, and her mother was not far away in the living-room, drinking a cup of tea after coming home from the hospital. Everything was normal and as it should be.

Marigold's eyes snapped open. She wasn't at home! Home was miles and miles away. Her throat tightened and the tell-tale stinging in her eyes threatened tears. She swallowed hard. She'd cried this morning when they'd left her mother behind at Liverpool Street station. She hadn't been able to stop herself, because she didn't want to come here. Marigold had told her mother this same thing, but she hadn't listened.

Why couldn't she stay, she had kept asking. Hadn't they survived the Blitz together? All those bombs raining down, night after night, while they'd tried to sleep deep down in the Underground. Her mother hadn't sent her away back then! Marigold could have been evacuated at the start of the war – lots of her friends from school had gone. But she'd stayed, and they'd got through it together. So why did her mother want to send her away now?

Her mother had explained it all to her. It was be-

17

cause of Hitler's doodlebugs, those rockets which came buzzing through the air like angry wasps and made everyone stop and hold their breath, listening for the engine to cut out. You waited. Hoping and praying it would miss you. Waiting for the roar and flash to come from somewhere else. Then you knew you'd survived ... that time. No-one knew when they'd come next, or where they'd fall. After what happened to Daddy, her mother had said she couldn't risk losing Marigold as well. It was too dangerous for her to stay in London now.

Her mother should leave, too, in that case! What if a rocket fell on her? Marigold shuddered at the thought and hugged Blue tighter. She could have left with Marigold, but she wouldn't – she'd said she had to stay in London and do her job because they needed nurses more than ever now. Her mother couldn't even bring Marigold to Norfolk herself, so she'd travelled with her mother's friend, Mrs MacDonald, who was coming here to visit her husband who was in the RAF. She'd handed Marigold over to Bessie at the station and then left.

Marigold stuck out her chin, trying hard to stop it from wobbling, but she couldn't stem a rush of tears from spilling down her cheeks and soaking into Blue's fur. She'd never been this far from home before, or even stayed with anyone else except her parents and Mrs Fox. Now, she was here with strangers. Her mother knew them and said they were good, kind people who'd look after Marigold well. But they weren't her mother, and where they lived wasn't her home. And it never would be!

'She's out for the count,' Bessie said to her husband soon after, slipping into bed beside Harry. 'Curled up with her arm around her rabbit. She was worn out, poor mite.'

Harry nodded.

'Being evacuated is hard on children.'

'I hope she'll soon settle in and feel like it's her home.'

Bessie paused for a moment. 'What do you think of her?'

'Just like her mother to look at, when I first saw her.'

Bessie nodded.

'I knew what you were thinking from the look on your face. I thought exactly the same when I saw her at the station. I wanted to hug her, Harry, but I knew I couldn't.'

Harry opened his arms and Bessie snuggled up, resting her head on his chest.

'We've got to respect Grace's wishes, even if it's not what we'd want. At least Marigold's safe here with us and we've got the chance to get to know her, and for her to know us.'

'It's not the same, though, is it? Her not knowing who we are?'

'It's not as it should be, it's as it is, Bess. Try not to worry about it. Maybe she will know, one day. Marigold has the chance to get to know us for ourselves, doesn't she? Hopefully that will count for something, and make it easier for her if Grace ever decides to tell her the truth.'

'I suppose.' Bessie hugged Harry tightly. 'I'm glad Grace turned to us. It can't have been easy for her to send her daughter away. Things must be bad in London.'

'We never thought we'd have to go through it again, not after last time, did we?' Harry sighed. 'Yet here we are again, the world torn up with fighting each other.'

'And Robert out there, somewhere in France.' Bessie shuddered. 'Please God he makes it through and comes back!'

'He will, Bess, he will. Wouldn't it be grand if we had them all home again? Robert, Grace and Marigold, too? We've got to hope it will happen one day.'

Grace hesitated on her front step. Now she was home, it was finally going to sink in that Marigold was gone, leaving a great gaping hole where she used to be. She wouldn't be tucked up in bed asleep, as she usually was when Grace got home from a late shift. There would be no warm arms around her neck in the morning. Her daughter had gone, and by now would be miles away from here, in a safer place.

'Is that you, dear? Come on through and I'll make you some tea.'

Grace closed the door behind her, glad to hear her landlady's welcoming voice. Ma Fox had already poured the tea by the time Grace had taken off her coat and gone through into the cosy living-room where the old lady spent most of her life.

'Thanks, Ada.' Grace sat down at the table and warmed her hands around her cup.

'I thought you could do with it, love, after a hard

20

shift at the hospital and then coming home to...' she waved her hand in the air '...the quietness. I can feel she's not here, you know. The old house feels empty without Marigold, and I'm going to miss looking after her while you're at work. She's been a right little ray of sunshine in my life.'

Grace reached out to Ada's hand and gently patted it.

'I know. I kept myself extra busy all day so I didn't have to think about it, but coming back here – it's hit me.' Grace swallowed hard to stop herself from crying. 'I had no choice but to send her away, Ada! If she'd have been hurt, or...' her voice caught and she stopped to compose herself '...or killed by a doodlebug, I'd never have forgiven myself. She's all I've got left after losing John!'

This war had robbed her of her husband, leaving her a widow at twenty-nine. She'd already paid a high price, and wasn't prepared to risk her daughter's life, too.

'You did the right thing.' Ada clasped Grace's hand. 'What's missing her, compared with knowing she's safe and out of harm's way? She'll come home when it's all over, just you wait and see.'

Grace blinked hard.

'Marigold will be safe in Norfolk with Bessie and Harry. They're good, kind people and I know they'll look after her.'

'You're lucky you were able to send her there – better than her going away to live with complete strangers, like most children have to.'

'Marigold's never met them, though.'

'Yes, but you know the people, so at least you know she'll be fine with them. It's a lot more than most mothers have. They've had to send their children off into the unknown, not knowing where they'd end up, or with whom.'

Grace nodded.

'I know you're right, Ada, but she cried so hard this morning at the station, I nearly said she didn't have to go. Still, I had to send her. I had no choice.' Her voice wobbled. 'But I'm going to miss her so much!'

'Well, you can go see her when you get a bit of leave.'

Grace smiled tearfully.

'Not for a while. She'll need time to get used to being away, and if I go too soon it might unsettle her.'

It wasn't just the fear of unsettling Marigold that would stop her from going, Grace thought. It was far more complicated than that. If she went to see Marigold, it would mean returning to the place from which she'd once run. The place she'd been too ashamed to go back to when things went wrong.

Bessie and Harry were welcoming Marigold to their home, but would they be as happy to have her mother back in their lives? Grace couldn't be sure.

'I'll write to Marigold as often as I can, starting tonight,' she told Ada. 'It'll make her feel a bit closer and I'm sure she'll be glad to get a letter from me.'

Ada smiled.

'Send her my love, and tell her I'll write to her in a day or two as well.' She nodded towards Grace's cup. 'Drink your tea before it goes cold.'

22

# Life On The Farm

The sound of thrumming engines seeped into Marigold's dreams. Through the fog of sleepiness, she wasn't sure at first whether they were just in her dream or real. Then her instinct kicked in. They were real!

Marigold woke with a start and immediately sat up. The air above the house was throbbing with the noise of planes. They were going to be bombed! She let out a shriek and leaped from the bed, then rushed into the living-room.

'Bessie!' she yelled, running over to the sink where the woman was washing up. 'The bombers are coming! We need to get in the shelter!'

'It's all right.' Bessie put her hand on Marigold's shoulder. 'You're shaking!'

'We need to go to a shelter – now!' She grabbed hold of Bessie's hand and started tugging her towards the door.

'Hold on! It's the Americans' planes taking off, Marigold, not the Germans. They won't hurt you. They're just a bit late leaving this morning.'

Marigold's body sagged with relief and tears trickled down her cheeks.

Bessie put her arms around her and hugged her tightly.

'It's all right, my girl, you're safe here.'

'I thought we were going to get bombed,' Marigold whispered, resting her head against Bessie's flowery apron. 'Like at home.'

'They don't usually come this far. That's why your mother knew it was safer for you.' Bessie smiled at her. 'We're all glad you're here with us. Peter was just saying so this morning.'

Marigold looked around the room. She'd been in such a panic she hadn't noticed only Bessie was in there.

'Where is he?'

'Gone to school. You were so tired last night I left you to sleep this morning. Dottie and Prune have gone to the woods, and Harry's outside, working. You'll see them all later. Are you hungry?'

Marigold nodded.

"I'll make you some porridge. You can have honey in it from Harry's bees, if you like. Sit yourself down.'

'Thank you.' Marigold pulled out a chair and sat down at the table, glad to be off her legs, which had suddenly gone all shaky with relief that it hadn't been German bombers after all.

The honey tasted of sunshine and flowers. Marigold scooped up another spoonful of porridge, dipped it into the golden pool of honey in the middle of her bowl and then ate it. It was warm, sweet, soft and lovely.

'Do you like it?'

Marigold nodded and smiled.

As Marigold ate her breakfast Bessie worked on the dough, stretching and pulling, folding and kneading. Marigold looked around the room.

'Is there an upstairs?'

'No, it's all on one level. The only stairs we've got are the ones leading up to the front and back doors. Remember we went down the back-door steps last night, to the closet?'

That was another thing different here, there was no indoor bathroom like at home. Marigold had had to go outside to the toilet in a little wooden hut, where there was just a wooden seat with a hole in it and a bucket underneath and no chain to pull. She had been frightened she was going to fall in!

'The house is made from two old railway carriages lined up side by side, with a brick bit built in between them.' Bessie divided the dough and gently laid the portions into two loaf tins.

Marigold looked around. Now Bessie had told her she could see tell-tale signs, like the curved ceiling. The doors on the opposite side of the room were like those she'd climbed out of from the train when she arrived at the station yesterday, only these were painted a pale butter yellow.

'When you've finished your porridge, go and get dressed and then I'll show you around.'

Back in her room, Marigold dressed and did her hair, brushing it out carefully and then weaving it into two long plaits. She tied the ends off with ribbons. She wondered what her mother would think of this strange house. Would she like it?

Marigold liked her room. It led off the living-room through an arched doorway which was closed off with a long curtain. There were two sets of windows. Cream-coloured muslin curtains hung at all the windows. Underneath the outside windows there was a long table top with a sewing machine on it. Her bed was tucked in beneath the windows facing inwards.

'Are you ready?' Bessie's voice called.

'Yes.' Marigold pulled the curtain aside.

'Good girl.' Bessie smiled at her. 'So, do you think you'll be comfy in here?'

'Yes, thank you. Was this Dottie or Prune's room?'

Bessie shook her head.

'No, they've always shared a room. This was my sewing-room. I work as a seamstress as well as working on the farm.' Bessie smiled. 'I didn't think you'd want to share a room with Peter. Nicer to have somewhere of your own.'

'Thank you.' Peter seemed nice, but Marigold was glad she didn't have to share a room with him.

'Right, I'll show you the other bedrooms.' Bessie led the way across the living-room and opened what looked like an ordinary carriage door.

'This is Dottie and Prune's room.'

When Marigold peered in, she expected to see the familiar inside of a compartment. But the seats and luggage racks were gone and the room was light and airy inside, with white painted walls. There were two patchwork-covered beds, one on each side, with a chest of drawers between them at the far end. All the windows, the ones facing outside and those looking into the main room, were covered with cream muslin just like in her own room.

'Peter's room's next door.' Bessie closed the door and moved on to the next one.

In Peter's room there was only one bed, a chest of drawers and a large table which was covered

26

with a map of Europe with small flags set out on it.

'Peter follows what's going on with the war.' Bessie gently touched one of the small Union flags. 'He and Harry listen to the news on the wireless, then move the flags about, going by what they hear is happening. Right, one last bedroom to see.' Bessie showed Marigold into her and Harry's room.

Marigold stared around her at the big double bed, drawers and wardrobe. Then two pictures of soldiers in uniform, hanging on the wall opposite the bed, caught her eye.

'That's Harry, taken in the last war.' Bessie came to stand beside her and pointed to the older-looking picture. 'The other one is of our son, Robert. He's somewhere in France.'

'Is he a soldier?'

'Not a fighting one. He's in the Army Medical Corps, looking after wounded soldiers. He's always liked caring for people and would have been a doctor if he'd had the chance.' Bessie turned to Marigold and smiled. 'Just a bit more to see, then we'll go outside.'

Marigold followed Bessie across the main room where everyone lived and ate. At the heart of the room was a black cooking-range built into a brick fireplace, where Bessie had cooked Marigold's porridge. There was a kitchen area in one corner, with a sink and cupboards, and just to the side of it another door.

'This is the pantry.' Bessie opened the door and stepped aside so Marigold could look in.

Marigold gasped when she saw the well-stocked

shelves. There was a lot more food here than they had in their kitchen cupboards back at home! There were jars of jam and honey, bottled fruits, pickled onions and beetroot, a metal meat safe and stone bread crock and a cold slab with butter and milk sitting on it.

'We don't do so badly for food here. It's a lot easier living on a farm than in London.'

Marigold nodded. How she'd love to show Bessie's pantry to Mrs Fox, who spent hours queuing up to buy food, and not much of it, at that. Marigold suddenly shuddered. This was all so different from home – the people, the house, everything.

'Are you OK, my girl?'

'Yes.' She couldn't tell Bessie what she was thinking and feeling, not when she'd been so kind.

'Come on, we'll go outside and collect the eggs, and then we can find Harry and see what he's up to.' Bessie picked up a basket from behind the pantry door and held out her other hand for Marigold to take.

Marigold forced a smile, slipped her hand in Bessie's and followed her outside.

The swallows came swooping out of the open shed doorway as Bessie led Marigold into the cool, dusky interior.

'See, up there?' Bessie pointed to a nest moulded on to a beam under the roof. 'It's a swallows' nest. You can see the chicks' yellow beaks resting on the edge.'

Marigold craned her neck, staring upwards.

'Won't they fall out?'

'No, they'll be all right. If you keep coming in

to have a look every day you'll see them growing. They'll be out of the nest and flying around soon. Their parents will have another brood before they fly off in the autumn.'

At that moment a swallow came flying in the door and, seeing Bessie and Marigold standing there, did a lightning-quick about-turn and darted out again, chattering loudly.

'They want to feed again. Come on, we'd better leave so they can come in.'

Bessie took Marigold across the yard and through a small gate in a hedge leading into a large orchard, where reddish-brown chickens were running around or pecking at insects in the dappled, shaded grass. Strutting around amongst them was a large, brown cockerel with a puffed-out chest and curved, glossy green tail feathers.

'That's Hector, our cockerel,' Bessie said as they walked across the grass towards the chicken coop. 'Harry's beehives are over there.' She pointed to five hives standing at the far end of the orchard. 'Best not to go near them, or you might get stung.'

Reaching the chicken coop, Bessie lifted up the lid of the nest box and motioned for Marigold to look inside.

'Eggs!' Marigold looked at Bessie, a look of wonder on her face.

Bessie smiled back, relieved to see, after Marigold's upsetting start to the day, she seemed to have settled down. She was talking, too, unlike last night.

'Will you collect them for me?'

Marigold nodded and reached her hand in to

the nest box.

'This one's still warm!' She carefully picked up the egg, cradling it in the palm of her hand and gently stroking the pale brown shell with one finger.

'Freshly laid and still warm from the hen. You can have it for your dinner, if you like.'

'Can I?' Marigold's eyes were wide.

'Of course. We have a lot more eggs here than you get from rations.'

'Do you get eggs every day?' Marigold placed the egg in the basket and reached back into the nest box to collect another.

'Yes, though not so many in winter.'

A harsh cawing call made them both turn to see a black bird flying straight towards them. It came to land on the hen-house roof and then side-stepped along to get closer to them.

'Hello, Hana.' Bessie stroked the bird's glossy black feathers. 'I wondered where you were.'

'Is Peter back?'

'No, not till nearly five o'clock. Hana stays here with us while he's at school. I don't think the grammar school would like a jackdaw in class! She's usually with Harry somewhere on the farm when Peter's not around.'

'Harry's over there.' Marigold pointed to the gate, where Harry was standing looking at them.

'Come and see the calf, Marigold!' he called.

'Where is she?' she asked Bessie.

'In the barn. The other cows are grazing down in the bottom meadow. I'll take you to see them later.'

Marigold looked uncertain.

'I've never been close to a cow before.'

'They're lovely and very gentle, so there's nothing to be frightened of. And Daisy's only small. We'll go and see her first.'

They walked towards Harry who opened the gate for them. Hana flew after them and landed on Harry's shoulder.

'You've plenty of eggs there, Marigold,' Harry said. 'We ought to send some to your mother in London.'

'Can you send eggs in the post?'

'If you wrap them well enough. Do you think she'd like some?'

Marigold's face lit up.

'Yes, she loves eggs, and we hardly have any because of rationing!'

'Then we'll send her some,' Bessie promised.


'I dip my hand in the milk like this, and then put my fingers to her mouth. See?'

Marigold watched in fascination as the calf sniffed Harry's fingers and then started to suck on them.

'I'm going to slowly lower my hand into the milk, and she'll follow.'

Daisy, the beautiful little calf, followed Harry's hand down to the pail. Once her mouth was in the milk Harry eased his fingers out of her mouth. Daisy kept her head down for a few seconds then jerked it up out of the pail, sending streams of milk dribbling off her mouth.

Harry chuckled.

'It takes them a while to learn how to do it properly. She's been used to feeding from her mother, so drinking from a pail is strange. Do you want to have a go, Marigold?'

She stared at Harry. Did he really think she could?

'Go on, have a go,' Bessie encouraged her. 'She won't hurt you.'

She'd try once, Marigold decided, and if she didn't like it she wouldn't do it again. She kneeled down in the clean straw next to Harry.

'Ready?' he asked.

Marigold nodded.

'Dip your hand in the milk first.'

Marigold did as Harry said and put her hand into the warm milk.

'Now, bring it up to her mouth and put your fingers on her lips.'

Harry took hold of her hand and put it in the right place. As soon as Marigold's fingers touched Daisy's mouth, the calf, started to suck strongly on them, drawing them into her mouth.

'Her tongue's rough,' Marigold said. 'She's sucking hard.'

'Good. Now we'll draw her down to the milk.' Gently and slowly, Harry guided Marigold's hand down, Daisy still sucking on her fingers, and into the pail of warm milk. Marigold felt Daisy begin to draw the milk into her mouth.

'Now, ease your hand away. Nice and slow.'

Marigold did as he said and, to her delight, Daisy kept her head down and sucked steadily from the pail.

'There you go.' Bessie squeezed Marigold's shoulder. 'You did it!'

'Well done,' Harry told her. 'You did a good job.'

Marigold smiled. She'd never done anything like this before. Until yesterday she had never been near a cow, and now here she was, helping a calf learn to drink milk from a pail!

'Daisy will need some help again tonight, just to help her get the hang of it,' Harry warned.

Marigold nodded then turned her attention back to Daisy, gently stroking the calf's soft ears as she drank the milk. Peter was right – she was beautiful, with big brown eyes. Her coat really was the colour of toffee. Marigold didn't feel so worried about meeting the other cows now, not if they were as lovely as Daisy!

## She Must Go Home!

Bessie's knitting needles made a gentle clicking noise. Her fingers seemed to work of their own accord, moving in a steady rhythm, weaving the wool around the needles, in and out, every stitch making the sock grow.

She loved this part of the day. The day's work was done, the tea finished and cleared away and she could sit down for a while. They'd listened to the news on the wireless earlier, and now Harry and Peter were poring over the map spread out on the table, talking about the latest news from France and moving the flags around to mark the Allies' latest position.

At the other end of the table, Marigold, her tongue sticking out in concentration, was drawing a picture to enclose with the letter she'd written to her mother.

'How do you spell Hana?' Marigold asked Peter. Peter looked up from the map.

'It's H. A. N. A. Why do you want to know?'

'I need to write Hana's name on the drawing I'm doing for my mother. See?' She held up the paper, which was packed with drawings of the people and animals living at Orchard Farm.

Peter took the paper from her and studied it closely. 'You've done a good job.'

'It will help her get to know about everyone who lives here,' Marigold explained. 'I've written about Daisy and the chickens and everything, too.'

'Did you tell her about teaching Daisy to drink from the pail?'

Marigold nodded.

'And about how rough her tongue was!'

Bessie smiled. It was good to hear Marigold sounding so happy and at home. Over the past couple of days since she'd arrived, they'd shown her how life at Orchard Farm worked. Bessie had spent a lot of time taking her around the farm, introducing her to the rest of the animals and showing her their wood, and the stream running through the bottom meadow.

Marigold had settled in well, and so Bessie had told Grace in the short letter she'd written to her. She would put it in with the parcel of eggs, along with Marigold's letter and drawing. They would go and post them in the village tomorrow. Bessie hoped it would give Grace some peace to know her daughter was happy, reassuring her she'd been right to put her trust in Bessie and Harry.

The front, door opened and Dottie and Prune came in from cleaning their boots outside.

'Look at your drawing.' Dottie leaned over Marigold and examined her picture. 'Aren't you good!'

Marigold beamed.

'It's for my mummy. So she'll know all about Orchard Farm.'

'I'm sure she'll be pleased with it,' Prune said. 'I expect she's missing you.'

'I miss her, too.'

'She can come and visit you here,' Dottie comforted her. 'Can't she, Bessie?'

'Yes, of course she can. Any time she wants. I've already asked her to come in my letter, Marigold.'

'That would be a nice holiday for her, out in the countryside.' Dottie put her arm around Marigold and gave her a hug. 'Make a lovely change from London.'

'She might not be able to come,' Marigold said sadly. 'She can't get away from work very easily. Not with the doodlebugs.'

'Don't worry, my girl, she'll come when she can,' Bessie said.

Although how Grace would feel about coming to Orchard Farm and seeing her and Harry, Bessie didn't know. All they could do was invite her, and she'd made it plain in her letter that Grace could come and visit any time she wanted.

Now it was up to Grace whether she would accept their invitation. She must, some time, as she wouldn't be able to keep away from her daughter

35

forever. When she did come, they'd welcome her with open arms. Now was what was important, not dwelling on what had gone before.

What was done was in the past. And it would have been forgiven and forgotten years ago, if only Grace had given them the chance.

Marigold couldn't sleep. She lay on her side with Blue, her rabbit, safe in her arms. Writing the letter to her mother tonight had made her seem so far away. A letter and a picture didn't seem enough to tell her about what it was like at Orchard Farm.

Marigold would rather have told her face to face. It made her feel as if her mother wasn't part of her life any more, not her everyday life. Her mother was still there at home in London, but it was miles away, and Marigold didn't get to see her each day like she used to. She didn't even know when she'd next see her!

Since she'd arrived here, Marigold's days had been busy, and she hadn't had much time to think about home, not since the first night here. But now, thinking about her mother and home brought a heavy weight of misery pressing down on her. She missed her mother so much! She started to cry, muffling her sobs with Blue so no-one would hear her.

Thoughts started to crowd into her mind. Was her mother safe? Where was she now? At home, or working at the hospital?

It was nice here in this little house on Orchard Farm, and Bessie and Harry, Peter, Dottie and Prune were all kind to her. But they weren't her mother, and that was who Marigold wanted to be with. The need to go home was tugging at her heart, making it ache painfully inside her chest.

Marigold sat up in bed. She couldn't stay here! She had to go home, and as soon as she could. Only she didn't know how. When she'd come to Rackbridge her mother's friend, Mrs Mac-Donald, had brought her, but she wouldn't be there to take her back again.

Marigold knew if she asked Bessie to take her home, she'd say no. She'd have to go on her own. When or how, she'd have to work out. But she would go. Marigold was determined.

Later on, when Bessie popped her head around the curtain to check on her before she went to bed, Marigold pretended to be asleep. Her eyes were heavy and all her body wanted to do was sleep, but her mind kept going over and over how she was going to get home. By the time she eventually fell asleep, she still didn't have an answer.

### *Missing*

It was late afternoon by the time Bessie and Marigold left the farm to walk into Rackbridge. Bessie carried the parcel of eggs for Grace in her shopping basket. They'd carefully wrapped up each egg in a strip of torn-off cloth and packed them all securely in an old OXO tin. The letters went on top of the closed tin lid and the whole thing was wrapped in brown paper and tied up with string.

37

'How long do you think it will take to get there?'

'A day or two.' Bessie looked at Marigold who'd been very quiet and subdued all day. Maybe she was overtired from the excitement and newness of everything over the past few days, and it had finally caught up with her. 'Perhaps your mother will read your letter to Mrs Fox. I'm sure she'd like to hear how you're getting on, too.'

'She'll laugh when she hears about me feeding Daisy!'

Bessie nodded.

'Life is very different here compared with London.'

They walked along in silence for a few minutes.

'Have you ever been to London, Bessie?'

'No, I've never needed to go there. I might, one day.'

'You could come and visit me when I go home, then.'

Whenever that would be, Bessie thought. Grace hadn't said anything about how long Marigold would stay with them. While London was still being targeted with doodlebugs it was safer for the child to be in Norfolk.

Perhaps she'd stay till the war ended. When that would be, nobody knew. If Bessie had her way it would be over today– now. Every day more people were being injured and killed, but there was still no sign of it ending. The Allies might be battling their way across France, but the Nazis were putting up a fight and weren't going to give in easily.

Bessie sent up a silent prayer that soon there

would be peace again, and all those far from home would come back safe. She touched the envelope which lay in the bottom of her basket alongside Grace's parcel. It was for Robert. 'Somewhere in France,' was all he could tell her, but Bessie hoped it would reach him. Writing to him every week helped her, and made him feel a bit closer.

'So this is your little evacuee?' Nora Chambers peered at Marigold from behind the post office counter.

'Yes. I'd like to send this to London, please, Nora.' Bessie handed Nora the parcel of eggs. 'And can I have a stamp for a letter to Robert as well?'

Nora dealt with the parcel and found the right stamps, but kept taking quick, furtive glances at Marigold.

'Here, you can stick this on the letter for me.' Nora passed a stamp to Marigold, who did as she was asked and stuck it on Robert's letter.

'Looks like you've got a good one there.' Nora took the money Bessie had put on the counter.

'Thank you, Nora.' Bessie put the coins in her purse.

'Of course, not all evacuees are like yours.' Nora leaned forwards across the counter, her thin lips pressed so tightly together they almost disappeared. 'You'll have heard about those at Mrs Potter's, I expect? Causing a lot of trouble.'

Bessie quickly turned to Marigold.

'Why don't you go and put the letter in the postbox just outside for me? I won't be a minute.' She watched Marigold leave, then turned back to face Nora. 'It's hard for children, coming among strangers so far from home.'

Nora closed her mouth and sniffed.

'It must be bad in London, with all those doodlebugs falling on it,' Bessie went on. 'Terrifying when nobody knows where or when they'll fall next.'

'Your girl didn't come with the new lot of evacuees last week, then?'

'No, it was a private evacuation. Her mother asked us to look after her.'

'She's lucky she came to you and Harry, then,' Nora probed. 'How did her mother know you?'

'Oh, from way back.' Bessie looked Nora directly in the eyes. 'I knew her in the last war.'

Nora's eyebrows rose above her horn-rimmed glasses.

'Not family, then? I did wonder...'

Bessie forced a smile.

'I'd better go and find Marigold. She's settling in well, but she doesn't know her way around the village yet. I don't want her getting lost. Cheerio, then, Nora.'

Not waiting for an answer, she turned and strode towards the door, her heart thudding loudly. Nora Chambers didn't need any encouragement to sniff out gossip and spread it around. Her probing about how Marigold had come to them made Bessie uneasy. She didn't want the likes of Nora spreading around the village who Marigold might be. Not when the child didn't know it herself.

Marigold was waiting for her by the postbox not far from the post office door.

'Did you post it?'

Marigold nodded.

'Good. Your mother's parcel will soon be there and she'll be able to have eggs for tea again. I just need to do a bit of shopping, then we can head home. You could wait for me on the seat under the tree there. It'll be cooler in the shade.' Bessie pointed to the wooden seat circling the old chestnut tree standing on the village green. Its wide canopy cast a cool shade which looked inviting in the heat.

Marigold considered for a moment.

'OK.'

Bessie watched Marigold cross the road and settle herself down on the wooden seat.

'Won't be long!' Bessie called.

It took longer than Bessie expected to be served – there were several people in the shop already and all the ration books had to be dealt with. There was the careful measuring out of cheese or butter, making sure everyone had the correct amount. No more and no less. Bessie looked out through the paper-crossed window and saw Marigold was sitting swinging her legs to and fro. Her head was down looking at the ground. It wasn't a happy pose.

'Marigold? That's a lovely name.' Edith Turner, the grocer's wife was checking Marigold's ration book. 'How's she's settling in?'

'It's so different from London, but I think she's enjoying it. She's sitting outside on the old seat in the shade.'

'I don't blame her, in this heat.' Edith fanned her red face with her hand. 'So, what would you like today?'

Bessie read her list and Edith started with the

tea ration.

'Any news from Robert?'

'Not for a couple of weeks, but I'll probably get a bundle of letters in one go. That's how it is sometimes.'

'We get the same with our Stan. I write to him every week. He said he likes to hear what we're doing and what's going on in the village.' She carefully tipped a little extra tea on to the scales to reach the exact weight. 'I suppose it's a bit of normal life for them, while they're living through war.'

Bessie nodded.

'It makes me shudder when I think of what's going on in France, and our boys out there mixed up in it. I suppose it's got to be done.'

'Yes, if we don't want that man over here telling us how to live! Hitler's time is running out.'

'Sooner the better,' Bessie replied.

Bessie stepped out of the grocer's a short while later, her basket full of packages. She looked over at the seat under the tree. It was empty. She hurried across the road and circled the tree, but Marigold wasn't there. Bessie looked up and down the street. Where was she?

Perhaps Marigold had gone to look for her and somehow they'd missed each other? Bessie dashed back across the road and into the grocer's.

'Edith, has a girl with blonde plaits been in?'

'No, love. Is it your Marigold you're looking for? I expect she's not far away – something probably caught her eye and she went to have a look.'

Bessie hoped so. Grace had trusted her to look after her daughter. Keep calm, she told herself, Marigold couldn't be far away. She went outside again and hurried up and down the street, searching in the shops and around the village green, but there was no sign of her. Marigold wasn't there.

Could she have gone home on her own? But she wouldn't have left without telling Bessie first, would she? And where else would she have gone?

Peter was in a hurry. Much as he'd loved his first year at grammar school, he couldn't wait to start the summer holidays. He wanted to spend more time with Hana and help Harry with some work, and then there were the silver B24 Liberators to watch from the American airbase. So much to do! He wanted to get started as soon as possible.

The train pulled into Rackbridge station. As soon as it jolted to a halt, Peter opened the door and jumped down. Slinging his satchel over his shoulder he rushed along the platform towards the booking hall and out through the exit to collect his bike. But then he stopped. Turning on his heels, he went back through to the platform and looked at the lone figure sitting on a bench.

Marigold.

'What are you doing here?' Peter called out as he went over to her. 'Have you come to meet me?'

Marigold looked at him and shook her head.

'I'm going home.'

'So am I. Come on!'

'No. I'm going to my home. My proper home in London, to be with my mother.' Her lip trembled.

Peter sat down on the bench beside her.

'Do Bessie and Harry know you're going home?'

'No.' Marigold sniffed and several tears escaped.

'Here, have my hanky.' Peter pulled a folded

white handkerchief from his blazer pocket. 'It's clean.'

Marigold took it and gave him a watery smile.

'Thank you.' She blew her nose. 'I don't know which train to get, or if I've got enough money.' She held out a couple of pennies in the palm of her hand.

'That's not enough to get you to London.'

Marigold sighed.

'I need to get back.'

'Why? Don't you like it at Orchard Farm?'

'Yes.' She wrung the handkerchief tightly between her hands. 'But I'm not with my mother. I worry about her and miss her. I want to go home!'

Peter touched Marigold's arm.

'I'm sure she misses you, too, but it's safer here.'

She turned to face him, her eyes flashing with anger.

'You don't know what it's like to miss your mother and be in a strange place with people you've never met before!'

Peter's face clouded.

'Yes, I do. I know exactly what it feels like, Marigold.'

'How can you, when you're still living at home with Bessie and Harry?'

'They're not my parents. Did you think they were? I don't call them Mother or Father, do I?'

She looked confused.

'No, you don't.'

'I'm Austrian. I haven't seen my parents since they put me on a train years ago.' Peter took a deep breath. 'I haven't heard from them since, and I don't know where they are now.'

44

'I'm sorry. I shouldn't have said what I did.'

He shrugged and smiled at her.

'It's all right, I understand how you're feeling. You're upset and you miss your mother. I miss my parents, too.'

'You don't sound foreign.'

'I was only seven when I came here. I didn't know much English, so I had to learn it from scratch.' He frowned. 'Now I can't remember much German.'

'Why did your parents send you away?'

'So I'd be safe. My family is Jewish, Marigold, and the Nazis don't like us. After they invaded Austria, they started making rules for Jewish people. They made life very difficult for us. I wasn't even allowed to go to school any more.' Peter sighed. 'Then our apartment was taken away from us. My parents decided it would be safer for me to leave them and come to England.'

'On your own?'

He nodded.

'By train to Holland, first, then we got a boat to England. I travelled with lots of other Jewish children. We all had to leave our families behind.'

'Did you know Bessie and Harry before?'

Peter shook his head.

'They'd heard what was going on and wanted to help a child. Bessie says she couldn't stop a war coming, but she could get a child away from it. She came to meet me from the boat, then brought me back to Orchard Farm.'

'Will you go back home after the war?'

'I don't know. It depends on what my parents want to do.' He paused for a moment. 'Before I

45

left, my papa told me to look at the moon every night, and know it would be shining down on them, too. They would be looking up at it, thinking of me. I do that, and it makes them feel a little closer. You could try it, too.'

They fell into silence for a few moments.

'What do you think I should do, Peter?' Marigold spoke so softly he could hardly hear her.

He looked at her firmly.

'I think you should stay here and not give up. Your mother sent you here for a good reason. She'd rather you were at home with her, but it's too dangerous there now.'

Tears welled up in Marigold's eyes again.

'She said she couldn't risk losing me as well as Daddy. He died on D-Day in France.'

Peter squeezed her hand.

'You've got stay here, for your mother. It's what she wants you to do, and Orchard Farm's a good place to be if you have to be away from home.' He smiled at her. 'There's plenty to do and see here. I've finished school for the summer now, so I can take you around. Show you the American airbase, and see the planes taking off. Come on.' Peter stood up and pulled Marigold to her feet. 'Let's go home, they'll be wondering where you are.'

'I ran off while Bessie was in the grocer's,' Marigold admitted. 'Do you think she'll be angry with me?'

'I think she'll be worried.'

Peter led Marigold out through the booking hall and collected his bike. As they walked out of the station yard they ran straight into a frantic-looking Bessie.

'Marigold!' Bessie cried. 'Where have you been?'

'I found her on the platform,' Peter said.

Bessie stepped back from Marigold, her hands resting on the girl's shoulders.

'What were you doing there? I came out of the grocer's and you were gone. I've been looking for you. I was so worried!' She hugged her again. 'Your mother trusted me to look after you. When I couldn't find you...' Her voice caught and she stopped.

'She was trying to go back home,' Peter explained.

'To London?' Bessie looked horrified.

He nodded.

'But she didn't have enough money or know which train to get.'

Bessie took both of Marigold's hands in hers.

'Why do you want to go back? Don't you like it here?' She shook her head. 'You've been getting on very well and I thought you were settling in.'

'I – I miss my mother so much!' Marigold stammered, her words punctuated with sobs. 'I worry about her.'

'Of course you miss her! It's only natural, my woman. But she wants you to be here so you're safe. Lots of children are living away from home now because of the war.'

'Like me,' Peter put in.

Bessie smiled.

'Peter knows just how you feel, Marigold. We all understand how hard it is for you. You can write to your mother as often as you like, and she can come and visit whenever she wants.'

'Writing a letter's not the same,' Marigold said.

'I know, but it's the best way to keep in touch when you're apart. The good thing about letters is you can read them over and over again. Reading them makes you feel a bit closer to the person who wrote them. I do that with Robert's letters.'

'Do you?'

Bessie nodded and smiled.

'I probably know them all off by heart!'

'I'm not very good at writing letters. I don't know what to write in them,' Marigold complained. 'The first one was easy, because there were so many new things to tell her, but I can't write that every time, can I?'

'No, but all you have to do is tell your mother what you've been doing,' Peter said.

'I'll forget what I've done.'

'You could keep a diary,' Peter suggested. 'Write in it what you do every day. Use it to help you write your letters.'

'I kept a diary a long time ago,' Bessie put in. 'I liked writing in it at the end of the day. How about if I gave you a little book to use as a diary? Would you like that?'

Marigold nodded.

'Could I draw pictures in it, as well?'

'Of course. You could draw Beauty and Buttercup, and Daisy.'

'And Dottie and Prune,' Peter added.

'Shall we go home, then?' Bessie asked.

Marigold nodded.

'Peter, will you ride ahead and tell Harry we're on our way, please? He'll be wondering where we've got to.'

Peter swung his leg over his bike, pushed off and

rode out of the station yard. He was relieved Bessie had met them and had sorted Marigold out. Now he could get home and properly start his summer holidays.

## The Diary

Bessie rummaged through the bottom drawer, feeling between folded clothes and reaching into the furthest corners with her fingers.

'What are you looking for, Bess?' Harry climbed into his side of the double bed.

'My old diary.'

'I thought you already gave Marigold a book to use as her diary?'

'I did. She took it to bed with her to write in but it got me thinking about my own one. Ah, here it is!'

She pulled out a cloth-bound book and waved it in the air.

'You haven't written in that for years.'

'I know.' Bessie pushed the drawer shut and climbed into bed beside Harry. 'It was an important part of my life for a while.' She lay back against the feather pillows. 'Helped me get through hard times.'

Harry put his arm round her and she snuggled into him.

'I just felt like reading it again.' She stroked the faded cloth cover and then opened it and looked at the inscription inside.

'Who gave it to you?'

'Sergeant Harmer. See here.' She pointed to his signature.

'*To dear Nurse Carter,*' Harry read aloud. '*With warmest wishes and thanks for all your care, Sergeant Frederick Harmer; March 4, 1918, Marston Hall, Auxiliary War Hospital.*'

'You were a good nurse.' Harry plopped a kiss on her hair. 'The men used to enjoy drawing and writing verses in the nurses' autograph books. What verse did he use?'

Bessie cleared her throat and read aloud the neat copperplate handwriting.

'*Whatever you are, be that.*
*Whatever you say, be true.*
*Straightforwardly act,*
*Be honest in fact,*
*Be nobody else but you.*
*All that is best for thee,*
*That best I wish for thee.*'

'He picked the right one for you. You're as honest and straightforward as the day is long, Bessie Rushbrook. True to yourself more than anyone I know.'

Bessie's insides squirmed. The verse was anything but true for her. Her thoughts drifted off to a place she seldom dared let them go.

A place Harry knew nothing about, and never would.

'Are you going to read it, then?'

Harry's words dragged her back to the present. 'Beg your pardon?'

'The diary. Are you going to start reading it?'

'Do you want me to read you some?'

50

'No. It's your private diary, with your thoughts, for your eyes only. I meant are you going to read some tonight, or shall I blow out the candle and we'll get some sleep?'

'I'd like to read a page or two. You settle down, I won't be long.'

Turning the page, Bessie began to read words she'd written more than 25 years ago when another war was raging. The one they called the Great War, the War To End All Wars.

Only it hadn't.

*March 4, 1918*

*My name's Bessie Carter and this is my diary. I think that's how I should start, but I don't know if it's the right way or not, because I've never had a diary before. This was given to me by Sergeant Harmer, one of my patients. He told me writing a diary had helped him, and it would be a good place to put my thoughts and feelings.*

*Perhaps I should say something about myself. I'm twenty-one years old and I'm working as a VAD – short for Voluntary Aid Detachment nurse – at Marston Hall Auxiliary War Hospital.*

*I do some seamstress work for Lady Heaton when I've got the time. That's what I used to do here before the war, working as a seamstress for her. When she turned the Hall into a hospital at the beginning of the war, most of her staff started working in the hospital, too.*

As Bessie read on, it felt as if the years in between dissolved away, and she was back at Marston Hall...

'It's for you, Nurse Carter. Please, I want you to

take it.'

Sergeant Harmer folded Bessie's hands around the clothbound notebook he'd just given her.

'I'm sorry, I can't. You know the rules – nurses aren't supposed to accept gifts from patients.'

'Who's to know? It's my spare one, and I don't need it. If you don't take it, I'll just leave it there on that seat!' He nodded towards a bench on the platform, then looked at her and smiled with a mischievous glint in his eye. 'Would be such a waste.'

Bessie sighed and returned his smile.

'It's kind of you, but I can't.' She handed it back to him.

'I think you can. It's for you to use as a diary, to write in what you've done, think and feel. I kept one all the time I was in France, and it helped me.'

'I'm not in France. This is England, and it's safe here.'

Sergeant Harmer nodded.

'I know, but you young women see things you never ought to see, and deal with the horrors of what war does to a man. That's hard.'

Bessie pondered this.

'Come on, Nurse, we need to get all the men on board. No time for long goodbyes!' one of the orderlies said, grinning at the pair of them as he wheeled a patient in a bathchair towards the waiting train.

'We need to get you on board, and then you'll be on your way home and out of the war for good.' Bessie took hold of the sergeant's arm and started to walk him slowly towards an open carriage door, her own stride shortened to match his slow, dragging limp.

He stopped at the carriage door and turned to Bessie.

'Please take it with my warmest wishes and thanks.'

Before Bessie could say anything, he slipped the diary into her pocket and climbed slowly into the carriage.

'It's yours now.' He settled back into a seat.

Bessie nodded and tapped her pocket.

'All right, I can see you're not going to give in. I appreciate your gift. Thank you.'

'Nurse Carter?' One of the orderlies called to her from the doorway of another carriage. 'Can you help here?'

'I'm coming. Goodbye, then.' Bessie smiled at him. 'Remember to take care.'

Walking back to Marston Hall with the rest of the nurses and orderlies, Bessie mulled over what had happened that morning. She always enjoyed taking the men to meet the train. It was satisfying seeing them on their way again, her job done and the men healed.

The lucky ones like Sergeant Harmer were going home for good – the war was over for them – but other patients would be going back to France. Some would get a short leave at home, but if they were badly needed out there, they'd be straight back to the war. Knowing men would be sent back was hard for the nurses, because some wouldn't be so lucky next time. Bessie wished the war was over, and everyone back home safe where they belonged.

The wind was picking up, so Bessie turned up

the collar of her coat and quickened her pace. It was good to be out of the wards for a while, but there would be plenty to do when she got back. Everything had to be cleaned and prepared for the next lot of incoming patients.

Pushing her gloved hand into her pocket, she touched the diary Sergeant Harmer had given her. He'd told her to write down her thoughts and feelings, but that wasn't the sort of thing she was used to doing. A fanciful thought, her mother'd call it, and the best way to cure that was hard work.

But her mother wasn't here, and she'd never seen the things Bessie had, nor had to deal with the things she did every day. Perhaps the Sergeant was right and she should write these things down, let her thoughts free.

But it would have to wait until later, judging by the look on the face of one of the orderlies who came running down the Hall drive to meet them.

'Telegram's just come. More patients on their way!' John Bishop gasped between breaths. 'On the early afternoon train, so Matron wants you back at the double!'

Bessie picked up her skirts and hurried with the others back to the hospital.

'Did they reach the train in one piece?' Ethel, Bessie's friend and fellow VAD asked as they worked together stripping empty beds.

'Yes. They were in fine form.'

'Sounded like it, from all the cheering and whistling when they left!' Ethel tipped another armful of sheets and pillowslips into the laundry basket. 'They don't make that sort of noise when they arrive.'

54

Bessie smiled at Ethel.

'We did a good job.'

'Yes, but there's always more to fill their place.' Ethel sighed. 'And always will be while we're at war.'

'We'd better hurry up, or Matron will want to know why the ward's not ready.' Bessie added the last of the sheets to the basket. 'If we're lucky there will be time for some bread and jam and a cup of cocoa before the ambulances arrive. Do you know where they're coming from?'

'Matron didn't say,' Ethel replied. 'Let's hope they're not straight from the Front this time.'

As Bessie started on the next job of disinfecting the beds, her thoughts drifted to her brother, Robert. He was out there, at that place they called the Front, somewhere in France, and she hoped and prayed he was safe. She'd seen enough injured men to know how badly soldiers could be hurt.

If, God forbid, Robert was injured, Bessie hoped a good nurse would be looking after him, giving him the best care they could. That's what she tried to do. Every man who came to their hospital was someone's son, brother or husband, who'd done their bit and been hurt and deserved nothing but the best.

Swallowing hard to fight back the tears stinging her eyes, Bessie wiped faster and worked harder. It was the best way to deal with worrying about Robert. Keep herself so busy she only had time and energy to think about the job in hand, not the 'what ifs' and the worst that might never happen. She'd had to deal with it once before and, God willing, she'd never have to face it again. The best thing to do was concentrate on what had to be done.

By the time Bessie and Ethel had the ward ready, beds made up with hot-water bottles warming them ready for the next occupants, it was past one o'clock. They'd only been sitting down for 10 minutes, and were ravenously eating bread and jam and drinking hot cocoa, when one of the orderlies put his head round the kitchen door.

'The ambulances are on their way up from the station. Be here in about ten minutes.'

'Thanks,' Bessie said. 'Come on, Ethel. Eat up quick. We don't know when we'll next get a chance to have something.'

It all depended on what was coming in the ambulances. If the men were straight from the Front they'd be in a sorry state, still wearing their muddy, lice-ridden uniforms, and their Blighty wounds would only have been dressed quickly in a field hospital. After travelling so far they'd be exhausted, shocked and in pain. Bessie still found it upsetting to see the men arrive like this, but she'd learned not to show it. Outwardly she was calm and professional, for the men's sake. But it wasn't easy.

Bessie and Ethel joined Sister Williams, Matron and the other VAD nurses and orderlies waiting at the front door, watching as the ambulances came slowly up the drive. Jolts and bumps would send pain searing through wounded men, so the drivers always did their best to give them a smooth trip by taking it slowly.

As soon as the first ambulance came to a halt,

everyone snapped into action. They all knew what needed to be done to get the men inside and comfortable as quickly as possible after their journey. Bessie loved the way they all worked together – VADs, Sister, Matron and the men from the RAMC – everyone knowing what to do after plenty of practice. Together, they worked like a smoothly oiled machine.

Bessie gave an inner sigh of relief when the back doors of the first ambulance were opened and a soldier wearing hospital blues was helped out. These men had already been treated in a bigger war hospital and hadn't come straight from France.

'Where have you come from?' Bessie asked as she guided a patient walking with the aid of crutches in through the front door and along the short distance to the ward in the old ballroom.

'Norfolk and Norwich hospital, Nurse. It's good to be sent out here to convalesce. Fresh air, peace and quiet.' He grinned at her. 'Just what the doctor ordered.'

'I hope you'll find it that way.' Bessie smiled at him and steered him towards one of the empty beds. She looked down at the notes the soldier had brought with him from the hospital. 'Private Dennis, this will be your bed and locker. We'll soon have you settled in and comfortable.'

'Nurse Carter, as soon as you've finished there, hurry along and tell cook to organise some tea, and bread and butter. The men could do with some refreshment after their journey. Then straight back and start on the observations,' Sister Williams ordered as she bustled past, guiding some orderlies carrying stretcher cases to their beds.

'Yes. Sister. Right, Private Dennis…'

'I'll be all right now. You go and get tea organised. I could do with a cup, and I'm sure the rest of the lads are the same.'

Bessie looked at the young soldier who smiled back at her, his brown eyes crinkling at the corners.

'Well, if you're sure. We don't want you keeling over from lack of tea! I'll be back to check on you soon.'

Passing other new patients being helped into the ward, Bessie hurried down to the kitchen, going as quickly as she could without actually running. Matron was strict about that. They must walk, never run.

Down in the kitchen the VAD cook and kitchen hands were already busy preparing the evening meal, and looked up when Bessie walked in.

'Tea and bread and butter?' Mrs Taylor, the cook, asked.

Bessie nodded.

'Sister's orders.'

'We've got the kettles on ready.' Mrs Taylor nodded at the big black kettles coming to the boil on the big range. 'Put them on as soon as the ambulances drew up. Agnes,' she said to one of the kitchen maids, 'you get started on the bread and butter.'

'Thank you, Mrs Taylor, the men are gasping for a cup. It'll warm them up after their journey.' Bessie smiled at the woman, who always reminded her of a friendly little bird in her pale-brown cook's uniform.

'Where are the new men from?'

'Norfolk and Norwich War Hospital,' Bessie said. 'I must go, or Sister will wonder where I've got to.'

'You can tell us about them later. Have a cup of tea.'

'I will. But it won't be for a while. We've lots to do.'

That was always true, Bessie reflected as she hurried back to the ward, and not just on days when a convoy arrived. Every day was busy. The arrival of new patients just increased the load, and everyone would work hard to get the men settled and comfortable. Her next job was to get the temperatures and pulses taken, because the new men couldn't have their cups of tea until it was done.

*It's been a busy day and I'm tired. New patients arrived, from Norfolk and Norwich, though, so no lice-ridden uniforms or mud to deal with today. It is strange to see new faces in the beds; I still expect the old ones to be there. But they've gone on their way again, our job with them is done.*

*I wonder what this new group of men will be like? It's always interesting to get to know the characters who come our way. They're all different and keep us VADs on our toes.*

*Must sleep. Good night.*

Bessie closed the diary and leaned back against her pillows. She could still remember the bone-aching feeling of tiredness at the end of a long shift, when her only desire had been to fall into a deep, dreamless slumber.

'I needed that.' Dottie replaced the stopper in her bottle of cold tea and tucked it back in the shade under a bush, then lay down on the grass, her hands behind her head and let out a huge sigh. 'This is lovely!'

'Sure is.' Prune was sitting on the grass nearby with her arms wrapped around her knees, looking out over the meadow from their picnic spot at the edge of the wood where they were working.

Dottie started to giggle.

'Hark at you! You sound like an American.'

Prune's cheeks flushed.

'I don't!'

'Sounded like one to me. "Sure is" is the sort of thing a GI would say. You're picking up the language from Howard.'

'Not intentionally.' Prune plucked a daisy out of the grass and twirled it around between her fingers.

'No, but I suppose it's only natural. The more time you spend with someone, the more you pick up from them. The Americans get things from us, too, you know. Look at Clem, he loves learning our different British words. Did you know he writes them down? Remember when he called Harry's waistcoat a vest?'

Prune laughed.

'He didn't know a vest's a totally different thing

for us. They speak English, but it's not the same as ours.'

They fell into silence for a few minutes and closed their eyes in the warm sunshine, listening to bees drone from flower to flower. A skylark was hovering above the meadow, filling the air with its crystal-clear song.

'The fact is, Prune,' Dottie said, breaking the silence, 'you are spending a lot of time with Howard. Every chance you get.'

'I like spending time with him. What's wrong with that?'

Dottie rolled over on to her side, her head propped up on one hand, and smiled at Prune.

'Nothing, nothing at all, but I think you might be falling for him.'

Prune shrugged.

'Perhaps.'

'Come on, Prune, can't you be more exact?'

'Well...' Prune strung out her reply. 'Yes, I like him very much. I enjoy his company and he makes me laugh.'

Dottie let out a long whistle.

'You're not giving much away, are you? Have you fallen in love with him?'

'I think I might have.'

'He'd better watch out. You'll be taking him home to meet your mother next!'

'No,' Prune snapped. 'Definitely not!'

Dottie held up her hand.

'I was only joking, Prune. There's no need to get upset.'

Prune sighed.

'I'm sorry, Dottie. I shouldn't have spoken so

rudely.' She leaned back on her hands and looked up at the clear blue sky. 'It's just my mother wouldn't approve. If she knew I was spending time with a GI she'd be furious! She doesn't agree with them being here.'

'Well, they're not here on holiday, are they? Who knows where we'd be now if the Americans hadn't joined the war!'

'Unfortunately, she doesn't think that way.'

'She doesn't know what she's missing.' Dottie looked at her watch. 'Right, five more minutes, then we'd better get back to work.'

She rolled on to her back again and closed her eyes against the sun.

'What about you? Wouldn't you like to find a nice GI to fall in love with?'

'Me?' Dottie opened her eyes and shielded them from the sun as she looked over at Prune. 'No. I'm staying carefree, not getting romantically involved with anyone. I've got plans for a career after the war's over, and I don't want to get sidetracked by any man.'

'Doesn't Clem count?'

'Not in that way. He's a good friend and a great dancer. We enjoy each other's company. But because he's an honourable, married man, that's it. No romance involved.'

'Don't you wish, deep down, you could find someone to love?'

Dottie's stomach twisted. She swallowed hard and forced a bright smile

'That's for you, Prune, not me. Trust me when I say I know what I'm doing. Now, be quiet and let me have a rest before we start work again.'

Grace slipped quietly through the door at the end of the ward and stepped out on to the balcony. As her eyes adjusted to the London blackout she could pick out familiar landmarks which were bathed in pale moonlight. The full bomber's moon of a few nights ago was waning, but it still radiated enough light to lift the city from complete darkness.

Grace took a deep breath, leaning forward on the cold stone of the balcony balustrade and drawing in fresh air which had a slight salty, tarry tang to it. She often escaped out here for her break while she was on night duty.

From its position overlooking the Thames, St Thomas's hospital boasted a fine view of the river, where coal barges floated gracefully past along water which was streaked with faint, silvery ripples of moonlight. Across the river stood the Houses of Parliament, which were still standing even after all the Luftwaffe had thrown at the city.

Leaning a little farther over, Grace picked out the dome of St Paul's which curved against the sky, standing proudly amongst the jagged ruins littering the skyline. She loved that the grand old church was still standing – it was like a symbol of Londoners' resilience against the German attacks. They hadn't managed to destroy St Paul's, nor the spirit of the people who had lived through the Blitz and had come out the other side still strong, still there.

But there was one thing missing from London, Grace thought. Marigold. She wasn't here any more. Grace felt in her pocket and touched

Marigold's letter which had arrived that morning.

She didn't need to read it now, because she almost knew it by heart after reading it so many times. The words had salved Grace's worries about sending her daughter away to a strange place. Marigold was safe and enjoying her new life, which was all Grace wanted for her, though she missed her daughter with every ounce of her body. Not knowing when she'd see her again made Grace's heart ache, but her feelings must come second to Marigold's safety. She'd lost John and she couldn't face losing her daughter, too.

Grace smiled as she recalled the things Marigold told her about in her letter – collecting eggs, teaching a calf to drink from a pail and the description of the house. Grace could picture all of it, the smells and tastes, the feeling of a calf's rough tongue.

She closed her eyes and was there. Then she sighed. All of that was a long time ago, in another lifetime.

The parcel of eggs Bessie had sent was a lovely surprise, and typical of Bessie and Harry's kindness. Grace had rushed to show Ada and together they'd carefully unwrapped the precious brown eggs, which had arrived still as perfect as when they were laid. Eating them would be such a treat, so much nicer than the awful powdered egg.

Bessie's letter told Grace all she needed to know, even down to the little details of how Marigold was eating and sleeping. It helped her to know her daughter was happy.

Bessie had invited her to come and visit any time she wanted, but when she'd be able to accept

Grace didn't know. It wasn't that she didn't want to see Marigold. She did. She was desperate to see her daughter. But it would mean facing up to her past, and that wasn't so easy.

Grace sighed and checked her watch. A couple more minutes and she'd have to get back to work. With all the windows bricked in and the glass in the balcony doors boarded over, the wards felt closed in, with no fresh air and artificial light.

Escaping outside on to the balcony helped. Work on the ward was hard, with the never-ending stream of patients injured by doodlebugs. Soon after a flying bomb exploded the first casualties would start to come in. It didn't matter if Grace was just about to go off-duty, she would stay and do her bit like all the other nurses and doctors. But it made for long, hard shifts.

Grace filled her lungs with fresh air and, with a last glance at the moon shining down on the city, she opened the balcony door and went back to work.

'They are huge!' Marigold shouted. She stood beside Peter staring at the queue of silver B24 Liberators waiting to take off. The air around them and the ground they stood on seemed to throb and shake from the roar of the engines.

She'd never seen planes so close up before. They looked big and heavy and it was a miracle they ever got off the ground!

'We're lucky to see them take off – they're going late this morning!' Peter shouted back. 'See that one?' He pointed to the plane closest to where they stood on the road outside the boundary hedge. 'That's the Peggy Sue. Prune's Howard is the navigator on her.'

'Are they full of bombs?'

'If they're going on a bombing mission.'

Marigold swallowed hard. She'd been on the other end of many bombing missions – the sharp end, where the bombs landed with a sickening crump and killed people. Her bones seemed to turn to jelly inside her as she recalled the siren's wail and then the urgent rush to reach the safety of a shelter before the droning German bombers arrived overhead to drop their load.

Afterwards, when the all-clear sounded, there'd be the anxious walk home the next morning, emerging out into the street again, picking their way through damaged streets, never knowing whether their house would still be there. They'd been lucky. Their home had escaped the bombs when others only a street or two away had been flattened.

Peter touched her arm.

'Are you all right, Marigold?'

She nodded.

'Just thinking about what it's like to be on the side getting bombed.'

'You were bombed?'

'Yes.' She took a deep breath. 'The Blitz was really bad. The Germans bombed us night after night.'

'Were you scared?'

'Of course I was. Wouldn't you be?'

Peter nodded.

'So, what do you think about these planes going to bomb the Germans?'

Marigold worried a stone with the toe of her shoe. She didn't know what to say. Part of her thought, because they bombed us, then we should bomb them. An eye for an eye. But she knew what it was like to feel the fear. The way it made your heart race and the adrenalin pump through your veins, because you didn't know if it was going to be you who got it this time. If a bomb had your name on it or not.

It should all stop, Marigold thought. Everyone should stop fighting each other. The British and the Germans, the Americans and the Russians, the Japanese and the Italians. Everyone.

Children weren't supposed to fight. Teachers always stopped children from fighting at school, pulled them apart and sent them to the head-master. So why was it right for adults to fight when they tell children not to? Their fighting was worse – it killed and injured people.

'I wish the war would end,' Marigold said. 'No more bombs dropped anywhere.'

'We all do. Especially those men in there.' He gestured towards the planes.

'Then why are they fighting?'

'To stop Hitler.' He laid a hand on Marigold's shoulder. 'Trust me, you wouldn't want the Nazis to come here to England. It would be terrible. We have to fight back until it's safe again.'

'Was it very bad at your home before you came here?'

'Yes, and it was getting worse all the time. My parents tried to hide it from me, but I listened to them talking. They were scared, and tried to get us out of the country. They wrote to England to try to get jobs here, but couldn't find any. They were desperate, so when the chance came for me to leave on the train with other children, they grabbed it.'

'Did you want to come here?'

Peter shrugged.

'Yes and no. It seemed exciting to come to England. An adventure, my parents called it. But I had to come alone and leave my family behind.'

She smiled sympathetically.

'I know how that feels.' She turned her head. 'Hey! What's that?' She pointed to a green flare shooting up in the air.

'It means they can go.'

The noise increased as the lead plane revved its engines harder and harder. It started to hurtle down the runway, faster and faster, until Marigold thought it was going to run into the field at the far end of the runway, if it didn't stop. It slowly began to climb upwards like a heavy swan taking off.

'Here goes another!' Peter shouted.

'But the first one's only just gone!'

'They leave about forty-five seconds apart.'

'Don't they hit each other?' Marigold worried.

'They try not to, though that sometimes happens in bad weather. But not today, I hope.' He pointed upwards, to the clear blue summer sky which, after a misty start, had cleared.

They watched as, one by one, the planes took off. The Peggy Sue moved to the left and joined the queue of planes waiting to take off. Peter counted each one as they left the ground. The children could see them climbing higher and higher, circling round and around as they went.

'That's the last one,' Peter said as it sped down the runway and took off. 'That makes twenty-nine up today.'

'What happens now?' Marigold asked, her voice back to a normal level.

'They'll join up into a huge formation with planes from other bases, then head off over the North Sea to wherever they're going for today's target. They've flown nearly a hundred missions from here since they arrived, and there's going to be a big party soon to celebrate.'

'Do you know where they're going to today, Peter?'

'It's a secret.' He turned and looked behind him, first to the right and then the left, and pressed his finger to his lips. 'Shh! Careless talk costs lives. There could be a spy around.'

Marigold giggled.

'Do you?'

'No. They only tell the crews just before they fly. They have a big map on the wall and point to where they're going.'

'When will they be back?'

'This afternoon some time. I'll come back and watch them come in. Do you want to come along?'

Marigold nodded.

'You can help me count them back in. All twenty-nine, I hope.'

## *Nightmares*

Bessie's arm was starting to ache. She let go of the churn handle and opened the lid to see how far off the butter was. Inside, small granules of yellow butter bobbed in the pale milk, so it was nearly there. She shut the lid firmly and had just started churning again when the door opened and Marigold walked in.

'Hello, Bessie, we're back. Peter's gone to find Harry.'

'Did you see the planes?'

Marigold nodded.

'They were huge – great big silver things! And full of bombs.' She sighed. 'I didn't like thinking they were going to bomb people, like the Germans bombed us in London.'

'I know, but it's what Churchill thinks we must do to win the war.'

'I wish it was over.'

'So do I, Marigold, and so do millions of people.' Bessie turned the churn handle faster. 'You should write about seeing the planes in your diary.'

Marigold nodded and pulled out a chair and sat down at the table near where Bessie was working.

'What did you used to write about in your diary?'

'About things I did every day, like you do. I was a nurse, you see, during the Great War. So I wrote

70

about my work in the hospital and, sometimes, about what I thought and felt.'

'My mummy's a nurse, too,' Marigold said. 'At St Thomas's Hospital in London. Which hospital were you at?'

'Marston Hall Auxiliary War Hospital. It wasn't a big hospital like St Thomas's. It was in Marston Hall, a big house where I used to work as a seamstress before the war. When the war started there were so many wounded men, they needed more hospitals. Lady Heaton, who I worked for, volunteered her house to be used as a hospital, and I became a nurse there. A VAD.'

'VAD?'

'Voluntary Aid Detachment. I wasn't a proper medical nurse, trained like your mummy. I did have some training, but my job was to help look after the men and run the ward.'

'Did you like it?'

Bessie stopped churning and smiled at Marigold.

'Yes, I did. It was very hard work, and I was on my feet all day, rushing around. It was hard to see the men with such terrible wounds, but I enjoyed caring for them and helping them to get better.'

'Mummy says her feet ache at the end of her shift. Did yours?'

Bessie nodded.

'Oh, yes, and I'd be so tired all I'd want to do was sleep. But I always wrote in my diary first, let all my thoughts out and then I'd sleep. I suppose, by writing them down, it was a bit like letting them go so I didn't lay awake worrying about things so much. It helped me.'

That's what Sergeant Harmer had said would happen when he'd insisted she take the diary, Bessie realised. He'd been right.

*March 6, 1918*

*A letter from Robert today. He says he's well, in good spirits and having a few days' rest from the Front, with a chance for a bath and clean clothes. I can imagine what he's like from the state of the men who come here straight from that place.*

*He got the socks I knitted him and the scarf from Mother, too. He's worrying about them all at home – Mother, our little sister, and Father especially, now he has to manage the forge on his own. Robert's concerned about me, too, seeing the wounded men. That's typical of him, to be worrying about us when he's the one in danger.*

*But I can manage perfectly well. I'm used to it now, and like doing my bit to help.*

'Here we are, Nurse.' Private Dennis placed his empty mug on Bessie's tray. 'Lovely cup of tea, thank you.'

'You're welcome.' Bessie smiled at the young private who'd quickly made himself at home in the ward and fitted in as if he'd been there for ever. She liked that, she thought as she carried on around the ward collecting more empty mugs and adding them to her tray.

Each time they had a convoy of new patients arrive it shook the ward up, and it took a while for things to settle down again and for everyone to get to know one another and feel comfortable together. The new group of patients who'd arrived a week ago seemed to have settled in well. They

72

were a happy and talkative bunch, except for one.

Sergeant Rushbrook was an amputee, with one leg gone below the knee and still bedbound. His bed was at the far end, facing the window, and he seemed to spend most of his time staring out of it, not joining in with the cheerful banter of the other men. He was quiet and withdrawn, though always polite when they changed the dressing on his leg. Bessie had the feeling he was far away somehow, and was intrigued by him.

She watched him as she approached his bed to collect his mug. He was staring out of the window again with a look of sadness on his face.

'Sergeant Rushbrook?'

He started at Bessie's voice and turned to look at her.

'I've come for your mug. Have you finished?'

He reached over and picked it up from the top of his locker. It was still half full and he quickly finished off the contents and handed the mug to Bessie.

'Was it cold?'

'It was fine, thank you.'

Bessie nodded and half-turned to leave, but then she looked back at Sergeant Rushbrook.

'Would you like a book to read, or a paper?'

He shook his head.

'No, thank you.'

Bessie regarded him for a moment.

'I've noticed you often look out of the window. What are you looking at?'

'Trees, grass, birds. The sky.'

'Spring will soon be here. The daffodils are coming up in the garden and there are some snowdrops out already. You'll be able to go outside and see them for yourself, once you're up.'

Sergeant Rushbrook nodded but didn't say anything. Bessie wasn't going to push him. She'd learned that men would talk when they wanted to, and not before. She'd keep talking to him, and hopefully he'd become less withdrawn and begin to enjoy being on the ward with the other men.

'If you change your mind and want me to fetch you a book or something, just give me a call.'

He nodded and resumed staring out of the window. Bessie carried on collecting up the rest of the empty mugs.

'Nurse Carter!' one of the other new bed-bound men called as Bessie walked past with her laden tray. Both his arms were bandaged from fingertip to shoulder.

Bessie stopped by the end of his bed.

'What can I do for you, Private Wade?'

'I'd like to write a letter to my girl, only...' He held up his right arm and shrugged. 'I can't hold a pencil at the moment. I know what I want to say, it's just that I need someone to write it down for me.'

'I'll be happy to help you,' Bessie said. 'I'll just take these along to the kitchen, then I'll be straight back.'

Five minutes later, Bessie drew up a chair alongside Private Wade with a pencil and paper in her hand. The first time she'd written a letter to someone's sweetheart she'd felt awkward, as if she were intruding in their private world, but now she'd done it so many times it no longer bothered her. She was just acting as a secretary and, besides,

74

all the men were used to their letters passing through the censor while they were in France.

Every word they'd written to loved ones back home had been scrutinised for anything which might prove useful if the letter fell into enemy hands. The censor's stamp was on every letter Bessie had had from her brother.

'I'm ready.' She smiled at Private Wade. 'You just dictate to me and I'll write in my best handwriting.'

'Dear Lizzie.' He stopped, looking awkward.

Bessie smiled at him encouragingly.

Private Wade cleared his throat and continued. 'Nurse Carter is writing this for me...'

The ward was winding down for the night. All the men were in bed. Some were reading and others were already dozing off. Bessie glanced at the clock on the wall. Fifteen more minutes and she'd be off duty.

She was more than ready for her own bed. Since she'd come on duty at midday it had been almost non-stop except for those few minutes sitting beside Private Wade's bed while she'd written his letter for him. She was happy, though. She loved doing this work, helping the men who had been through so much.

'No!' A loud shout came from the far end of the ward. 'No! No!'

'It's Rushbrook, Nurse!' Private Dennis called from his bed. 'He's asleep. He does this sometimes.'

Bessie nodded and strode down the ward to the end bed where Sergeant Rushbrook was still sleeping. His face was contorted in anguish, with beads of sweat standing out on his brow. His eyes twitched rapidly under their eyelids.

Bessie pulled up a chair and sat down beside his bed, then gently took hold of one of his hands in hers.

'Sergeant Rushbrook? It's Nurse Carter.'

Her voice must have broken through into his dream. He woke with a jolt, his eyes darting around as if checking where he was, then he sighed heavily.

'Everything's all right – you're safe. You were dreaming.' Bessie gently squeezed his hand. She'd seen plenty of men have bad dreams. Some would thrash about in their beds, scream and cry out as they relived the terrors of the trenches from the safety of their hospital beds. The best thing to do was hold their hands and be there for them.

'A dream?'

She nodded.

'You were crying out.'

'What did I say?'

'"No",' several times over.'

Sergeant Rushbrook sighed heavily and glanced down at the space in the bed where his right leg should be. Was that what he was dreaming of? The time when his leg was injured? She knew she shouldn't push him, so she waited quietly for him to speak, holding on to his hand which, to her surprise, he hadn't snatched back when he woke up.

'My leg,' he said eventually. 'It was about my leg.' His blue eyes caught hers for a few seconds and then he looked away again. The glance had been brief but Bessie had caught the look of pain in them.

'About when you were injured?'

He shook his head.

'When they told me they'd amputated it.' He swallowed hard. 'I need it! One leg's no good to me!'

Bessie's heart ached for him.

'Better to lose your leg than your life.' She tightened her hold on his hand. 'I know the doctors wouldn't have removed it unless they had to. Trust me, you wouldn't have wanted gangrene.'

'But one leg is no good for…'

'There you are, Nurse Carter!' Sister William's voice interrupted them. 'It's time you were off duty.'

Bessie looked at the sergeant who was now staring at the foot of his bed. What bad timing.

'Yes, Sister. I'll be along soon.'

Bessie waited until her footsteps retreated to the other end of the ward and then quietly spoke.

'What's one leg no good for, Sergeant Rushbrook?'

'You should be off-duty, Nurse,' he said abruptly. 'You've been on the go since midday.'

How did he know how long she'd been on duty for?

'I watch what's going on,' he said, a hint of a smile playing on his lips. 'You started duty at midday today, and brought me my dinner.'

'I did, but you're trying to distract me. You haven't answered my question. Tell me what one leg's no good for,' Bessie coaxed.

'For my old life.' He stared up at the ceiling as he spoke. 'I can't go back to it now.'

'What did you do?'

'Worked on a hill farm in Cumberland, where I come from. Up on the fells with the sheep. You need two good legs to walk about up there. A wooden leg's no good.'

'The artificial legs are good for walking on, but I don't think they'd stand up to jumping around the fells,' she agreed. 'Isn't there something else you can do?'

'I love farming!' he countered. 'It's all I ever wanted to do, right from when I was a lad. I like looking after the animals and working outside.'

'Then perhaps you could think of another way to do it?'

'My old boss would never employ a one-legged man.' His voice was tinged with bitterness.

What could Bessie say? It was true. She knew all the farmers around her home village wouldn't take on a man who couldn't do the job as well as a man with two legs, even if he had lost a leg fighting for his country.

'It is hard for you, Sergeant Rushbrook. But you are alive, and you still have your whole life ahead of you,' Bessie said gently. 'It might not be the one you hoped for, but you mustn't give up. Something will appear for you to do. But you need to get fully better first – up on crutches, and then learning to walk again with an artificial leg.' She fixed her eyes on Sergeant Rushbrook's face. 'Nurse's orders!' she added with a smile.

His face was still as he looked downwards towards the hump made by his remaining foot under the covers. Then he turned to face her.

'It's time you were off-duty, Nurse Carter.

Thank you for talking to me.' He smiled at her. 'And for holding my hand.' He squeezed her hand. 'Goodnight.'

He didn't want to talk about it, that was clear. She had done all she could for now. But she wasn't finished with him. She would do all she could to get him up out of bed and on to crutches, then well enough to go on to St Mary's in Roehampton to be fitted with a new leg. There would be a life worth living for him. Not the one he'd planned, but Bessie had the strongest feeling he would find a role in life which made him happy.

'Goodnight, then, Sergeant Rushbrook.' She stood up. 'I'll be back on duty at midday tomorrow, so I'll see you then. Sleep well.'

### Counting Home The Planes

Peter paced up and down the road, stopping every now and then to listen, straining his ears for the sound of approaching engines. But there was nothing, only the distant caw of a crow.

He glanced over at Marigold who was sitting on the bank making a daisy chain. She looked so relaxed and calm, unlike him. Waiting for the planes to return was always a bittersweet time. Peter loved being there to welcome them home, but at the same time, he dreaded it, too. What sort of condition would the planes be in? Would they all come back?

He sighed. They'd already been waiting nearly

an hour because he could only guess what time the planes might be back. It all depended on where they were sent. The farther away, the longer it took and the later they'd be back.

Over in the distance, Peter could just see the top of the control tower where small figures were standing on the high balcony around the top. If they were out watching and waiting, the planes should be back any time now.

Then it came, the first droning. Peter searched the sky in the distance and could just make out some small specks heading towards them.

'They're coming, Marigold! Look!' He pointed to the specks which were growing bigger by the second.

Marigold jumped to her feet, scattering daisies. 'Where?'

'See, there! We need to count them back.'

Marigold nodded.

'There were twenty-nine went out. Let's hope twenty-nine come home.'

Peter hated it when they didn't all come back. He'd got to know some of the crews and when they didn't make it home after a mission it made him so sad he'd cry about it. He wanted everyone to get through their 30 missions safely so they could go home to America. Not all of them made it – it was a bitter fact of war.

'Here comes the first one!'

Marigold grabbed hold of his arm as a B24 descended down towards the runway. It landed with a bounce and rushed along the runway so fast it looked like it would plough into the corn-field at the far end, but it slowed, turned in time and headed in their direction around the perimeter track on its way back to its own hardstand.

'It's the Laughing Jenny. See the picture and name painted on the nose, Marigold? It looks fine. No holes.'

That wasn't always the case. Sometimes the planes came back damaged, with ragged tail planes, holes in the wings, engines not working or worse.

If they were really badly damaged the landing could be a problem. Peter had once seen a plane land with no wheels! It had skidded along on its belly and ploughed off the runway at the far end. The men had been lucky that time.

'Here comes another,' Marigold said. 'Number two.'

They watched as each plane they came down, and made their way back to where they'd started that morning. Some of them were damaged, with chunks missing out of tails and holes peppered in the fuselage. But at least they'd made it back.

'Twenty-eight. One more to go.' He looked around for a sign of the last plane, but the sky in the distance was empty. His stomach tensed.

'Where's the last one?'

'I don't know!' Peter snapped.

Marigold stared at him, her eyes wide with surprise.

'I'm sorry, I didn't mean to snap at you, I'm just worried.'

'Is Howard's plane back?'

Peter shook his head, gesturing his hand towards the empty hardstand in front of them. Then he listened.

'There!' In the distance a small speck had appeared and was slowly coming towards them. 'Is that them?'

Marigold grabbed hold of his hand and they watched as the plane came in. She was flying lower than the others and just skimmed over the trees in the far distance before she touched down on the runway.

Peter let out a sigh of relief.

'Twenty-nine, Marigold. Twenty-nine out, and twenty nine back, safe!'

As the Peggy Sue rolled down the runway and turned to head back to her hardstand Peter could see what the problem was. Two of her propellers were still. She'd had two engines knocked out, which had made her slower than the others, but she'd got back in one piece.

'Don't forget Bessie's message. You need to tell Howard,' Marigold reminded him.

'Of course. I'll tell him as soon as he gets out, before they go off for debriefing.'

'What's that?'

'It's when they talk about what happened on the mission. If they saw German planes, if they hit the target ... that sort of thing.'

Like all the other boys he knew at school, Peter was fascinated with the planes which filled the skies above Norfolk, and the men who flew them. He'd often talked to Howard about how things worked when he'd been to Orchard Farm to visit Prune.

Peter wanted to know what the men did before and after a mission. What it was like, flying thousands of feet up over enemy territory.

Howard had told him what he could.

Howard was the fourth to climb down out of the plane.

'Hey, Peter!' he called, striding across to talk to them, still wearing his thick sheepskin flying jacket and boots. 'School vacation's started, then?'

'Last Friday,' Peter said. 'What happened to the engine?'

'Had a spat with a Focke-Wulf 190 as we were coming back over the Dutch coast. Nothing to worry about, though, the Peggy Sue brought us safely home. You must be Marigold?' Howard held out his hand to her. 'Prune's told me about you. I'm glad to meet you.'

'Hello,' Marigold said, shyly shaking his hand.

'Hey, Howard, time to go!' one of the Peggy Sue's crew called over as they piled into a jeep brought out to meet them.

'OK!'

'Bessie said to remind you and Clem about tea on Saturday,' Peter told him.

'Thanks, I'm looking forward to it. So I'll see you guys soon.' He smiled and jogged over to the waiting jeep and climbed on board with the rest of his crew.

Marigold laid the last of the knives and forks in their places and stood back to look at the table in case she'd forgotten anything. She'd had to lay eight places instead of the usual six, because they were having visitors.

'You've done a good job.' Bessie put her arm around Marigold's shoulder. 'There's just the bread to slice and then I think we're ready.

Howard and Clem should be here any minute. Are you sure you don't want to go with the others to meet them?'

'No. I'll stay here.'

Marigold had met Howard for a few minutes, but she still felt shy, and there was another one coming, too.

Marigold hadn't met any American servicemen before she came to Rackbridge. She'd seen some in London, but had never spoken to any of them. The only Americans she'd ever seen before had been at the pictures.

'Go and tell Harry to come in for tea,' Bessie said.

'Where is he?'

'In the garden. He wanted to check something before tea.'

Marigold slipped out of the back door and ran quickly past the wash house, with its big copper for heating water where Bessie did the washing, then along the path to the large garden where Harry grew all the vegetables and fruit they ate.

'Harry!' she called.

'Over here.' He was standing in the row of cabbages examining the leaves.

'What are you doing?'

'I'm checking for caterpillar eggs. If they hatch out, they'll eat the lot.'

'Are there any?'

'Not yet, but I've seen the cabbage whites flying around, so I'm keeping an eye out for them.'

'Bessie said to tell you to come in for your tea. The visitors will soon be here.'

'Howard and Clem? It'll be good to see them.

84

You'll like them, Marigold, they're full of fun.'

'I met Howard when his plane landed.'

'Peter told me. They were lucky to get back.'

'He said it was nothing to worry about.'

'He would say that.' Harry patted Marigold's back. 'Come on, then, or there'll be nothing left for us.'

Marigold could hear strange voices coming from inside as she and Harry climbed up the steps to the house. The Americans were here.

She held back behind Harry, lingering in his shadow as she followed him into the house.

'Hello, sir.' Howard and the other American both came over and shook Harry's hand.

'Hello, Howard, Clem. Good to see you both.'

'Here's Marigold, Clem.' Howard smiled at her.

'I'm glad to meet you, Marigold.' Clem held out his hand to her. 'My daughter's about the same age as you.'

'Hello,' Marigold whispered, shaking his hand.

Clem was different to Howard, older and he wore glasses, but both of them were dressed in the smart American uniform.

'Look what Howard and Clem brought us!' Bessie's arms were full with cans of peaches and luncheon meat, and bags of sugar.

'And they brought these for us!' Peter waved some comics and two Hershey bars in the air. 'There's "Superman" and "Captain Marvel"!'

'That's very kind of you,' Harry said. 'We don't expect you to bring us something if you come to tea.'

'We appreciate you having us in your home,' Clem said. 'It means a lot to us.'

'Come on, then, sit yourselves down, everyone,' Dottie said. 'Howard, you sit next to Prune there. Clem, you go next to Peter.'

'Can I get your chair for you?' Clem asked Marigold as she started to pull her own chair out from under the table. She nodded and smiled at Clem.

'Thank you.'

Marigold watched as he and Howard did the same for Bessie, Dottie and Prune before sitting down themselves. The Americans had nice manners and were friendly and polite. Marigold decided she was going to like getting to know them.

## Cowboys

'What do you think of her?' Peter leaned over the side of the pen and scratched Daisy's ears, making Hana flap her wings to keep her balance as she sat on his shoulders like a pirate's parrot.

'She sure is a fine calf.' Howard ran his hand appreciatively along the calf's back.

'A heifer, too,' Harry said. 'We were pleased.'

'Will you keep her?'

'I'd like to, if we can,' Harry said.

'Tell us about your cows in America, Howard,' Peter pleaded.

'What would you like to know?'

'Are they like ours?'

Howard stroked under Daisy's chin and the calf stretched out her neck, enjoying his touch.

'No, our cattle are a bigger, hardier breed. They're used to being outside most of the time. Your girls are much prettier, but they wouldn't do well on our ranch.'

'Do you lasso your cows?' Peter asked.

Howard grinned at him.

'Sure do, when we need to. I guess you don't with these ladies, do you?'

'I don't think they'd like it,' Harry said. 'They're so friendly they'll come to you, so we don't need to catch them.'

'Would you show me how to lasso?' Peter asked. 'Not on Buttercup or Beauty, though, it would scare them.'

'Sure. We'll find something else to lasso. Have you got some rope?'

Peter thought it looked as if the Wild West of the cinema had come to Rackbridge as, five minutes later, Howard stood in the middle of the farmyard effortlessly circling the lasso around his head. The sight of the twirling rope had spooked Hana and she'd flown up to the safety of the barn roof and was watching what was going on.

Round and round the rope went, then effortlessly Howard flung the lasso away from him. It slipped cleanly over the end of Harry's sawing stool, and with one swift movement he pulled the noose tight.

'There you go.' Howard grinned. 'That saw-horse is not far off a cow shape. It's got the four legs, horns, but no tail. You want to have a turn next, Peter?'

'I'll try, but I've never been able to do it before.'

Peter said. He'd love to be able to swing the rope as effortlessly as Howard had, and if he could get it to actually go over what he aimed for, well, that would be swell. Real swell, as Howard and Clem would say!

'No problem. I can soon teach you how, and Harry, too, if you like, sir?'

'Turn us into cowboys?' Harry laughed. 'Why not?'

'OK, first up, you need to hold your rope like so.' Howard held the loop in one hand and the other end coiled up in the other. 'Stand in front of your target, let your wrist relax and slowly start to swing the rope, right to left, like this.' Howard brought the rope up and swung it above his head. 'Cast the loop forward.'

Peter watched as he swung the loop forward and once again sent it straight over the sawhorse's horns.

'Then pull the loop tight.' Howard shrugged his shoulders. 'Nothing to it, once you know how. Whose turn first?'

'Let's see you have a go, Peter,' Harry suggested.

Howard guided Peter, helping him to start off holding the rope the right way.

'You've got it,' Howard said. 'Remember, relax your wrist and swing it above your head.'

Concentrating hard, Peter brought the rope up and started the swinging motion. He didn't have to look at it to know it wasn't as good as Howard's had been.

'You're doing fine. When you're ready, cast the loop forward on to the sawhorse.'

Peter launched the loop in the direction of the

sawhorse, but it landed short with a thud on the ground.

He sighed. Howard made it look so easy, but it wasn't.

'Good try, Peter. Have another go!' Howard encouraged him. 'It took me weeks of practice to get it right. You'll get there if you keep at it.'

Howard and Harry leaned against the gate leading into the orchard and watched Peter practising over and over again.

'He's getting the hang of it better than me,' Harry said. 'He won't give up until he gets there.'

'Practice is the only way. That's what I did after my pa taught me – kept on practising until I could do it every time.' Howard looked at Harry. 'I'd like to ask you something, sir. You know the Peggy Sue lost two engines on our last mission?'

Harry nodded.

'She's being fixed up, and we'll have a trial flight in a day or two to check her out before we go on the next mission. I wondered if Peter would like to come with us. We'd only be flying up to the coast and back, and I know he'd love it, but I didn't want to ask him without checking with you first. I'd take real good care of him.'

'I don't doubt that.' Harry smiled. 'But it's Bessie. I know what she'd say about it. No!' He rubbed the back of his neck. 'But it's a grand chance to fly and I think the lad should take it, if he wants to.'

'What about Bessie? I don't want to upset her,' Howard said.

Harry patted him on the shoulder.

'You leave her to me. If Peter's happy to do it,

we'll keep it between ourselves, and she'll only know afterwards when it's over and done with.'

He would deal with the aftermath when it came. This was too good an opportunity for Peter to miss.

'You sure?' Howard asked.

'Yes. Come on, you'd better tell Peter...'

'Really? You'll take me flying in a Liberator?' Peter stared at Howard, hardly believing what he'd just heard.

'You bet, Peter.'

'Yes, please, Howard! Thank you. Thank you!'

All the times he'd stood and watched the Liberators take off and come back, he'd never imagined he'd get the chance to fly in one. It was wonderful!

'There's one thing you must promise me, Peter,' Harry said. 'You mustn't tell Bessie what's going on. If she knows, she won't let you go.'

'But...' Peter began.

'She'd be too worried about it, lad. I think you should grab the chance to do it, if it's what you want to do. We'll tell her when it's over and you're back. I know Howard will look after you.'

Grace opened her eyes, shielding them from the bright sunlight, and saw Helen coming towards her smiling and waving, her auburn curls bouncing as she walked. She got up from the bench where she'd been sitting overlooking the lake in St James's Park.

'Helen!'

This was the first time she'd seen her friend since she'd taken Marigold to Norfolk in July. Helen had been back for a few days now, but with their conflicting shift patterns at the hospital, they hadn't yet had a chance to meet.

'It's lovely to see you.' Helen put her arms around Grace and gave her a hug. 'How are you?'

'I'm fine. Glad to have the day off.'

She stepped back and looked at Grace.

'You should take a holiday, too. I feel like a new woman now.'

'It was good?'

Helen smiled.

'It was marvellous! I didn't want it to end, but, of course, it did.' She shrugged. 'We both have work to do to fight this war.'

'Shall we walk around the lake?' Grace linked her arm through Helen's and they walked in the warm August sunshine.

They weren't the only ones enjoying the park on a Sunday afternoon, there were plenty of families out with their children. Just like she and John used to do with Marigold. St James's Park had been one of their favourite places.

'Have you heard from Marigold?' Helen asked.

'Yes, she's settled in well and seems to be enjoying it. She's been helping out on the farm. She even taught a calf how to drink milk from a pail.'

Helen laughed.

'It's a wee bit different from round here, then.' She stopped walking and her eyes met Grace's. 'You did the right thing sending her to live in Norfolk. I know it wasn't easy for you, but she's safe there.'

Grace's throat tightened and she swallowed hard, forcing back the swell of emotion threatening to overwhelm her. She nodded and waited until she was sure she could talk without crying.

'I miss her so much, Helen!'

'I know.' Helen squeezed her arm. 'Let's walk.'

They walked in silence for a short way, before Helen spoke again.

'Bessie seemed like a lovely woman. I only met her for a few minutes, but she had a real warmth about her. Her face when she saw Marigold! I thought she was going to scoop her up in her arms there and then and give her a huge welcoming hug.'

'Did she?'

'No.' Helen laughed. 'But I could see in her eyes she wanted to. She just shook Marigold's hand instead.'

Grace took in a sharp breath. What had Bessie thought when she saw Marigold? It must have been hard to hold back, not to let Marigold know who she was. Bessie was such a warm-hearted, loving person, it must have been dreadful for her.

'You've no worry about Marigold not being cared for properly with Bessie,' Helen affirmed.

'What about Marigold? How was she when you left her?'

'Quiet. I think she was resigned to it by then. After we left you at Liverpool Street, there was no going back and she seemed to accept it.'

'I hated seeing her so upset.'

'I know, but she soon settled down once we were on the way. It's not easy for wee children being evacuated, but thousands of them have been, and it's the safest thing for them right now.'

Grace nodded.

'I keep telling myself that. I'll go and see her eventually.'

'Why...' Helen began and then stopped. 'Listen!'

They both stood still, hardly daring to breathe, and listened to the ominous droning sound which was coming nearer and nearer. All around them, other people were stopping and listening, too.

'Doodlebug!' someone shouted.

Grace scanned the sky looking for it, her heart beating harder and faster.

'There!' Helen pointed as it came into view travelling fast over them heading north. 'It's still going.'

Seconds later, the doodlebug's drone altered to a 'phut, phut' sound, and then the engine cut out, and it started its deadly glide downwards to somewhere out of sight of them, behind trees and tall buildings in the distance

Grace closed her eyes. They were safe from that one, but some poor souls were about to have their world blown apart. She clung on to Helen's arm tightly as they waited for the explosion.

Then it came. Whoomph! They couldn't see the flash as it exploded, only the pall of smoke rising high into the air marking the spot where innocent people would have been killed or injured.

'Grace?' Helen's voice was shaky.

Grace looked at her friend, whose face had gone chalk white.

'Are you all right?'

Helen nodded.

Grace put her arms around her friend and held her close. It was a harsh reminder of why she'd

93

had to send Marigold away. With things like that falling out of the sky, London wasn't a safe place for her daughter.

### *Flying Lessons*

Peter stared up at the Peggy Sue. She was beautiful, and so much bigger close up! He could still hardly believe he was going to fly in her, and had had trouble sleeping the night before for thinking about it.

'OK, Peter, are you ready to fly?'

He nodded.

'I just wanna double-check your harness and 'chute.' Howard tested the buckles on the parachute harness Peter was wearing. 'Remember, I promised Harry I'd take good care of you. Bessie still doesn't know about this?'

'No. I didn't like not telling her about it, but Harry said she wouldn't let me come if she knew.'

'It's because she cares about you. My mom's just the same, she worries about me.'

'Bessie's not my mother.'

'No, but she's looking after you for your mother. I guess that's even harder, in a way, because she feels responsible for you.'

'All aboard, you guys!' Walt Stewart, the pilot, called over to them.

Peter's heart was beating fast, and his legs suddenly seemed to go soft as he followed Howard to the belly of the Peggy Sue, where the bomb-bay doors lay open.

'This is where we get in, Peter. You have to remember it's where we'd get out if we needed to. Understand? We'd jump from here and parachute down.'

Peter nodded. He hoped they wouldn't need to jump, but he'd remember, just in case.

Howard climbed in first, and held out a hand to help Peter as he made his way inside. Standing upright, Peter was surprised at the difference between the smooth outside skin of the Peggy Sue compared with the inside. It was a network of joins, looking like ribs, where each part of the plane was attached to the next bit and riveted strongly together.

'OK?'

'It looks so different in here.'

'Yup, I guess so. You kinda get used to it. Walt wondered if you'd like to go to the cockpit for take-off?'

'Yes, please!'

'First, we need to fix you up with some head-phones and a throat-mike. Then you'll be able to hear us and talk back, once we're airborne.'

Peter couldn't stop smiling as he followed Howard along the length of the Peggy Sue to the cockpit a few minutes later. He was dressed up with his harness and parachute, and had the headphones and throat-mike on to complete the set of an airman. He'd have so much to tell Harry about when he got home!

'Welcome aboard, Peter,' Walt said when Peter arrived at the cockpit. 'John's flying co-pilot with us.'

'Thanks for letting me come.'

'It's a pleasure. If you want to stay in here for take-off you can kneel down here between our seats. OK?'

Howard laid a hand on Peter's shoulder.

'I'll go back to my base for take-off, and I'll see you once we're up.'

Peter nodded and kneeled down where Walt had indicated. He watched every move the pilots made as they prepared to take-off.

When the four engines roared into life the whole plane seemed to come alive, shuddering from the throbbing engines. Peter listened in as Walt talked to the control tower and, once they'd been given clearance to go, they started to move. They were the only plane going out on a check-out flight that afternoon. The others had left on a mission earlier in the morning.

At the end of the runway they turned to face the long ribbon of tarmac. Walt applied the brakes and revved the engines hard. The whole plane thrummed and throbbed with the noise of the engines, and it seemed as if she were straining to go, like a dog desperate to be off its lead.

Then, on word from the control tower, Walt released the brakes and they were off. The Peggy Sue hurtled down the runway, faster and faster. When it seemed as if they could go no faster, Walt eased back the control column and the plane's nose tilted skyward.

Peter felt the strangest feeling as they swung upwards, a sudden lightness. His stomach felt like it had been left behind on the ground. It quickly caught up with him and then Peter knew he was actually flying! There were clunks and whirrs as the undercarriage came up and the flaps came in. Peter felt his ears tighten and pop. Howard had warned him he'd need to keep swallowing as they went up and down, but he'd forgotten with the excitement and wonder of it all.

'Peter, how are you doing?' Walt's voice came through the headset.

'Great. It's wonderful!' He smiled at Walt, who grinned back and gave him the thumbs-up sign.

'We're going to take her out for about an hour, do some circuits round the base first, then go up to the coast and you can see the ocean. Howard said you'd like to buzz your folks?'

'They're going to look out for me.'

'You live on the farm to the east of the base, right?'

'Yes. Orchard Farm.'

'I know it. Howard will take you down to the nose turret. You'll get a good view and they'll be able to see you, too.'

Sitting in the nose turret a short while later, with just the Plexiglas between him and the air, made Peter feel he was as close to flying as a bird could be. He had the sort of view Hana would see if she flew high enough. Everything looked so small and neat, the tree tops green and the fields and hedges spread out like the patchwork quilt on his bed.

'OK, Peter, we're on approach,' Howard told him. 'Orchard Farm's just up ahead. I can see the elms on the lane. Where did Harry say they will be?'

'In the yard. He should be there with Bessie and Marigold.' Peter fished in his trouser pocket and pulled out a scarlet scarf. 'Dottie gave me this to wave. She wanted to make sure they could see me. She and Prune are going to look out for us in the field near the woods where they're working.'

Howard grinned.

'I told Walt we should give them a buzz, too. You'd better start waving, Peter, we're going in!'

'Bessie! Marigold! Come out here, quick!'

Bessie stopped turning the handle of the mangle and turned to Harry, who had stuck his head around the wash-house door.

'What's the matter?'

'Just come, or we'll miss it.' He beckoned them. 'Come on!'

'What on earth's going on, Harry?' Bessie repeated.

'You'll see. Just hurry up.'

Bessie and Marigold followed Harry out into the cooler air. It was a relief to be out of the steamy heat of the wash house.

'What are we supposed to be looking at?'

'You'll see, any minute now,' Harry said. 'All we have to do is stand here and wait.'

'Harry Rushbrook, I've got a lot of washing to get through! If you think I've got time to play silly games you've got another thing...'

Her words failed at the sound of engines approaching. Loud, fast engines. She whipped round to face the direction from which they were coming, and gasped. A Liberator was heading towards them, so low it would only just have cleared the church tower. Was it going to crash?

'Harry!' Bessie gasped and clutched his arm tightly.

'It's all right, love. Look!' He pointed to the front of the plane where they could see someone waving something red in the front nose turret.

Harry waved back, laughing and smiling.

'Wave, Bessie, Marigold! Come on, wave at the lad!'

Bessie glanced at Harry's face, which was beaming as he looked up at the plane. Had he taken leave of his senses?

Marigold jumped up and down, waving madly.

'Who's in there?'

Harry's reply was drowned out by the noise of the Liberator bearing down. As it flew straight over the top of them, they all instinctively ducked down.

Harry laughed.

'Did you see him?'

Bessie's heart was hammering.

'What's going on here, Harry?' Her voice came out wobbly. 'Who was waving at us?'

'Peter!'

Bessie's knees went soft and she thought for a moment her legs were going to buckle.

'Peter? Peter's up there? Flying in that thing?'

Harry nodded.

'He had the chance to go for a trip in the Peggy Sue.'

'When was this arranged?' Bessie's voice sounded surprisingly calm. 'Why wasn't I told?'

'Here they come again!' Marigold shouted, jumping up and down and waving as the huge plane came rushing towards them, barely higher than the elms lining the lane. 'Look at Peter, he's waving to us!'

Bessie stood, her arms hanging limply at her side, while Harry and Marigold both waved their arms above their heads. She could just make out Peter's face looking down at them as the plane passed over. When the plane was lost from view, Bessie stalked back to the wash house without saying a word.

She slammed the door shut behind her and leaning back against the door she closed her eyes. Harry had a lot to answer for when she could trust herself to speak to him.

She grabbed the handle of the mangle and started to turn it with far more force than it needed.

'Here he comes!' Dottie squealed, grabbing hold of Prune's arm tightly.

'Ow, let go!' Prune pushed off her friend's hand and stared at the plane bearing down on them.

'Come on, wave!' Dottie pulled the pink scarf off her hair and waved it in the air. 'Look at the red up in the nose turret. That's Peter waving my scarf!'

Prune swallowed down the bubble of unease welling up in her throat and joined in, waving both her arms over her head back and forth in a cross motion. Howard was in the plane, too. Although she couldn't see him, no doubt he could see her and would tell her so next time she saw him.

As the plane thundered towards them Prune had to fight the urge to throw herself on the ground for fear it was going to hit them. But it didn't – it roared overhead with its four engines making the air and ground around them throb.

'Did you see his face?' Dottie asked.

Prune nodded.

'Just for a moment.'

They stood in silence watching the plane head northwards, growing smaller and smaller, until it was gone.

'I bet Peter's loving it,' Dottie said. 'It was good of Howard to arrange this for him.'

'He's a kind man.' They turned and started to walk back up the track to the woods where they were working. 'I wish it was the only sort of flying he did, Dottie. No more dangerous missions over the Germans, with their big guns pointing at them.'

Dottie put her arm through Prune's.

'I know. We all wish they didn't have to do it.'

'You know what some of the men call the planes, don't you? Flying coffins.'

'There's only one way to deal with it, Prune.' Dottie stopped and turned to look back in the direction the plane had gone. 'You've just got to take it one day at a time.' She gently squeezed Prune's arm. 'Cheer up. Remember, we've got the Hundredth Mission party to look forward to.'

Prune smiled.

'I know, you're right, but it's the way I am. I care about Howard very much. Sometimes I wish I could be like you, carefree and easy, but I'm not.'

Dottie shrugged.

'Well, we're all different.'

'But don't you wish for...' Prune paused. 'A

proper beau? To marry, even?'

Dottie shook her head.

'No. Come on, we've got work to do.'

Was Dottie's attitude the right way to be, Prune wondered. She certainly saved herself the worry and heartache which Prune went through every time Howard flew on a mission.

But knowing Howard brought her a great deal of happiness, too, and she couldn't have one without the other, at least while the war was on. If it hadn't been for the war they'd never have met. Howard was worth every minute of worry, even if it was hard.

Bessie was folding a sheet into four, ready to put it through the mangle, when the wash house door opened and Harry stepped inside.

'Are you all right, Bess?'

Bessie ignored his question.

'Where's Marigold?'

'She helped me take the cows out of the barn and then I sent her to collect any eggs.'

'What were the cows doing indoors at this time of day?'

'I thought they might get frightened by the plane if they were outside. They're fine.'

Bessie fed the sheet into the mangle and started turning the handle so it ran between the rollers and out the other side.

'So what have you got to say for yourself?'

Harry looked at Bessie, concerned.

'Firstly, I'm sorry I upset you. I knew how you'd feel about Peter going flying. I knew what you'd say.'

102

'No!' Bessie interrupted him. 'I would have said, no.'

'I was right, then.' A smile flickered across Harry's mouth. 'But I said yes. The lad was desperate to go, Bess, and it was a good chance for him. You know I'd go, too, if I got the chance.'

Bessie shook her head.

'I thought Howard was a nice, sensible young man. Wait till I see him!'

Harry held up his hand.

'Hang on a minute. You've got the wrong idea. Howard wanted to ask you, too, but I told him not to. He wasn't happy about you not knowing.' He paused for a moment. 'Howard will take great care of Peter. We can trust him.'

Bessie stopped turning the handle and stared at Harry.

'That's not the point! Things can go wrong. Planes don't have to get shot at by Germans to crash, they can do it all on their own, Harry! You've seen the smoke going up when they do, the same as me.'

'Nothing's going to happen.'

'It could, though.'

'And I could get run over next time I go into the village. Sometimes you've got to take a risk.' Harry rubbed the back of his neck. 'It was a chance for Peter to do something he really wanted. Goodness knows what's going to happen to him in the future, or if he'll ever see his parents again.'

'Don't you understand?' Bessie gripped the handle so tightly her knuckles turned pale. 'I gave my word to his parents I'd look after him. Who knows what's happened to them, or where they are.' She took a deep breath. 'Or even if they're still alive. But I promised them I would look after Peter! If anything happens to him...'

'It won't.' Harry reached out to touch Bessie's hand. 'I know you promised to take care of Peter, and you do, very well. But he's got to have the chance to live his life to the full, too. Sometimes you've got to let things go.'

Bessie sighed. There was no point in being angry now. Peter was up there, flying in the Peggy Sue, and all she could do was wait and hope he came back in one piece.

'If there's a next time, I want to know about it, Harry. No more hiding, understand?'

'Yes, ma'am.' Harry gave a mock salute and held his arms out wide to her. 'I'll go to the base and meet Peter if you like.'

'No, I'll go.' Bessie walked into Harry's open arms and leaned her head against his chest as he wrapped his arms around her.

### A Promise Made

Peter couldn't take his eyes off the sea. It was a deep sapphire blue and had just the hint of waves rolling across its surface in lines towards the shore. It was perfect, and so beautiful. He'd spent most of the flight looking down on the world from inside the Plexiglas nose of thse Peggy Sue, loving the way everything looked from up there.

'Peter? We're going to start heading back to base

now.' Walt's voice came through the headphones as the Peggy Sue began to bank around and turned towards the shore. 'Would you like to come up to the cockpit and have a go at flying for a bit?'

'Me, fly? Really?'

'Sure, if you'd like to.'

Walt didn't have to ask twice. With a last look at the sea, Peter made his way back up to the cockpit, where John, the co-pilot, got out of his seat and beckoned for him to take his place.

Peter's heart was pounding as he climbed into his seat. Did Walt really think he could fly the plane?

'OK, Peter, you take hold of the control column, like me.' Walt nodded towards the co-pilot's controls.

Peter tentatively took the column in his hands and held it just like Walt.

'Great, Peter. Now, hold it steady and keep your eye on this.' Walt pointed to the artificial horizon indicator. 'It will keep us straight and level. OK?'

Peter nodded.

'Right, then, you have control.'

Walt took his hands off his control column and grinned at Peter.

'You're flying the Peggy Sue, Peter. No looping the loop, though, this old ship couldn't take it.'

Peter could hardly believe it, he was flying a plane. He was terrified, but so happy at the same time. He held on to the column as if his life depended on it, sitting completely still in case he jogged the controls.

'You're doing a great job.' Howard patted Peter gently on the shoulder. 'You can relax a bit;

nothing will happen.'

Peter nodded and tried to relax, loosening the tension in his shoulders.

For the next five minutes Peter was in control of the Peggy Sue. He flew her straight and level, concentrating hard on the artificial horizon indicator and keeping the column still. If he hadn't been so focused on what he was doing, he'd have been smiling so hard his face would have ached!

Part of him was relieved when Walt took back control and he slipped out of the co-pilot's seat. His arms and legs were stiff and aching from holding them so still while he was flying, even though he'd tried to relax.

'How was that?' Howard asked.

'I loved it,' Peter said. 'But I was scared!'

Howard clapped him on the back.

'You did a great job.'

Peter stood between the pilots as they headed back towards the base. They made flying the Peggy Sue look so easy. One day, he thought, he'd like to be able to fly like them.

As they neared the base, Walt heard over the radio that they should join the incoming formation of Rackbridge Liberators on their way back from a mission. Peter watched out of the window as they seamlessly joined the formation and began the circuit around the base as they waited their turn to land.

He'd watched these formations many times from the ground, but flying as part of one was something else. It made Peter feel part of something, like a big creature made of many parts, doing its best to fight off the enemy.

The first Liberator landed just as Bessie arrived at the place where Peter always came to watch the planes, close by Peggy Sue's hardstand. She heaved her bike on to its stand and stood by the hedge watching them land. She'd seen the planes coming in the distance as she'd biked along. They'd looked like a flock of huge birds coming home to roost.

Bessie watched as each Liberator came into land, some of them battle-scarred with bullet holes and ragged tails, or with knocked-out engines, but at least they'd made it home. Had they all come back? Bessie wondered.

She shuddered. The thought of men going out and not coming back was heartbreaking, but she knew it happened. There were ten men in each plane, all of them someone's son, husband or father, making too many lives lost every time a plane didn't make it home.

Where Peter was, Bessie had no idea. Howard had told Harry the flight would be about an hour, and that was almost up now. She'd arrived early, desperate to see Peter and know he was safe.

The sight of him in the nose of the Peggy Sue had been such a shock, she'd had no idea what was going on. It was only her and Marigold who hadn't known, Harry had admitted. Marigold wasn't told because they thought she might let the secret out, and Bessie knew very well why he hadn't said anything to her. She would have said no.

But would that have been the right thing to do? Perhaps it was better she hadn't known...

Bessie's protectiveness of Peter had started the instant she saw him coming down the gangplank off the ship which had carried him away from the clutches of the Nazis. He was a seven-year-old with grubby, crumpled clothes, carrying a single brown suitcase. Bessie's heart had melted at the sight of him.

The first few months had been hard for Peter. He'd only been able to speak a few words of English and they knew little German, only a few phrases which Harry had picked up in the trenches. But Peter had been determined to learn English and now no-one would suspect he hadn't spoken it all his life.

At first, Peter's parents had kept in touch by letter, telling him they were safe and well. They'd always sent a note to her and Harry in each letter, too, thanking them for looking after their son. But the letters suddenly stopped coming. They had no idea why his parents stopped writing, where they were or what was happening to them. Bessie thought about them often and desperately hoped he'd be reunited with them one day, when all this was over. Until then, it was her job to look after Peter for them.

The sound of engines turning into the hard-stand near Bessie brought her thoughts back to the present. It was the Peggy Sue.

Peter was back.

Howard and Peter were the first ones out of the plane, appearing feet first from its underbelly. They headed straight over to where Bessie stood waiting on the other side of the hedge. As they got closer she saw they both looked guilty.

She crossed her arms and waited for them to speak first.

'Good afternoon, Bessie,' Howard said. 'I owe you an apology.'

'I'm sorry I didn't tell you,' Peter added, his grey eyes wide with concern. 'Harry told me not to, because you wouldn't have let me go.'

'He was right. I wouldn't have.' Bessie looked hard at both of them, the expression on their faces told her they were bracing themselves for what she had to say.

'But Harry told me all the reasons why he thought you should. Firstly, because you wanted to.' She smiled. 'Secondly, because it was a good chance for you to fly, and thirdly, because Howard would be with you and take care of you. They're all good reasons. But I would still have said no, because I worry and care what happens to you.'

'It was all right, though, Bessie. Nothing happened to me. I'm back safe and in one piece.' Peter held out his arms wide and grinned. 'It was wonderful up there! Everything looked so small and neat. We even went out over the sea and I flew the Peggy Sue for a bit on the way back.'

'It's true, ma'am,' Howard said. 'He took control of her and did a fine job.'

'I want to be a pilot when I'm older,' Peter said. 'And fly a Liberator to help win the war.'

'I hope this war will be over long before you're old enough to fly.' Bessie caught Howard's eye. He nodded briefly to her, no doubt thinking the same thing. 'But you could still learn in peacetime, though, and fly people around for pleasure.'

'I could take you flying, Bessie. You'd love it.'

'Me? I don't know. It frightened me enough seeing you waving down at us.'

'I guess you'd like it if you tried, Bessie,' Howard said. 'It's beautiful up there.'

'Perhaps, one day, I will.' Bessie smiled.

## The Worst Of News

Bessie woke from a dream in which Peter had been madly waving the red scarf, trapped inside the nose of a Liberator as it spiralled downwards, smoke trailing from its engines. It was only a dream, Bessie kept telling herself, one which played on her fears from the day before, when thankfully nothing had gone wrong. But the fear of what could have happened had haunted her, and kept rattling around her mind, stopping her from going back to sleep.

Beside her, Harry breathed deeply in his sleep, oblivious to her wakefulness. She should get up, Bessie thought. Read for a bit until she was tired. She hadn't had a chance to read her old diary again for a while. Now the house was quiet was a good time and it would take her mind off the dream.

Swinging her feet out of bed, Bessie pushed her feet into her slippers and wrapped her dressing-gown around her. She took the diary from the chest of drawers and padded out of the room, carefully closing the door behind her.

Bessie lit the lamp and settled down in an armchair by the stove. Opening her diary at the place she'd marked with a piece of ribbon, her eyes fell on the first words and her stomach instantly clenched into a tight knot.

*March 23, 1918*
*Terrible, terrible news.*

Bessie snapped the book shut. She didn't need to read on. That day was etched in her memory.

'Nurse Carter?'

Bessie stopped tucking in the clean sheet and looked at Sister Williams who'd come to stand by her side.

'Matron wants to see you in her office.'

Bessie caught Ethel's eye across the bed. What did Matron want to see her for?

'Hurry along. I'll take over this for you,' Sister said, stepping into place and tucking in the rest of the sheet.

'Yes, Sister.' Bessie smiled at Ethel then walked out of the ward and along the hallway to the small sitting-room which was Matron's office.

Bessie stopped outside, checked her cap was straight, smoothed down her apron and then tapped on the door.

'Come in!' Matron called.

Taking a steadying breath, Bessie opened the door and stepped inside. Her gaze immediately fell on the person sitting opposite Matron in one of the armchairs in front of the fire. Her father! What was he doing here? She noticed her father didn't look her directly in the eye as he normally did. Something was wrong.

'Nurse Carter, your father...' Matron tilted her

head briefly towards him '...has come with some bad news, I'm afraid.' She cleared her throat and continued. 'I'm sorry to tell you, Nurse Carter, your brother has been killed in France.'

Bessie heard the words come out of Matron's mouth. Saw her lips move. But she didn't want to take them in. These weren't words she ever wanted to hear, not about Robert. Never.

'I'm so sorry, my dear.' Matron stood up and laid her hand on Bessie's arm. 'Your mother needs you home.'

Bessie looked at her father. His eyes now held hers for a few moments before he looked down at his hands again, which were clasping his hat so tightly his knuckles had turned pale. Bessie saw how shadowed and bleak with sorrow his eyes looked. It was written on his face for all to see. He'd lost his only son. Robert had gone to France and wouldn't be coming back. Just like...

Bessie's legs suddenly felt like they were made of jelly.

'Come and sit down for a moment.' Matron held Bessie's arm in a firm grasp and led her over to the armchair she'd just vacated. 'Stay there until you're ready. I think some tea's in order here.'

Matron didn't wait for an answer. She bustled out of the room, closing the door quietly behind her.

Bessie's throat was tight with emotion.

'How? When?' She sounded hoarse.

'The twentieth. We don't know how yet. I expect there will be a letter telling us more.'

Bessie reached out and touched his hands.

'How's Mother?'

'She wants you home, Bessie. Just for a bit.' He paused. 'I know you're doing good work here, but we need you to come home for a while. Matron's given her permission.'

Bessie nodded. If her mother needed her at home, then she had to go. But she feared there was precious little she could do to make her mother feel better. Nothing she could do or say would bring Robert back.

The first thing Bessie noticed as they reached home was that the curtains were drawn. It was only one o'clock, yet they were closed shut. She'd seen this so many times. Parents who received the dreaded buff-brown envelopes telling them their sons were no more shut the curtains and blocked out the world, because they were in mourning.

Bessie glanced at her father who walked silently along beside her. He hadn't said much all the journey. Not on the walk to the station, or on the train, and not now on the final leg home as they walked through the village back to their blacksmith's forge. Her father was a quiet man, but he seemed to have retreated inside himself.

The door flew open as Bessie raised her hand to turn the doorknob, and the sight of her mother standing in the shadowy inside shocked her. She had aged. Her usual upright stance was bowed. She looked haggard and weary.

'Bessie!' Her mother's voice was raw, and her blue eyes were red and puffy from crying.

'Mother.' Bessie stepped inside and reached out and touched her mother's hands.

Her mother pulled her towards her and began to cry, huge heaving sobs which shook her whole body.

'I'll get through to the forge.' Her father closed the front door behind him, plunging the room into a gloomy dusk befitting the atmosphere of grief filling the room.

Bessie looked over her mother's shoulder and nodded at him. He looked relieved to go. He would feel safer amongst the familiar heat and smell of the forge, where he could deal with his own feelings. And he still needed to work if the family were to eat. Keeping busy was the best way to deal with it, Bessie understood well enough.

'Bessie?'

A tugging at her skirt drew Bessie's attention down to her little sister who stood staring up at her, her eyes wide and glistening with unshed tears. Poor little mite, Bessie thought. Grace was only three, and wouldn't properly understand what was going on.

'Hello, my girl.' Bessie reached out her free hand and ruffled the little girl's wavy blonde hair. 'Come on, Mother. Let's get you a cup of tea. Sit down, I'll see to it.'

She led her to the armchair by the stove and helped her sit down. Then she checked the fire was banked up and pushed the kettle on to the hotplate to boil. The best thing she could do was be practical. As much as she wanted to cry herself, she mustn't. Not now, not here. She'd save her tears for when she was alone. She had to be strong for the sake of the family. Robert would

114

have wanted her to do that.

Swallowing hard to try and relieve the tightness in her throat, Bessie forced herself to smile.

'I'd best take my coat off, then.' Her voice sounded artificially high, but no-one seemed to notice. Her mother was bowed in the chair, silent tears running down her cheeks, and little Grace had settled down on the rag rug in front of the stove and was playing with her raggy doll at their mother's feet.

Two days later, Bessie watched her mother as she read the letter the postman had just brought. It was the one they'd been waiting for.

Her mother's pale face sagged, then crumpled as she let the letter drop on to the table.

'My boy!' she wailed, her shoulders shaking as she slumped forward in her chair, her head on her arms.

Her father picked up the letter and read it in silence, his mouth a grim straight line. When he'd finished, he drew in a sharp breath.

'Stay with your mother, Bessie.' He handed her the letter and laid his hand briefly on his wife's shoulder, then went out of the door back to the forge. They could hear the sound of hammer beating iron, over and over again.

Bessie steeled herself and looked at the letter.

*Dear Mr and Mrs Carter*, she read.

*It is with my deepest sympathy that I write you this letter. Your son, Robert Carter, was a fine young man who was well liked by all the company. He was a conscientious worker who shall be greatly missed by all of us all.*

*Robert was killed by a sniper while digging out a*

115

*fellow soldier who had been buried in a shell explosion. Rest assured he did not suffer in any way.*

*Yours sincerely,*

*2nd Lieutenant Charles Pearson.*

A sniper. Killed by a sniper while helping someone else. Bessie bit hard on her bottom lip. It was so typical of Robert to help others, only this time he'd paid a high price for it. Bessie tasted blood. She wouldn't cry; she mustn't. At least it would have been over quickly for him.

'He didn't suffer, Mother. We can be grateful for that.'

Her mother's shoulders stiffened.

'He's dead. How can you expect me to be grateful for a sniper's bullet?' She spat out her words and glared at Bessie. 'Get out of here, I want to be alone.'

Her mother was in no state to reason with. Bessie couldn't tell her there were far worse ways for a soldier to die. Slow, painful deaths. From wounds that maimed a soldier, took him through painful operations, brought him back to Blighty and still killed him in the end. Her mother didn't want to know that. If Robert had to die, then a clean sniper's bullet was the kindest way.

'Come on, Grace. Let's go out for a walk.' Bessie held her hand out to the little girl who looked from Bessie to her mother and back in confusion. 'It's all right, my dear. Mother just needs some time on her own.'

Grace nodded and slid off the armchair where she'd been sitting watching the whole proceedings, her raggy doll clasped tightly in her arms.

116

At the forge, a shower of tiny molten sparks flew off the metal as Bessie's father's hammer hit it. Again and again he hammered, working at the metal, moulding and forming it. He was so focused on his work, he wasn't aware of Bessie and Grace standing in the doorway.

'Father,' Bessie said when he eventually stopped hammering and plunged the hot iron into a bucket of cold water, making it sizzle and hiss.

He looked up and Bessie saw the pain in his eyes.

'Mother wants to be alone, so I'm going to take Grace out for a walk. I think she could do with some fresh air.'

Her father nodded and wiped his brow with his sleeve.

'I'll look in on her in a while. She's taken it hard.'

'I know.'

'Don't fret yourself, Bessie. It's the shock of it...' His voice wavered. He cleared his throat. 'You run along now.'

Bessie felt her hand being tugged and looked down at Grace. She'd been such a quiet and patient little girl since Bessie had arrived home, playing quietly on her own, making no demands on anyone, clearly aware of the atmosphere in the house.

'Are you ready, Grace?'

The little girl nodded.

'We'll see you later.' Bessie smiled at her father. 'Come on, then, Grace.'

For the first time since she'd come home, Bessie was aware of the birds singing. There was the smell of spring in the air, and a sense of the world reawakening after the winter. She breathed in deeply, filling her lungs with fresh, clean air. It felt such a relief to be outside again.

It seemed Grace felt the same. The further they'd walked from the house the more talkative she became, speaking about the things they could see, clumps of frogspawn in the pond, white clouds dotting the blue sky. Grace stopped often, looking carefully at anything which caught her interest. Walking at Grace's slow pace gave Bessie a different view of the world, one in which life was still going on outside the gloomy room where their mother sat, wracked with grief for Robert.

What did Grace make of it all, Bessie wondered. Did she fully understand what had happened? She had no idea what Grace had been told.

'Grace,' Bessie began as they started walking again after looking at smashed snail shells scattered around a thrush's anvil. 'Do you understand what's happened to Robert?'

Grace looked up at Bessie and nodded.

'He's dead.'

'Yes, he is.' Bessie put one hand on the little girl's shoulder. 'Do you know that means he can't come home again? We won't see him any more?'

'Never again?'

'Yes, never again. He's buried in France now. He'll stay there for ever.'

Grace stared at Bessie, her deep blue eyes wide, while she absorbed what she'd been told. Bessie expected her to say something, but she didn't, she just nodded and put her hand in Bessie's.

She kept quietly by Bessie's side for a few

minutes until something in the hedge caught her attention, and then let go of Bessie's hand and skipped over to it, looking as if they'd not just had a conversation about their dead brother.

Bessie sighed. Thank goodness she seemed to accept it. Whether Grace fully understood the meaning of what had happened Bessie couldn't be sure. But at least she'd explained it to her. She hoped it made sense.

Grace hadn't seen much of Robert for the past year since he'd been called up. Just a few fleeting visits before he'd been sent to France. Did she really remember him? Would she remember him as she grew up? She wouldn't have the memories of him to look back on that Bessie had. Robert would become a faint shadowy memory for Grace. Just a brother in a photo on the mantelpiece.

But he had been so much more, and Grace would never know. Bessie's throat tightened. A sniper's bullet had stolen Robert from them all, taken away their parent's son and their brother. Bessie didn't even try to top the tears running down her cheeks...

Martha Carter's back looked ramrod straight as she walked out of church, arm-in-arm with Bessie's father, after the service on Sunday morning. Walking behind with Grace, Bessie was glad to see it. The days since they'd found out about how Robert had died had been long and painful. Her mother's grief had been raw and she'd sunk into a deep, dark pit.

But suddenly this morning she'd been first up, with the table set and breakfast made when

Bessie had come down. Her mother had come back almost to her former self, except for a veil of sadness about her eyes.

Bessie held Grace back, watching her parents accept the kind words from their friends. People who'd briefly come to the house, bringing with them plates of food to eat, caring that the family shouldn't starve while they grieved for Robert. Those same simple kindnesses Bessie knew her mother had done for other families who had been unfortunate enough to receive a telegram telling them their son or husband wouldn't be coming home.

They would be all right. They would carry on. Robert was gone, but he'd never be forgotten. Bessie's chest squeezed tight. One day, she promised herself, she would go out to France, see the place where he lay and put flowers on his grave.

Tomorrow she would go back to Marston Hall and help the Tommies who were still alive. It's what Robert would tell her to do. Keeping busy, banishing her thoughts and worries, was what she needed now more than ever. Working hard had stopped her worrying about Robert before, and now it must stop her from thinking about the huge gap he had left in her life.

## Carry On

Closing the front door quietly behind her, Bessie soaked in the familiar atmosphere of Marston Hall Auxiliary War Hospital. The pervading smell of carbolic was comforting, and she could hear the sound of a cheery song being played on the gramophone in the ward. She closed her eyes. It was good to be back.

'Nurse Carter!' Bessie opened her eyes and saw Matron bustling towards her. 'You're back so soon?'

'Hello, Matron. It was time for me to come back.'

Matron raised her eyebrows.

'If you're sure. How are your parents?'

'They're fine, thank you. Carrying on as best they can.'

'It's the only thing they can do.' Matron shook her head. 'Too many families are losing their sons.' She sighed. 'I'm glad to see you back, Nurse Carter. We've missed you. I'm sure the men will be delighted to see you in the morning.'

'Oh, but I'd like to start work straight away.' Bessie looked down at her clothes. 'At least, when I've changed into my uniform.' She needed to be busy.

'Well, there's plenty to do. But you're not to start until you've had something to eat. Come along this way.' She indicated for Bessie to accompany her.

Bessie knew better than to argue with Matron and fell into step beside her. She was hungry. The train had been delayed and it felt a long time since she'd eaten her breakfast.

'I'm sure Cook can find you something warm and filling. Then, and only then, can you start work.'

Reaching the door of the kitchen, Matron opened it and stood aside, motioning for Bessie to go in.

'I've found a stray who needs feeding, Mrs Taylor,' Matron announced. 'Something warm and filling, please.'

She laid a hand on Bessie's arm.

'Take your time and we'll see you on the ward when you're ready.'

'Thank you, Matron.'

Matron went out closing the kitchen door behind her.

Bessie looked around the kitchen at the faces staring at her. They looked as if they were frozen on the spot – Mrs Taylor, her hands floury from the pastry she was rolling out, and the two kitchen maids who were at the sink.

'Bessie!' Mrs Taylor broke the silence and came towards her wiping her hands on her apron. 'How are you, my dear? We were all so sorry to hear about your brother.'

Bessie nodded, her throat tightening.

'Thank you,' she managed to say.

Mrs Taylor nodded, her eyes shining with sympathy.

'Right, how about some nice hot broth? It'll

warm you and fill you up in one go. And a nice slice of bread and butter to go with it. How does that sound?'

'Lovely, thank you, Mrs Taylor.'

'Sit yourself down, and I'll fetch you some.'

'I can do it,' Bessie protested. 'You're busy cooking.'

'My pleasure. Agnes will cut the bread and butter for you, won't you, Agnes?'

Agnes nodded and smiled shyly at Bessie.

'Thank you.' Bessie pulled out a chair and sat down at the table. 'It's good to be back here with everyone again.'

Mrs Taylor had just placed a bowl of steaming broth in front of Bessie when the kitchen door burst open and Ethel came rushing in.

'Bessie! You're back.' She rushed over and hugged her tightly. 'It's so good to see you again.'

She stepped back and held Bessie at arm's length.

'I'm so sorry about Robert.'

'Thank you, Ethel.' Bessie smiled at her friend. 'I'm sorry I didn't see you before I left. There wasn't time.'

'Matron told us about Robert.' Ethel frowned. 'I was worried you might not come back.'

'I had to come back. There are patients here who need to be looked after. My brother would have wanted me to carry on.' Bessie blinked back sudden tears threatening to spill over. 'I'll be starting again this afternoon.'

'Not until you've some food inside you,' Mrs Taylor said. 'Matron's orders. Have you time for a cup of tea, Ethel?'

Ethel shook her head.

'I'd love to, Mrs Taylor, but I can't. I should be sorting out some bandages, but when Matron said Bessie was back, well, I had to come and see her for myself.'

'I'm glad you did. I'll be back on the ward as soon as I've eaten my broth and changed into my uniform.'

'Everyone's looking forward to seeing you,' Ethel said, making her way to the door. 'The men all missed you. You'll see how well they're doing. Especially Sergeant Rushbrook. You're in for a surprise when you see him.'

Dressed in her familiar uniform again, Bessie glanced in the mirror on her chest of drawers to check her cap was straight. Her reflection seemed just the same as before she went home – same uniform, same face, same cap – but underneath it all she wasn't the same, and never would be again. It was as if there was a big hole somewhere inside her chest. A place Robert had filled, which now was empty.

For something empty it was strange it should hurt so much. The best way to forget about it for a while was to be busy. So busy she didn't have time to think or feel as she cared for men still living. It was how she'd coped before.

With a final tug of her cap to make sure it was secure, Bessie left her small attic bedroom and made her way down to the ballroom where 20 men needed looking after. Pausing outside the door, she took a deep breath, plastered a smile on her face and went in.

The gramophone at the far end of the ward was

trilling out one of the men's favourite songs.

'If you were the only girl in the world, and I were the only boy...'

Some of the men were playing cards, others drawing or reading. Bessie's eyes were drawn to a figure slowly making his way down the ward towards her, with a smiling Ethel walking along beside him.

Sergeant Rushbrook was up! Bessie could hardly believe it. He was out of bed and walking towards Bessie on crutches, with a look of determined concentration on his face, his eyes focused on the floor ahead of him. He was tall. Much taller than Bessie.

Ethel caught Bessie's eyes and grinned at her. Bessie smiled back and nodded her head. She watched Sergeant Rushbrook's every move, silently willing him on. She dared not speak in case she broke his concentration.

Every swing of his crutches brought him closer. His one good leg stepped through and his arms worked in coordination to propel him along.

When at last he was within a couple of feet of Bessie, Ethel gently laid a hand on his arm.

'Stop there. Well done.'

Sergeant Rushbrook came to a rest and stood in front of Bessie and looked her in the eye with a gentle smile on his face.

'Welcome back, Nurse Carter. We missed you.'

'It looks like you've been busy while I've been gone,' Bessie said. 'I'm happy to see you upright, Sergeant Rushbrook. You were still flat on your back when I left.'

Sergeant Rushbrook nodded.

'I decided it was time I got up.'

'He's been working hard at this,' Ethel said. 'Started the day after you left. He practised getting his balance and since then there's been no stopping him. Could you walk alongside him for a while? I need to do the observations.'

Bessie nodded.

'I'd be delighted. Where shall we go?'

'He's been practising up and down the main hall,' Ethel said over her shoulder as she headed towards the first patient. 'It's quieter out there.'

'Lead the way, Sergeant Rushbrook, I'm right beside you,' Bessie said. She slowed her pace to fit in with his, walking alongside him, ready to catch him if he faltered.

Outside in the hall, Sergeant Rushbrook stopped and looked down at Bessie, his clear blue eyes meeting hers.

'I'm sorry to hear about your brother. Truly I am.'

'Thank you.' Bessie's voice came out in a whisper.

'If there's anything I can do to help...'

'You already have.' Bessie blinked back sudden tears. 'Seeing you up is a real tonic. I didn't expect to see that when I got back.'

'I'm not surprised. I was a right miserable so and so, feeling sorry for myself.' Sergeant Rushbrook shook his head and looked cross with himself for a moment. 'Got a kick up the backside, beg your pardon, and it made me stop and think about things' He paused. 'I decided it was time to get going again.'

'What made you change your mind?'

126

'You did.'

'Me? How?'

'What you said to me about finding another way. Then I heard that your brother had been killed. It made me realise how lucky I am. I'm still here.' He looked down at his foot and then up at Bessie again. 'After you disappeared, we all wanted to know where you were. Matron said you'd had to suddenly go home for family reasons. But she wouldn't tell us why. Ethel told me.'

'But she...'

'Hold on. Don't be angry with her. She only told me because I kept on badgering her to tell me. I gave her my word I wouldn't tell the others. They don't know.'

'Why did you want to know?' Bessie asked.

'Because I was scared you'd gone for good and I wouldn't see you again.' Sergeant Rushbrook's eyes held hers. 'I didn't know if I could cope without you here. You made it bearable.'

Bessie felt her cheeks flush.

'All I did was care for you like all the other nurses. I did my job.'

'You made a huge difference to me. When Ethel told me about your brother, I felt ashamed of lying there feeling sorry for myself. I'm alive. I've got a chance. A lot of men aren't so lucky. I've got to get on with my life and live it well, for those that don't have the chance anymore.'

'I think you're doing the right thing.' Bessie smiled at him. 'Life's never going to be the same again, without my brother and all the others that won't ever come home.' She bit her bottom lip. 'But we've all got to carry on and live our lives.

Live them well. It's what they would have wanted.'

Sergeant Rushbrook smiled warmly, crinkling up the corners of his eyes.

'Welcome back to life at Marston Hall, Nurse Carter. I'm glad you're here.'

'So am I. Now, are we going to stand here talking all day, or are you going to practise walking?' Bessie tried to sound firm, but she couldn't stop the smile from playing on her lips.

'Yes, Nurse,' Sergeant Rushbrook said. 'Your wish is my command.'


## The 100th Mission Dance

'How do I look?' Dottie twirled around, making the skirt of her dress swirl upwards and out.

Bessie looked up from where she was mending Prune's hem to watch. It was good to see her in something else other than the brown dungarees she usually wore for work. She was such a pretty girl, and looked beautiful tonight with her curly blonde hair shiny and bouncy.

'Lovely.' Bessie spoke carefully through a mouthful of pins.

'I'd whistle at you, if I could,' Prune decided.

'You look beautiful, Dottie!' Marigold said.

'Thank you, my angel.' Dottie plopped a kiss on Marigold's cheek. 'Whoops! I've left you a lipstick print on your cheek.'

'Where? Let me see.' Marigold jumped up from where she was sitting at the table drawing and

128

rushed across the room to look in the mirror, touching her cheek where Dottie's lips had left a pink print.

'Let me clean you up.' Dottie whipped a clean hanky out of her bag and gently wiped away the lipstick. 'There you are, as good as new.'

'I wish I could come with you,' Marigold said.

'I know.' Dottie put her arm around Marigold's shoulders. 'But it's not for children. I promise I'll tell you and Bessie all about it in the morning.'

'Will you tell us about everything; the music and the dances?'

'And the band,' Prune added.

Dottie laid her hand on her heart.

'I promise.'

'Will you be dancing with Clem?' Marigold asked.

'Definitely. He's a great dancer. We'll be on the floor most of the evening. Once the music starts it gets my toes tapping and I just can't stop myself dancing.' Dottie looked at her watch. 'Are you nearly done, Bessie?'

'Just a few more stitches.' She quickly passed her needle to and fro through the fabric, while Prune stood patiently on the chair towering above her

'I don't know how I didn't see it before,' Prune said. 'I'm glad you noticed.'

'We want you looking your best for Howard,' Dottie added, looking up at Prune with a broad grin on her pink-lipsticked lips.

'I don't think he'd have noticed,' Prune said.

'Probably not,' Dottie agreed. 'He's only got eyes for you, not what you're wearing.'

Prune blushed.

'There you go, all done.' Bessie put her needle and pins back in her work box, then smoothed Prune's skirt down, checking how it looked. 'It's as good as new.'

'Thank you, Bessie.' Prune steadied herself with a hand on Bessie's shoulder as she carefully climbed down from the chair and slipped on her shoes. 'Right, I'm ready to go, then, Dottie.'

'Have a lovely time,' Bessie said, following them outside once they'd gathered their jackets and bags. 'We'll want to hear all about it tomorrow.'

'You will – we'll be talking of nothing else for days!' Dottie said, running down the steps into the yard. 'Goodbye!'

Bessie and Marigold stood in the doorway and watched the two young women walk out the farm gate and turn in the direction of the base. It was grand to see Dottie and Prune looking so happy and off to have some fun.

And this wasn't just any old dance they were going to, it was the 100th Mission Dance. They'd been talking about it for days, planning what they were going to wear and how they'd do their hair. Celebrations had been going on all day at Rackbridge base to mark the first 100 missions, and this evening's dance promised to be wonderful.

Bessie put her arm around Marigold who leaned against her.

'Why don't we go for a walk? It's a lovely evening, and I fancy getting out for bit. We can go and see how Harry and Peter are getting on with that fence in the orchard.'

Marigold nodded and slipped her hand in Bessie's, and they went through the gate into the

130

orchard where the chickens were still scratching around, making the most of the light evening.

'Bessie, did you used to go to dances, like Dottie and Prune?'

'You mean during the Great War?'

Marigold nodded.

'Not very often, I was working most of the time. But we still had fun where we could.'

'How?'

'We put on concerts for the men. Held sports days...'

Bessie stood at the sidelines, hardly daring to watch as the blast from Matron's whistle started the race and the three men set off down the course marked out on the lawn. Each man had a look of concentration on his face that, combined with the egg and spoon tightly clamped, sideways on, between his teeth, made him look fierce and determined.

They'd jokingly called this the 'three-legged egg and spoon race', as each contender had just one leg of his own and two from the crutches.

All around Bessie, other patients in their hospital blue suits, nurses, orderlies and visitors cheered the men on, shouting out words of encouragement. Bessie's heart was thumping.

This must be how a mother feels, watching over her child when it first starts to walk, she thought. Worrying that it might lose balance and tumble on to something and hurt itself. Only, if any of these men fell, their injuries could undo weeks of healing.

'Look at them go!' Ethel said, coming up to

stand beside Bessie. 'Who do you think will win?'

'I just want them all to stay upright,' Bessie whispered.

Ethel turned and looked at Bessie her eyebrows raised.

'Don't worry, they will. Taking part in sports is good for the men's spirits. Look at that!'

The cheering around them grew louder as the three men drew abreast and deliberately crossed the finishing line together, side by side. Taking the spoons out of their mouths, they heartily congratulated each other on making it all the way. All of them were winners.

Bessie sighed with relief and her heartbeat gradually slowed to its usual steady rhythm. They had done it. All of them had finished in one piece and still standing on their three legs.

It would do all the men the world of good, boosting their confidence and raising their spirits. That was what today's event was all about, Bessie reminded herself. Raising men's spirits and money for the hospital funds.

Satisfied that the men were fine, Bessie headed back to the stall she'd been manning. It was full of hand-made goods, embroidered handkerchiefs, tablecloths, knitted socks and trimmed straw hats – some of which Bessie had sewn in the little spare time she had.

There had been a steady trade all afternoon, with visitors keen to buy something to support the hospital. Bessie had just sold a straw hat trimmed with silk daises to a woman when Sergeant Rushbrook appeared at the stall.

'Congratulations!' Bessie smiled at him. 'You

did a fine race. Finishing all together was perfect.'

'Thank you. We all thought it was the best way to do it. Didn't want anyone going daft trying to win and taking a tumble.' Sergeant Rushbrook's eyes met Bessie's. 'I looked for you afterwards. I wasn't sure if you'd watched the race.'

'I was there. I wouldn't have missed it for the world,' Bessie said. 'But I had to get straight back to the stall afterwards.'

Sergeant Rushbrook nodded and turned slightly as if to go, then changed his mind.

'I was worried in case I fell.'

'So was I. But I was proud of you – of you all, for doing it. You've come a long way, Sergeant Rushbrook.'

He smiled.

'Thanks to you, Nurse Carter. You've a special way about you.'

Bessie's cheeks grew warm. Before she could say anything, a shout went up for the tug-of-war to start.

'Are you planning on taking part?' Bessie asked jokingly.

'I would have, before.' Sergeant Rushbrook looked down at his one leg and shrugged. 'I have to make allowances now, so I'll just watch this one, give some moral support instead. Put my energy into cheering them on.'

'I'm glad to hear it. You'd best get over there and start cheering.'

Sergeant Rushbrook nodded and smiled at her, his blue eyes holding hers for a few moments, before he turned and made his way over to where the crowd had gathered to watch the two mixed teams of able-bodied patients and visitors pull against each other.

As Bessie watched him go, she considered how well he'd done since he first arrived at Marston Hall. Right from the start he'd intrigued her, then his determination to get himself going again when she'd returned after Robert's death had impressed her. He'd soon be ready to have an artificial leg fitted, and would leave here and start the next phase of his life. To her surprise, Bessie's heart clenched at the thought of not seeing him again.

She looked around at the men happily singing along to the music Ethel was coaxing out of the piano they'd pushed into the ward. The men always loved an impromptu concert and their spirits were still soaring after the afternoon's sports.

'What shall I play next?' Ethel called after she'd brought the last song to a close.

'"Long Way To Tipperary", Nurse,' Private Dennis shouted.

Ethel started to play, and the men sang along. Bessie added her own voice, but it was drowned out by the deeper tones of the men, which brought a lump to Bessie's throat and she had to stop singing for a moment. If only things could stay like this and none of the men would have to go back to France. If only the war would end.

The final notes of 'Tipperary' had just faded when Matron walked into the ward and came to stand by the piano.

'Beautiful singing.' She smiled warmly at the men. 'But it's time for cocoa and then bed, so just one more song.'

'What's it to be, then?' Ethel asked.

'"If You Were The Only Girl"!' a voice called out from the other side of the ward.

'Certainly, Sergeant Rushbrook,' Ethel said.

As the men sang Bessie joined in with the popular song. Taking her eyes off Ethel at the piano, she glanced round and saw that someone was looking at her. Sergeant Rushbrook. He was singing, his blue eyes twinkling as they caught and held hers. He nodded his head and smiled as they began to sing the second verse.

'If you were the only girl in the world
And I were the only boy.'

Bessie knew she should break his gaze but she couldn't.

'Nothing else would matter in the world today,
We could go on loving in the same old way.'

'Last verse,' Ethel called.

Bessie turned gratefully from Sergeant Rushbrook's gaze to look at Ethel who was playing the final verse with great enthusiasm. As she sang the final verse, Bessie knew he was still watching her, but she dared not look again. She concentrated on singing the words as her cheeks glowed warmly.

'Do you like it?' Howard asked.

Prune looked around at the inside of the huge hangar, which had been cleared of planes and for tonight, was turned into a dance hall. Straw bales had been set up around the side to sit on, and the whole place was decorated with bracken and lit up with blue lights.

At the far end, on a raised platform, a band was

135

in full swing, belting out 'In The Mood', which made Prune itch to get on the dance floor and join the dancing couples.

'It's wonderful.' Prune smiled at Howard and tugged at his hand. 'Come on, let's go dance.'

'Wait a moment. Take a good look at the band.'

It was hard to see them clearly, but they didn't look like the usual base band, The Galloping Gators, who played at the base dances.

'They look new to me.'

'It's Glenn Miller and his band!' Howard said. 'You can't get better than that.'

'Glenn Miller? Really?'

Howard nodded.

'So, come on, what are we waiting for? Let's dance!' Howard pulled her hand and led her on to the dance floor.

As they danced, Prune caught glimpses of Dottie and Clem who were also on the dance floor.

The whole atmosphere was electric, with everyone in a happy mood enjoying the climax of the 100th Mission celebration. The Americans knew how to relax and enjoy themselves, making the most of some time to have fun.

'Wanna have a beer?' Howard asked, leading Prune off the dance floor a while later, after the great bandleader had announced the band were taking a short break.

'I'd love one.' Prune's throat was parched from dancing and she was hot. Her cheeks felt like they were glowing.

'I'll grab us a couple. Wait here, I won't be long.'

Waiting while Howard pushed his way through the throng to the bar, Prune looked around for

Dottie and Clem and spotted them sitting at a table on the far side of the dance floor, sipping some drinks.

'Shall we go and join Dottie and Clem?' Prune asked when Howard came back with two beers a few minutes later.

'Later. I'd like to go and sit outside for bit and cool off.' He handed Prune her beer and took hold of her elbow guiding her out towards the doors.

They weren't the only ones spilling out of the hangar for some fresh air. The grass near the hangar was dotted with people sitting down resting after their vigorous dancing.

Howard led her to a spot a little way off from the others, who were chatting and laughing loudly.

Settling down on the grass, side by side, Howard put his arm around Prune's shoulders.

'Cheers.' He knocked his glass against hers.

'Bottoms up,' Prune said. They both took a long draught of the golden liquid. 'That tastes good.'

'Sure does.' Howard put down his glass and took hold of Prune's free, hand. 'I'm glad you're here, Prune. It wouldn't be half as good without you.'

'Thank you for inviting me.'

Howard laughed.

'I love the way you talk, Prune. So formal, sometimes.' Prune shrugged her shoulders.

'That's the way we British do things, you know.'

'I like it.' Howard stroked the palm of her hand with his thumb. 'I think about you a lot when we're flying, Prune. It keeps me happy. Makes me feel good and takes my mind off where we're going.'

Prune's chest tightened. She hated him flying on missions. The idea of him facing the possibility of being shot down terrified her, but she'd never tell Howard that. It wouldn't be fair.

She swallowed down her fear and took his hand in both of hers.

'So, tell me, then, what do you like about me?'

Howard's eyes met hers.

'The way you look. Your beautiful, big brown eyes. The way you make me feel. Your laugh.'

Prune's cheeks grew warm.

'You're having me on, Howard.'

'No, I'm not, Prune. I'm being totally honest with you.' He stroked her cheek gently. 'I love you, Prune. You've bewitched me with your funny, Limey ways, and I'm under your spell.'

'I love you, too.'

There, she'd said what she'd been feeling for weeks now. Prune's heart was thudding so hard in her chest that she was sure Howard must be able to feel it when he pulled her into his arms and kissed her.

## A Different Life

Grace put the letter down on the table and sighed. She'd thought it would get easier with time, but it wasn't happening. She still felt as if part of her was missing because Marigold wasn't there. Contact with her daughter through letters helped, but sometimes they could make it feel as if Marigold was a very long way away, living a different life. One which Grace wasn't an active part of. She was scared that Marigold might be slowly drifting away from her.

Shrugging herself out of her coat, Grace dropped down on to a chair and eased her shoes off. Her feet were throbbing and all she wanted to do was lay down and sleep, but she couldn't. Five minutes rest and then she'd have a quick wash and change, and go down to Ada's.

They'd taken to eating their meals together, as it made sense to pool their rations and Ada liked cooking for someone. It was company for both of them, too.

But Ada was sure to ask about Marigold's letter. She'd left it out on the hall table for Grace to see as soon as she got in from work. Usually she enjoyed sharing Marigold's news, but tonight Grace would rather not talk about it, as she wasn't sure she was strong enough to gloss over how she really felt.

She sighed and settled back in the chair, closing her eyes for a few moments. She'd just have five minutes and then she'd get ready.

A tapping on the door woke Grace with a start.

'Grace? The tea's ready.'

It was Ada. Grace glanced at the clock. It was nearly six o'clock, she must have fallen asleep. She shook her head to try to relieve the after-sleep muzziness in her head.

'Come in, Ada.' She smiled as the old woman's head appeared around the door. 'I'm sorry. I just sat down for five minutes and must have dropped off.'

Ada laughed.

'I thought you might have. And no wonder you're tired after a day on your feet. The tea's on the table, so come down when you're ready.'

'I won't be long,' Grace said. 'I'll just wash my hands and I'll be there.'

Grace was about to go out of the door a few minutes later when she spotted Marigold's letter where she'd left it on the table earlier. It was only fair to Ada that she should hear Marigold's latest news. She'd been such a support to Grace and she missed Marigold, too. Grace put the letter in her pocket. She would show Ada after tea.

'That was lovely,' Grace said, putting her knife and fork together on her empty plate. 'Thank you, Ada.'

'You're welcome, dear. If you cook it for long enough, even a tough bit of meat will soften up eventually!'

'Shall I start on the washing-up?' Grace pushed back her chair and stood up.

'Not yet. You can make the tea and tell me what Marigold's been up to.'

'Why don't you read it while I make the tea? She's got lots to say and I might miss something out.'

'You sure?' Ada asked.

'Of course.'

Grace usually told Ada snippets of Marigold's news from her letters, rather than giving her the actual letters to read herself. Marigold wrote to Ada separately so she received her own letters from her.

Standing with her back to Ada, waiting for the

140

kettle to boil on the gas ring, Grace mulled over how she'd felt earlier when she'd read Marigold's letter. It was just a reaction from being so tired, she reasoned. All mothers whose children were away in the country missed them. It was only natural.

It wouldn't be for ever, that's what she had to hold on to, keep telling herself. One day Marigold would be back home with her. She must focus on that and be glad that her daughter was safe.

But, then, most mothers would take the chance to go and see their children if they could, a treacherous thought whispered in her head as the kettle began to whistle. It wasn't as simple as that for her. She couldn't just go and see Marigold when she wanted to. She wished she could, but...

'Grace, the kettle!' Ada's voice made her jump.

'Oh!' Grace quickly turned off the gas, and poured the steaming water into the teapot.

'You really are tired tonight,' Ada said as Grace put the teapot down on the table and sat back in her place. 'Been extra busy today?'

Grace sighed.

'Every day's extra busy with those rockets falling on us.'

Ada shivered and waved Marigold's letter.

'It makes me thankful Marigold's out of it.'

'That's what I tell myself.'

'It sounds like she's settled in well at school and made some friends. She's got lots to say about it all.'

Grace nodded. Marigold was turning into a good letter-writer, filling pages with descriptions of what she did. This letter was all about her start-

141

ing school, her new friends, the teacher, what games they played at playtime. It painted a picture of a world far away from London and the life she'd had before.

Going to a new school was never easy. Grace knew Marigold would have been nervous about it. Her mind drifted back to when Marigold first started school and how she'd looked to Grace for reassurance. It would have been Bessie that she'd have looked to this time.

A pang of longing sliced through Grace.

She felt Ada touch her arm and stared down at the old woman's veiny hand.

'Grace, I don't think you've listened to a word I've said.'

'I'm sorry, Ada.' Grace looked at her friend's concerned face. 'The only thing I'm good for tonight is sleeping.'

She stood up.

'I'll wash up quickly, and then go to bed.'

Ada pulled her down into the chair again.

'Leave the pots, I'll do them. I want to know what you're going to do about Marigold's last line.'

'What do you mean?'

'Look.' Ada traced her fingers under the final row of handwriting.

Grace closed her eyes as Ada started to read it. She knew it by heart, because Marigold always ended her letters the same way.

'*I miss you, Mummy. When are you going to come and see me?*' Ada read. She put the letter down and looked at Grace. 'Have you picked a date yet?'

'No. It's been so busy on the ward with the

casualties from the rockets.' She shrugged. 'You know how it is, Ada. Look at me! I'm a wreck from tiredness.'

'I know that, love.' Ada patted Grace's arm. 'But everyone's entitled to some time off, even a couple of days. It's weeks since Marigold left here and she wants to see you. Norfolk's not that far away.'

'I will go and see her. I want to, believe me, but it's not as easy as you think.'

Ada looked at Grace, her shrewd conker brown eyes studying her face for a few moments.

'Are you making it harder for yourself than it need be?' She raised her eyebrows. 'I've got the feeling there's more to this than simply getting the time off.'

'We're short-staffed a lot of the time, so how can I go off and leave them with more patients than we've ever had?'

'I understand that, Grace. But if, by some magic means, I could wave a wand and you had no more patients to care for, plenty of staff, and time off, would you go straight away?'

Grace hesitated, then quickly said, 'Of course I would.'

'Call me an old fool, but there's something here that doesn't quite add up. No doubt you've got your reasons, and maybe you'll tell me, all in good time, but I think you're putting excuses in the way of going to see your daughter.'

'But–'

Ada put her hand up.

'Let me have my say, Grace, then I'll shut up about the matter. I know it's not because you don't want to see her. I can see from your face

143

how much you want to be with Marigold. So it must be something about where she is,' she probed, looking Grace straight in the eye.

Grace sighed and looked down at the teaspoon she was fiddling with.

'It's complicated, Ada, and best left alone. I know Marigold's safe where she is. For that I'm very grateful, and I just have to put up with missing her.'

'But she wants to see you!'

'I know. And I will go, but not just yet. I need a bit more time.'

Ada grasped Grace's hand.

'Just don't leave it too long, eh?'

## Christmas Day

'One, two, three, four, five, six.' Bessie hopped her counter along the board and landed on a snake's head. 'Oh, no, not again!' She slid her counter down the snake's curving body and landed on a square not far from the start of the board. 'Look! I'm right back near the beginning again.'

Harry, Peter and Marigold laughed. They'd been playing for a while, with no-one managing to reach the end before being sent back down again by a snake.

'That's snakes and ladders for you.' Harry picked up the dice and shook it in his cupped hands. 'You think you're getting somewhere, and then you land on a snake!'

'You might get a ladder next time,' Marigold said.

Bessie smiled. It was all part of Christmas, having time to play games and relax for a bit. She looked over to the kitchen where Dottie was washing up, Clem and Howard were drying and Prune was putting away. They'd insisted on doing it, saying Bessie should put her feet up after cooking such a lovely Christmas dinner.

It had been a good dinner. They'd eaten goose, crispy roast potatoes, batter puddings and vegetables. Nearly all of it they'd reared or grown on the farm. Even the Christmas pudding had turned out well, made with the dried fruit ration she'd saved up.

The house was looking beautiful, too, Bessie thought. They'd trimmed the living-room up with holly and ivy, draping sprigs over the mantelpiece and around picture frames. The Christmas tree Harry had cut down was laden with decorations. Old ones which they'd had for years, and the new ones made by Peter and Marigold.

They'd collected dropped Window from the bombers, the small metallic strips that were meant to create confusing signals on German radar screens and conceal the position of the actual bombers. It gathered in hedges, and the children had turned it into decorations which glittered and twinkled silver against the green tree.

'I've got a five!'

Peter's voice brought Bessie's attention back to the game and she watched as he moved his counter along, square by square, counting out five and finally reaching the end.

'I've won!' Peter beamed.

'Well done,' Harry said. 'At last someone's made it to the finish!'

'Shall we play another game?' Marigold asked. 'Do you want to join in?' She directed her question to the group who had just finished in the kitchen.

'I was kinda hoping Prune and I could go for a short stroll before Clem and I head back to base,' Howard said. 'Bessie, do you mind if we go out?'

'Of course not.'

She understood the young couple wanted some time on their own – a crowded house wasn't the place to be if you wanted to be alone together for a while.

'I'll play,' Clem said

'And me,' Dottie added.

They sat down at the table and each took a counter and placed it with the others on the first square on the board.

'Who's going first?' Marigold asked.

'Clem. He's our guest,' Bessie said.

'Thank you,' Clem said. 'You know, Bessie, Harry... Howard and I really appreciate you inviting us to spend Christmas with you all. You always make us so welcome when we come here. Orchard Farm's a real home from home for us.'

'We're glad you could come,' Bessie replied. 'We're pleased to have you with us. It can't be easy for you being away from your own families at Christmas.'

'No, ma'am. It isn't.' Clem smiled. 'But maybe we'll be home for the next one.'

'Let's hope so,' Harry said. 'Now, shake that

dice and let's get this game started.'

'Look at all those stars,' Howard said.

Prune looked up at the thousands of pin pricks of light in the inky blackness above them.

'They're beautiful.' She leaned back against Howard's chest, as he wrapped his arms around her, keeping them both warm.

'They sure are. Some of them are the same ones we see back home. See that one there?' He pointed to one group of stars. 'I used to be able to see it out of my bedroom window in Montana. I kinda like that it looks over here and there. Makes it feel connected and not so far away.'

'Do you miss home?' Prune asked.

'You bet. I miss lots of things about it. But I like it here, too.' He rested his head against Prune's. 'There's something I'd miss about here if I went home.'

'What?'

'You!' Howard laughed and loosened his arms around Prune, and spun her round until she faced him and then gently kissed her. 'There's something I want to ask you, Prune.' He paused and cleared his throat. 'Would you do me the honour of becoming my wife? Will you marry me, Prune?'

Her heart did a bunny hop. Howard had just asked her to marry him! She never expected that, they hadn't known each other that long. Just six months, and their meetings were snatched when they could. Nothing was ever guaranteed because Howard's life was ruled by the USAAF, and leave passes could be cancelled at a moment's notice. But six months in wartime wasn't the same as in

147

peacetime. Relationships were speeded up to make the most of every precious second.

'Prune?' Howard's voice sounded unsure. 'Are you OK?'

'I'm fine. You just surprised me, that's all.'

'Well, what do you think? Will you marry me? I love you, Prune, and I want to spend the rest of my life with you. Grow old with you.'

What should she say? Should she be sensible, and suggest they wait? Wait until the war was over and they'd known each other for longer? Or should she follow her heart and say yes to this man with whom she'd fallen in love? The old Prune, the one she used to be before the war, before she'd left home to become a timberjill, would have said wait. But she wasn't that Prune any more.

'Yes.' Prune's voice came out in little more than a whisper. 'Yes, yes. I'll marry you, Howard!' This time her voice was loud and clear.

Howard picked her off her feet and swung her round.

'We'll get married as soon as we can. There'll be forms to sign and your mother will have to give permission because you're not twenty-one yet. You'll have to meet the chaplain to show him you really want to marry me. Once we've got permission we have to wait sixty days till we can marry. So we need to get started as soon as we can.'

'How do you know all this?'

'I found out about it. Thought I should know what to do before I asked you in case you said yes.'

'Did you think I'd say no?' Prune asked.

Howard shrugged and grinned at her.

'I hoped you'd say yes, but I wasn't sure. I thought you might think it was too soon.'

Prune gently stroked his cheek.

'You make me happy, Howard. The happiest I've ever been. And I love you. Simple as that. I'd love to be your wife.'

Howard pulled her to him and hugged her tightly. Prune closed her eyes and savoured the moment. This Christmas Day had been the best she'd ever had and so different from the stuffy, rigid traditions of past Christmases at home with her mother.

Her mother. The thought of what she'd say about Prune marrying Howard was like dousing her flame of happiness with a bucket of water. Prune's stomach twisted for a few seconds before she took control.

No, she wasn't going to let anything spoil this moment. Howard wanted to marry her, to be with her for the rest of his life, and that made her heart sing with happiness. Nothing was going to spoil that feeling right now.

What would come, she'd deal with later. This was her moment now, hers and Howard's, with their whole lives together stretched out before them, and she was happy. Deliriously and wonderfully happy.

'Merry Christmas, Nurse.' A patient's visiting relative greeted Grace as they walked on to the ward.

'Merry Christmas to you, too,' Grace responded with a smile.

There was an air of jollity about the ward today as everyone made the best of being in hospital.

Grace was glad to be here, too, being on duty on Christmas Day was no hardship for her this year and she'd volunteered to do an extra shift today so nurses with families at home could be with them.

Grace didn't want to be at home today. It was better to be busy and useful at St Thomas's than to brood at home, desperately missing John and Marigold. They'd always made Christmas Day such a fun, happy family time.

Grace smiled at the memory of Marigold coming into their bedroom on Christmas morning, her face alight with joy that Father Christmas had been. She would climb up into their bed, snuggle down between them and delve into her stocking to pull out gifts. A doll, some chocolate, an orange, a handful of nuts and a sixpence in the toe.

When Grace had woken up this morning, she'd been alone. The flat was quiet and John and Marigold's absence seemed to echo around the rooms.

Grace sighed. She should be glad Marigold was safe in Norfolk with Bessie and Harry.

She'd sent a parcel to Marigold and knew Bessie would make sure she got it today. Marigold had sent her a present wrapped in brown paper with *To Mummy, Happy Christmas, Love from Marigold* written on it.

Grace had opened it in bed this morning. Inside was a lavender bag made from pale pink cotton with the word *Mummy* carefully embroidered on the front. Grace's eyes had misted with tears as she'd stared at the lavender bag, stroking the embroidered letters with a finger.

Marigold had made it all by herself, so the letter that came with it had told Grace. Bessie had taught her how to embroider and the lavender was from Bessie's garden. It smelled wonderful when she sniffed it.

Grace slipped her hand into the pocket of her dress and touched the lavender bag, her fingers skimming over the letters spelling out *Mummy*. Carrying it around with her while she was on duty today helped Marigold seem a little closer.

## Secrets Revealed

Something woke Bessie up, and she lay still, listening for it again. Beside her Harry was sleeping, curled up on his side as usual. The sound came again, a faint rattling as if someone was poking at the fire. Carefully pulling back the sheets so she didn't wake Harry, Bessie slipped out of bed, tiptoed to an inward-looking window and tweaked aside the muslin curtain.

She could just make out a silhouetted figure hunched over the fire, which gave out a red glow. Pushing her feet into her slippers, Bessie reached for her dressing-gown and put it on, then crept to the door, quietly opened it and slipped into the main room.

The figure in front of the fire started and turned round. It was Prune.

'Oh, Bessie! I didn't mean to wake you,' Prune whispered. 'I couldn't sleep. I was just trying to

151

poke the fire.'

Bessie sat down in the armchair opposite Prune and looked at her. Even in the faint red light from the fire, she could see something was wrong. Prune, who was usually so calm and collected, looked distraught.

'Are you all right, Prune?'

She shook her head and began to weep silent tears which splashed down on to her thick, tartan-patterned dressing-gown.

'I'm sorry.'

'It's all right.' Bessie touched Prune's hands which were tightly bunched up on her lap. 'I'll bank up the fire so we don't get cold, then we can talk, if you'd like.'

She busied herself adding some wood to the fire, taking care not to make any noise. The last thing they needed was anyone else coming in and seeing Prune like this.

'Are you feeling ill?' Bessie asked as she settled back in her armchair.

Prune shook her head.

'Nothing like that. It's ... it's just that Howard asked me to marry him tonight. And I said yes.'

'But that's good! Isn't it what you want? Or did you say yes when you meant no?'

Prune gave a watery smile.

'It's what I want more than anything.'

'Then I don't understand why you're so upset. Shouldn't you be happy?'

'The thing is, Bessie, I can't marry him. I'm supposed to be marrying someone else!'

Bessie stared at Prune.

'You're already engaged?'

'No.' Prune shook her head vehemently. 'Though, if Mummy had had her way, I would have been before I left home.'

'You've lost me, Prune. You'd better tell me the whole story. I never had you down for one who'd be involved with two men at the same time.'

Prune bit her bottom lip, suddenly looking very young.

'Mummy expects me to marry her best friend's son, Jeremy. I've known him all my life, we used to play together as children and grew up knowing each other and are now good friends. Only, Mummy and Jeremy's mother have this dream we'll marry, and foolishly Jeremy and I have let them go on thinking that, to keep the peace.' Prune sighed. 'But there's never been anything romantic between us at all.'

'Do you intend to marry him?'

'No! We're like brother and sister. When the war came along it gave us both an escape route from our mothers. Jeremy's escaped to the Navy and I'm a timberjill. Actually, Jeremy's engaged to a Wren, though his mother doesn't know yet.'

Bessie took one of Prune's hands in hers.

'You've got to marry who you choose, Prune, not who your mother wants. Write and tell her you've met Howard and Jeremy's met someone else. Simple as that!'

Prune sighed.

'You don't know my mother. She won't take this easily, after planning our marriage for years. And if I married a GI she'd never speak to me again!' Her voice wavered and she stopped to compose herself. 'She's all the family I've got left,

153

after Daddy died.'

'It sounds like she's trying to run your life for you, though. You've got to follow your heart, and trust where it leads you, even if it's against her wishes.' Bessie squeezed Prune's hand. 'Remember, it's *your* life. If she cares for you she has to understand that.'

'But what if she doesn't, and never speaks to me again? I'll have to choose between her or Howard.' Prune started to sob again.

Bessie stood up and put her arms around Prune's shaking shoulders.

'It's not going to be easy, but you've got to tell her. I suppose you haven't told Howard any of this?'

Prune shook her head.

'I never expected him to ask me to marry him.'

'He's a lovely young man,' Bessie said. 'Harry and I are very fond of him. Everyone is.'

'What's going on?' Dottie's voice made them both jump. She quickly crossed the room and came to kneel down in front of Prune. 'What's wrong?'

'You'd best tell her, Prune. Right from the start, like you told me,' Bessie advised.

After Prune had explained everything, Dottie let out a low whistle.

'You're a dark horse, Prune! You never let slip a word about this engagement!'

'It's. Not. An. Engagement!' Prune started to cry again, then calmed down after a few steadying breaths. 'Not a proper one, just our two mothers' understanding. Jeremy and I never agreed to anything, either to them or each other. It was something we just laughed at, behind their backs.'

Dottie shook her head.

'You should never have let them get away with thinking like that, especially now, with all this going on!'

Prune sighed.

'I know. But with Mummy, it seemed the easiest way. You don't know her.'

'I don't think I'd want to, either!' Dottie muttered.

'It's no good going over and over it,' Bessie said. 'You've got to do the right thing by Howard and Jeremy, and your mother. Write to her and tell her everything. Warn Jeremy, too. Then, when it's settled, you can get on with getting married.'

'Tell her you can't help who you fall in love with,' Dottie said. 'It hits you when you least expect it. Isn't that right, Bessie?'

Bessie nodded, smiling.

'It's true. Love often turns up when you least expect it.'

A flash of vivid blue and orange caught Bessie's eye as it sped off downstream in a blur, vanishing around a bend.

'A kingfisher!' Sergeant Rushbrook levered himself around in the wicker bathchair and looked up at Bessie, his face lit up with pleasure. 'Did you see it?'

She nodded and smiled.

'It was beautiful. Shall we stop here for a bit today, as usual?'

'Yes, please.'

'Right, but be careful how you steer. I don't

want to have to fish you out of the beck.' Bessie pushed the bathchair up the gentle slope on to the wooden bridge, while Sergeant Rushbrook steered with the T-barred handle which turned the small wheel underneath the front.

Satisfied the bathchair was safely parked so it couldn't roll off the bridge, Bessie leaned against the bridge's hand rail, still keeping one hand on the push bar at the back for security.

She closed her eyes and breathed in deeply, savouring the fresh smell of spring filling the air. The day had a gentle warmth, and the blue sky arched above them. Below them the water sounded as if it was gurgling with delight after fording across the road, and was free again to flow unhindered downstream.

Bessie sighed with pleasure.

'Was that a good sigh, because you're happy to be here, like me? Or a bad sigh, because you're tired of bringing me here?'

Bessie opened her eyes and saw Sergeant Rushbrook watching her, a warm smile on his face. She smiled back.

'Oh, definitely a good sign. I love coming here.' She looked across the ford towards the water meadows stretching along its banks into the distance. 'It's...'

'Lovely?' Sergeant Rushbrook suggested. 'Beautiful, gorgeous, marvellous?'

'All of those. It's just good to be outside, especially on a day like this,' Bessie said, throwing her free arm out to encompass the whole world around them.

The walks she'd brought Sergeant Rushbrook on

over the past few weeks had often brought them to the beck. They both liked it there and usually stopped on the bridge for a while, watching the water flow past while they talked and laughed. Their outings were always fun, with each of them seeming to find enjoyment in being away from the hospital together. It was part of the healing process, Matron often said. Men needed to be out of the hospital before they became too institutionalised.

'I'm going to miss this place when I go.' He glanced upstream and then turned to face Bessie, his eyes meeting and holding hers. 'Did you know I'll be leaving for Roehampton next week? Matron told me this morning.'

Bessie's stomach lurched.

'No. But that's good news, isn't it?'

'It is, and it isn't.'

'Your leg's healed up well enough to get an artificial leg fitted. That's marvellous! Think what you'll be able to do once you're walking again. You'll be able to start the rest of your life.'

'I agree, the thought of walking again is good.' He nodded. 'Very good.'

'It'll be wonderful for you.'

Bessie was pleased he had the chance to go to Roehampton. Walking again would give him back his independence, so he wouldn't have to rely on a VAD pushing him around in a bathchair, or hobbling along on crutches. But for that to happen, he had to leave Marston Hall. Their work with him would be finished and he'd be sent on his way, another successfully healed patient. The perfect outcome.

So why did her insides feel like they were being wrung out at the thought of him leaving? She would miss him, that was why.

'Have you decided what you'll do when you're finally discharged? I know you said you can't do hill-farming any more.'

'I've been giving it plenty of thought. I know what I want to do, it's just how I need to think about.'

'Is your father a farmer?'

'No. It was the last job he'd have done!' He laughed. 'My father was a shopkeeper. He was a neat and tidy man and kept his grocer's shop the same way. I grew up in the house behind the shop, and it was just me and my father after my mother died. He was more interested in weighing out blue bags of sugar than farming, and I was expected to follow suit and work in the shop after I finished school.'

'Did you?'

Sergeant Rushbrook pulled a face.

'No, I didn't. I had to work in there, helping out before I left school, but I was determined I would work on a farm when I left school. And I did. It's all I ever wanted to do, right from when I was small. I always loved animals and being outside and used to go and help on my aunt's farm – she's my mother's sister, who married a farmer. So I knew what farming was about, and that suited me. My father didn't like it, but he accepted it.'

He paused and a pained look crossed his face.

'In the end he did, though I think he thought I'd tire of being outside in all weathers and doing back-breaking, dirty work, and eventually go

158

back and work in the shop.'

'Is that what you're going to do?'

'I can't. My father died fairly recently, and I sold the shop and put the money in the bank for after the war. I'd planned to buy a hill farm of my own if I got through, only it's impossible now.'

'So what are you going to do?' Bessie asked.

'I've got a plan which will, I hope, make me happy.' Sergeant Rushbrook's blue eyes met Bessie's. 'I'll have a life I like. It's different from what I'd planned, but it'll still be right for me.'

'That's wonderful! What are you going to do?'

'I'm sorry, I can't tell you yet.' He smiled mysteriously. 'But I will one day, I promise. I'm not going to let the war stop me.'

Bessie smiled at him.

'Good. The war's changed things for all of us, making our lives go off in different directions from the ones we'd planned.' She hesitated for a moment. 'I would have been a married woman now, if it hadn't been for the war.'

Sergeant Rushbrook frowned.

'What happened?'

'My fiancé, William, was killed. We were engaged and planned to marry on his next leave, but he never came back.'

'I'm sorry,' Sergeant Rushbrook said gently. 'Was that when you joined the VAD?'

'No. I've been a VAD since Marston Hall was turned into an Auxiliary War Hospital. I was already working there as a seamstress and like the rest of the staff, I started working in the hospital.'

Falling into a silence for a few moments, Bessie recalled the last time she'd seen William and then the terrible news coming of his death. At least time had dulled the pain and she could look back and remember him with love, and hope he rested in peace.

'Enough about me.' Bessie stood up straight. 'I'm intrigued about your plan for the future, Sergeant Rushbrook, but if you're not going to tell me, I'd better get you back to the hospital or you'll miss tea and Matron will be on the warpath!'

Taking hold of the handle at the back of the bathchair Bessie prepared to pull it off the bridge.

'Steer straight back, if you please.'

Back on the road, Bessie expected Sergeant Rushbrook to turn right and head down the lane leading back to Marston Hall, but instead he kept going straight.

'We should have gone right,' Bessie reminded him. 'We'd better turn around.'

'No. I want to go this way, past the wood.' He turned in his seat, so he could see her face. 'Please, Nurse Carter. I just want to see if the bluebells are out. They were still in bud last time we came past there. It's been a long time since I saw bluebells.'

Bessie understood. She loved bluebells, too. She couldn't be sure when she'd have another chance to come out and see them and they might be over by the time she went that way again.

'Very well, but we mustn't be long or you really will miss your tea.'

Bessie smelled the bluebells before she saw them. A gentle breeze was blowing their subtle perfume towards them as they approached the wood where the beech trees were beginning to unfurl their fresh green leaves. Underneath the canopy a carpet of blue stretched out as far as they could see into the wood.

'Just look at them. They're so beautiful!'

'I want to go in there,' Sergeant Rushbrook said.

Bessie glanced at the uneven, rutted ground leading into the wood.

'I'm not sure if I can...'

'On these.' He held up the crutches which he'd insisted on bringing out with them today. 'Please. I want to stand among the bluebells again.'

Looking at his face, which was filled with hope and longing, Bessie nodded and took the crutches. Slowly and carefully, with Bessie's support and the aid of the crutches Sergeant Rushbrook levered himself out of the bath chair and stood upright. Then with slow careful steps, he made his way in through the gate, with Bessie right beside him her hand on his back.

'Easy here.' Bessie pointed at deep rut in the ground. 'Check each crutch is level and firm before you put your weight on it.'

A few minutes later they stood surrounded by bluebells, their perfume filling the air. Bessie gazed around at the blueness. It was beautiful, magical, and being there amongst the bluebells lifted her heart.

'Glad we came this way?' Sergeant Rushbrook's voice drew Bessie's attention back.

She smiled at him.

'Yes, I am. I love bluebells, they're my favourite flower.'

'Hold on to my arm, will you?'

Bessie quickly grabbed hold of his arm.

'Have you lost your balance?'

'No, I'm fine. I just want to do this.' He put both crutches under one arm and then slowly bent forwards, his weight still supported on his leg, and with Bessie holding onto one arm, he reached out with his free arm.

'What are you doing?' Bessie said. 'Be careful!'

'This.' He plucked a single bluebell stem and carefully stood upright again. 'For you, Nurse Carter.'

He held out the flower for Bessie to take, his eyes studying her face. She smiled and took the flower, bringing it up to her face to smell its perfume.

'Thank you.'

'It's a perfect match for your eyes, they're the same colour. I always thought so, but now I know for sure.' Sergeant Rushbrook glanced around at the bluebells carpeting the wood for a few seconds and then returned his gaze to Bessie's face, his eyes meeting hers and holding them. 'I've grown very fond of you, Nurse Carter. Forgive me if I speak out of turn, but I had to say something before I went.'

Bessie's heart quickened its pace. He was fond of her?

'It's all right if you don't feel the same way...'

'But I do, Sergeant Rushbrook. I do!' The words rushed out of Bessie's mouth before she had time to think. 'When you told me you were leaving I couldn't help thinking how much I'll miss you.'

He took hold of one of Bessie's hands.

'Harry, please. No more Sergeant Rushbrook.'

'But I have to call you that. It's hospital rules.'

'We're not at the hospital now.'

Bessie laughed, gazing round at the bluebell

162

wood, and then returning to look at Harry.

'No, we're not. My name's Bessie. Short for Elizabeth.'

'Bessie, I like it. Sweet Bess.' Harry reached out and gently stroked her cheek. 'Will you be my girl, Bess?'

'Nurses aren't allowed to be involved with patients. It's against the…'

'Rules. I know, but I won't be here much longer, and after that it won't matter because I won't be your patient anymore. Will you be my girl, Bess?' His blue eyes were filled with hope and tenderness.

'Yes, Harry, I will. But not properly, until you leave. You understand, don't you? It's not that I don't want to, but I have to keep to the rules.'

Harry smiled happily.

'I understand. I'll be back to see you as soon as I can. I'll walk back.'

'I'll be waiting for you.' Bessie gently touched his face.

She would see him again after he left. When he left to go to St Mary's it wouldn't be the end, but the beginning.


## Wedding Plans

Going sticking was a good antidote to Christmas Day feasting, Bessie thought as they marched across the meadow towards their wood. Peter and Marigold were running ahead, towing the small cart behind them, their breath coming out in steamy bellows in the crisp air, while she, Dottie and Prune followed on behind, their arms linked together.

'Have you decided what you're going to do about your mother, Prune?' Bessie asked.

'There's no way around it but to write to her.' Prune said. 'Until I'm twenty-one in February, I'll need her permission to marry.'

'Do you honestly think she'll say yes, when she expects you to marry Jeremy?' Dottie growled.

Prune shook her head.

'No, I don't.' She sighed. 'But what choice do I have? If I want to marry Howard before I'm twenty-one I must have her permission.'

'You could wait,' Bessie suggested.

'In normal circumstances I would, Bessie. But with the war on...' Prune shrugged. 'And Howard wants to get married as soon as we can. We won't be able to marry immediately anyway because of all the paperwork there is to do. I'd have to have an interview with his commanding officer or chaplain. Once we get permission, we'll still have to wait another sixty days until the wedding.'

'What's that for? To check you'd make a suitable GI bride?' Dottie giggled.

'I suppose they want to make sure you're not rushing into things lightly,' Bessie said. 'For some girls, marrying a GI is a one-way ticket to America.'

Prune shook her head.

'I promise you, Bessie, I've never been more serious about anything in my life. Howard is the man for me.'

164

'If your mother says no, what will you do?' Dottie asked.

'The only thing I can do. Wait until I don't need her permission. It's only a few weeks, I know, but time is precious these days. I'm going to marry him anyway, whether she gives her permission or not. She's got to realise that, so it would be better for us if she gave in and helped.'

'I hope she'll see sense and it won't come to that,' Bessie said as they reached the edge of the wood. 'Right, let's get this cart loaded up.'

The work of finding fallen branches and loading them into the cart soon warmed Bessie up. The others were feeling the same, from the look of their glowing cheeks as they scouted round for suitable branches and then dragged them back to the growing pile near the cart.

Prune and Dottie broke up long bits over their knees and loaded up the cart. It was a team effort, which would warm them again later when they burned the sticks in the stove.

'Have you thought about a dress, Prune?' Dottie asked, tipping an armful of short sticks into the cart.

Prune laughed.

'It's only been a few hours since he asked me! I'd rather wait until I know when the wedding's going to be.'

'You don't want to leave it too long; it's not easy to come by wedding dresses these days.'

'Who needs a wedding dress?' Marigold asked coming up behind them dragging a long thin branch behind her.

Dottie winked at her.

'You'd better ask Prune.'

'Are you getting married, Prune?'

Prune blushed and nodded.

'Yes. I think I am.'

'Who to?'

Dottie laughed.

'To Howard, who else?'

'Congratulations!' Peter said. 'Will you go and live in America after the war?'

'I suppose. I just want him to get through the war first.'

'We all do.' Dottie squeezed Prune's arm.

Marigold grabbed hold of Prune's hand.

'When are you getting married, Prune?'

'In a few months, I hope.'

'Bessie could make you a dress.' Marigold said. 'Would you, Bessie?' she called over to Bessie who was heading back to the cart dragging a fallen branch in each hand.

'What's this about?'

'Prune's getting married and she'll need a dress. You could make her one couldn't you?'

'I could, but it's up to Prune, and it would depend if we could get some nice material.'

'Can I be your bridesmaid?' Marigold begged. 'I've always wanted to be one.'

'I don't think Prune's even thought about that yet,' Bessie said, gently.

Prune laughed.

'I haven't. Howard only asked me last night, Marigold. But if I do decide to have one, I'll have to think hard who I might choose.' She looked hard at Marigold. 'Do you think you might be interested in the job?'

'Yes, yes!' Marigold jumped up and down. 'Please! I can, can't I, Bessie?'

'If that's what you'd like and, most importantly, if it's what Prune wants, then I don't see any reason why not.' Bessie put her arm around Marigold. 'I think you'd make a lovely bridesmaid.'

'What about Peter?' Marigold asked.

Peter grinned.

'I wouldn't make a good bridesmaid, Marigold!'

'Oh, it's going to be lovely to have a wedding to think about,' Dottie said. 'Give us something to look forward to.'

Bessie had brought men to the train station many times before, but none of those trips had ever made her feel the way she did now. Before, she'd always had a sense of happiness and satisfaction that the men were well again, especially if they were going home for good and the war was over for them.

Now, it was as if a tide of sadness was rising up inside and creeping around her heart. She felt chilly, despite the warmth of the beautiful summer's day with its clear blue sky arching overhead.

Sergeant Rushbrook – Harry – was leaving.

'Are you sure you've got everything?' Bessie stowed Harry's crutches in the corner of the compartment beside him, trying hard to be practical and ignoring how she felt.

Harry leaned forward from his seat by the window to speak to Bessie who stood on the platform.

'Nearly everything.'

Bessie frowned.

'But we checked before we left the hospital!'

'I did have everything I needed with me. But now I'm about to leave something behind. Something important.' He reached out and took hold of Bessie's hand. 'I'm leaving you, Bess.'

Bessie quickly glanced up and down the platform to see if anyone had noticed Harry was holding on to her hand. Fortunately, everyone else was occupied helping men into the train.

Swallowing hard against the growing tightness in her throat, Bessie met his eyes and smiled.

'You'll just have to come back for me, won't you?'

'I will, I promise you, Bess. And I'll write to you.'

The guard started slamming carriage doors shut, making his way towards them from the far end of the train. Time was running out.

'I'll miss you.' Harry raised Bessie's hands to his lips and kissed it. 'Thank you for everything you've done for me.'

Bessie nodded, not trusting herself to speak. She wanted to throw her arms around him and hold him tight. But she couldn't. Not here, not now.

'I'll miss you, too,' she managed to say, her voice sounding hoarse. 'Look after yourself.'

Harry gave her hand a final squeeze as the guard arrived at the door.

'All set, then?' he said. 'Mind your fingers.'

He quickly shut the door and moved on to the next compartment.

Harry pushed the door-window down and reached out his hand. Bessie linked her fingers in his.

'Have a good journey,' she said. 'Be careful on your crutches.'

'I will. Next time you see me, I'll be walking on two legs, Bess.'

'I look forward to it. Goodbye, Harry!'

The guard's whistle blew from the far end of the train and the engine up the front hissed and great chuffs of smoke started to puff out of the chimney.

'Goodbye, Bess.' Harry's eyes held hers as the train eased forward slowly.

Bessie walked with it, her fingers still on Harry's for a few seconds more, but then, as the train picked up speed, she let go and waved to him. Even after she lost sight of Harry's face at the window she kept waving and only stopped when the train rounded the bend and was gone.

## After The Bomb

Grace walked towards the two anxious-looking women waiting by the ward entrance. They were huddled together, their faces drawn and exhausted. But their eyes, as they watched her approach, still had hope in them that Grace would be able to tell them their missing relative was here, and would be all right.

But she couldn't always do that, and she hated that part of her job. It never got easier, no matter how many times she did it.

'Nurse, please!' The older, white-haired woman stepped forward and grabbed Grace's arm in a

169

firm grasp. 'Have you got my daughter Stella here? We can't find her nowhere. Red curly hair, blue eyes, thirty years old. Is she here?'

Grace patted the old lady's hand.

'If you'd like to follow me, please?'

She led them into one of the bathrooms just outside the ward they used to talk to relatives. It was somewhere quieter, more private and where they kept the brandy bottle and medicine glasses.

Taking a coat from one of the bundle of patients' clothes left in the bathroom for relatives to identify, she held it up. 'Is this your daughter's coat?'

The white-haired woman stared at the coat, which would once have been a smart navy blue, but now was stiff with dried blood and impregnated with dust and plaster.

'That's hers. That's my sister's coat.' The younger woman said. 'Thank goodness! Can we see her, please?'

Grace swallowed hard.

'I'm sorry, I'm afraid she died a short while ago. Her injuries were too bad.'

The old lady let out a soft moan and the younger woman grasped hold of her.

'Sit her down there.'

Grace nodded at a chair and unstoppered the brandy bottle they kept ready on a small table and poured some into two glasses, then handed them out to the two women.

'Drink this, it'll help.'

Grace stood back and gave the two women some time to gather themselves together as they sipped their drinks, wincing as the liquid burnt their throats. She'd do what she could to ease

170

their pain. At least their search was over – they'd found Stella. She wouldn't be a nameless victim of the latest V2 rocket any longer.

Stepping out of St Thomas's at the end of her over-long shift, Grace turned left instead of the usual right and walked to the middle of Westminster bridge and leaned against the parapet looking down into the water rippling underneath. She was exhausted, physically and emotionally. They'd been rushed off their feet dealing with a wave of incoming patients from a V2 blast. Many of them had been badly injured and several, like Stella, hadn't made it.

Grace sighed. This morning, all those people had been going about their business, and suddenly, without warning, boom, they were injured or dead. Young, old, children, it didn't matter, the V2s didn't discriminate. They hurt anyone.

A surge of anger flooded through Grace. It wasn't right or fair. But who said war was fair? How many more lives had been ruined just today? How many families had lost someone in this war? Not just away fighting, but here on home soil.

Normally Grace tried hard not to think about it too much. Dealing with what she had to do every day on the ward, it was the only way to keep going and cope with the things she saw. But sometimes, like today, it was hard not to think about it. Not to get angry.

How could she not get angry about Stella dying? She'd been so badly injured there was nothing they could do, and she just slipped away. She'd been the mother of two young boys, who were evacuated in Devon, so Stella's sister had told her.

Stella's husband had died on the North Atlantic convoys and now Stella was dead, her children were orphans.

'What if this happened to you?' a voice whispered in Grace's head.

What would happen to Marigold if she was killed by a V2? She didn't have a father to look after her any more.

Grace shuddered. She had to make plans, do something to ensure if anything happened to her, Marigold would be looked after. She would do it tonight.

## *January 1945*

Prune's fingers were numb and her cheeks had been whipped red by the raw wind, when she and Dottie turned their bikes into the lane leading down to Orchard Farm. The temperature was dropping fast now the sun had gone down and there would be frost over night.

'Last one in makes the cocoa!' Dottie shouted as she put on a spurt of speed and whizzed past Prune.

'Hey, I thought you were supposed to be tired after all the felling we've done today?'

'It's the sight of home and the thought of a warm fire!' Dottie called back over her shoulder.

Prune pedalled as fast as she could and had almost caught up when Dottie turned into the farm gate.

'I won.' Dottie panted as she jumped off her bike and skipped a few paces to a halt.

Prune brought her bike to a stop beside Dottie and leaned over the handle bars, breathing heavily.

'You had an unfair start.' She gasped, her breath misting like a cloud in the cold air. 'You caught me out. How about a fairer race tomorrow? One we both know when it's going to start, then we'll see who has to make the cocoa.'

Dottie grinned.

'You're on. But tonight the cocoa's on you. It might be tomorrow, too.'

Prune pulled a face.

'Is that a challenge?'

'Why not?' Dottie laughed. 'As long as you're not afraid of being beaten twice.'

Prune and Dottie were still laughing over their race when they went indoors. They peeled off their layers, hung them up in the porch and walked into the living-room to find there was a visitor waiting for them.

'Clem!' Dottie said.

Clem stood up.

'Hello, Dottie, Prune.'

'Hello, Clem,' Prune said, walking over to the stove and warming her hands above it. 'This is a nice surprise. Are you staying for tea? He can, can't he, Bessie?'

'Of course,' Bessie said from where she was working at the kitchen sink. 'As long as he likes rabbit stew.'

'It's very kind of you, Bessie, but I won't tonight.' Clem paused and took a sharp intake of breath. 'I've come with bad news. I'm sorry to tell you

Howard's plane didn't make it back today. He's officially Missing In Action.'

Prune's legs seemed to turn to jelly and she felt Clem grab hold of her and gently lower her into an armchair. She opened her mouth to speak but no words came out.

Bessie rushed over, wiping her hands on her apron. 'What happened?'

'All we know is the Peggy Sue went down. One of the other crews saw she was hit by flak and was losing height. They didn't see any 'chutes.'

''Chutes?' Prune shook her head. 'What do you mean?'

'Parachutes. They didn't see anyone parachuting out before they lost sight of her in the cloud.'

'So you don't actually know for sure what happened?' Bessie said.

'No,' Clem said. 'All we know is the Peggy Sue was hit by flak and was going down when she was last seen. Until we know more, the crew are all listed as Missing In Action.'

'But there's always hope. Isn't there?' Prune's words felt thick in her mouth. 'Howard might come back.'

She looked down at the engagement ring he'd given her. He'd to come back to her. She couldn't bear it if she lost him. Prune shut her eyes and concentrated hard. It didn't feel as if he was gone. He was still out there somewhere. He had to be!

Clem laid his hand on her shoulder.

'We'll keep hoping, Prune.'

A sudden loud sob made them all look at Dottie. Her normally pretty face was contorted with pain and her shoulders were shaking.

'Dottie?' Bessie moved, but before she could reach her, Dottie had thrown open the door and rushed out.

'I must go after her,' Prune said, struggling to her feet.

'No, you don't.' Bessie pushed her back down again. 'You've had a shock and you need to sit down. Clem, can you stay with her?'

He nodded.

'Of course.'

'You can make her some tea. Put sugar in it for the shock.' Bessie grabbed her coat. 'I need to find Dottie.'

'We were going to have cocoa, and I had to make it after Dottie won the race,' Prune said after Bessie had closed the door and gone out. 'That was before...'

She stopped. The words were in her head but they just wouldn't come out. That was before she knew Howard was missing. He might be back and he might not. If he didn't? Prune couldn't bear to think about it.

'Prune?' Clem said.

Prune's whole body started to shake and huge tears slid down her face.

Outside, it took a few moments for Bessie's eyes to grow accustomed to the darkness of the farmyard, but there was no sign of Dottie. It was too cold a night to be outside long without a coat on. Hurrying across the yard, Bessie wondered what had got into Dottie. Clem's news was bad, but there was still hope, after all. Why should Dottie run off? It wasn't as if Howard was her fiancé. She had always made it perfectly clear she had a career planned and wasn't going to get seriously involved with any man.

Bessie slipped in through the door of the barn, closing it quietly behind her. Inside, the white-washed walls were dimly lit by Harry's tilley lamp at the far end. The smell of warm cow and sweet hay filling the air around the cow stalls was familiar and comforting.

She hurried towards Harry and the children, who were by the cow stalls settling them in for the night. Marigold and Peter liked seeing to the animals with him after school. Thank goodness they'd been in here with Harry, and not indoors to hear Clem breaking the news to Prune, Bessie thought. They'd have to be told and it would upset them badly – especially Peter, as he'd flown in the Peggy Sue with Howard. But Bessie would deal with that later. Her first priority was to find Dottie.

'Are they all settled?' Bessie tried to sound normal.

'Nearly done,' Harry said.

'I'm looking for Dottie. Did she come in here?'

'No,' Peter replied. 'It's just us. Is it time for tea?'

Bessie smiled at Peter.

'Soon.'

Harry caught her eye.

'Is everything all right?'

'Yes.' She didn't want to say anything in front of Peter and Marigold. Not yet. 'I expect she's gone into the bike shed. Probably left something in her bike basket.'

She could tell from Harry's face that he knew something was wrong, but he just nodded.

Bessie tried the bike shed next, but there was no

sign of Dottie there, nor in the wood shed. Bessie eventually found her in the wash house. She could hear sobbing from outside, and when Bessie quietly opened the door and went in, she could just make out Dottie crouching on the little stool by the copper. There was still some warmth in the air radiating out from the copper, lit earlier for the washing.

'Dottie!' She closed the door behind her. 'Are you all right, my woman?'

Dottie shook her head and her shoulders heaved with sobs that seemed to wrench from deep inside her.

Bessie put her arm around her shoulders.

'We've got to hope Howard comes back, for Prune's sake.'

Dottie suddenly threw off Bessie's arm, stood up and turned to face her.

'It's a fool's game!' she snapped, her voice thick with emotion. 'You shouldn't encourage Prune to hope. He won't come back, and hoping will only make it worse for her in the end.'

Her anger left her and she sank back on to the stool and buried her head in her hands, sobbing loudly.

Bessie kneeled down in front of her.

'If Prune wants to hope, then she should, Dottie.'

'It's useless!' Dottie dropped her hands and drew in a deep breath. 'I hoped. I kept on hoping, day after day. But it was pointless. He died and won't be coming back. Ever.'

'Who?' Bessie asked, taking hold of one of Dottie's hands. 'Who didn't come back?'

'My husband!' Dottie's face crumpled and Bessie wrapped her arms around her while her whole body shook as more tears spilled out.

Bessie waited until Dottie's sobbing eased and then pulled back and held her at arm's length.

'I'm so sorry, Dottie. You're so young to have to lose your husband.'

Dottie shrugged.

'I'm not the only one. There's plenty out there like me.'

'Too many,' Bessie agreed, letting go of Dottie's shoulder and taking her hands in hers. 'I didn't know you'd been married.'

'I don't talk about it. It's too painful. After Jim died in forty-two, I joined the Timber Corps and thought it best to keep quiet about my past. It was easier if no-one knew and I didn't have to talk about it.'

'How did...?' Bessie paused. 'What happened to him?'

'He was a flight engineer on a Lancaster. They went down on a raid over Germany. I kept hoping he'd got out somehow and he'd come home. But then one of his friends wrote and told me he'd seen Jim's plane blow up in mid-air.' She halted. 'There were no survivors. They didn't have a chance to get out.'

'I'm sorry.' Bessie squeezed Dottie's hands. 'Hearing about Howard brought it all back to you?'

Dottie nodded.

'Prune loved him so much and I can't bear to think of her going through what I did. He was everything to her.'

'Your plans for the future to be a career girl – they are because of what you've been through?'

'I thought it was the best way forward. There's too much risk of losing someone all over again if you become involved. I've learned the hard way.'

'That's a shame, Dottie. You're only a young woman and you might meet someone one day who's right for you.'

Dottie shook her head.

'I'd rather walk a safe path, Bessie, and just look after myself and not get involved with anyone again. Look what a state I'm in, now, nearly three years since I lost Jim.'

'You've bottled this up for a long time.' Bessie smiled. 'No wonder you blew like a ginger beer!'

'I'm sorry.'

'Don't be. I understand.'

'I'll need to talk to Prune. Explain it to her.' Dottie sighed. 'I do hope Howard comes back, honestly I do. But the fact is most of them don't if their plane goes down.'

'I know. But if hoping helps Prune cope, then we've got to support her. It'll give her something to cling on to for now, anyway.' Bessie rose. 'Will you come in with me?'

Dottie shook her head.

'I need a few minutes.'

'Don't be long. You need to eat after a long day's work. The children are hungry.'

'Will you tell them about Howard?'

Bessie nodded.

'I think we have to, as they'll sense something's wrong. It's going to upset them.'

Leaving the wash house, Bessie hurried across

to the American whom she saw walking towards the gate.

'Clem, how's Prune?'

'She's quiet but OK. Harry and the children are indoors now, so I thought it was time to go.'

'Do Peter and Marigold know?'

Clem shook his head.

'Harry knows, I told him when he saw me out.'

'Thank you. We'll tell the children later.'

'Is Dottie OK? The way she rushed off...?'

'She'll be fine, Clem, this just opened up an old wound.' Bessie paused. 'Do you really think there's a chance Howard will make it back?'

Clem glanced up at the stars and then met Bessie's eyes.

'I don't know, ma'am. It happens. No-one saw the Peggy Sue actually crash because of the thick cloud, but there were no 'chutes seen, either. She couldn't have made it home.' Clem reached out and touched Bessie's arm. 'I hope and pray the whole crew comes back. Howard's a good friend of mine...' His voice wavered.

'We'll keep hoping and praying, too.' Bessie patted Clem's arm. 'Are you sure you won't stay and have some tea with us?'

'No, thank you, Bessie. It's kind of you to ask, but to tell the truth, I don't have a real appetite for food right now.'

Bessie nodded.

'Please let us know as soon as you hear anything?'

'Don't worry; I will. You can be sure of that.'

Peter stared at Bessie, not able to take in what

she'd just told him. He understood what she said, but he didn't want to believe it. Not Howard and the Peggy Sue!

'Peter?' Bessie's face was worried. 'Are you all right?'

He didn't know what to say, so he just nodded and picked up a flag marking the progress of the Allies across France from the table.

Twiddling it in his fingers he tried to make sense of what Bessie had told him. Every bit of him wanted to reject it, but it was slowly filtering through.

The bitter truth was that the Peggy Sue hadn't come back from today's mission and was last seen going down. Howard, Walt, Lieutenant Truman and the rest of the crew were missing. The Peggy Sue itself, too, that wonderful plane in which he'd flown. He'd felt so secure and safe inside her as she'd glided through the air. How could she, and all those men, be gone?

'Until we know otherwise, we'll keep hoping Howard will come back.' Bessie put her arm around his shoulders.

'Do you think he will?' Peter's voice was barely a whisper. 'And all the others?'

'The truth is, I don't know. All we can do is wait.'

The map on the desk started to blur as Peter's eyes filled with tears. A wave of sadness swelled through him. He'd been around the Rackbridge base long enough to know the chances of them coming back weren't good. He'd seen many crews go and never come back. Gone, just like that. Why should it be different with the Peggy Sue?

'Bessie?' Harry stood in the doorway. 'Marigold's asking for you.'

'Peter, I must go and see her. She's upset about Howard, too.' Bessie said. 'I'll come back soon.' She popped a kiss on his head and left.

'It's rough news for you and Marigold to hear,' Harry said, coming over to stand by the table.

'Do you think he'll come back?' Peter's voice came out in a croak.

Harry shrugged.

'I hope he does. I hope all of them will and that's all I can do. They might and they might not.' He sighed. 'It's what happens in wartime. It's not right, but it's life. People are seeing more of it in this war than the last, with the planes flying out from here instead of it all being over in France, like before.'

'Did many of your friends not come home?'

'Too many. I was one of the lucky ones. I came home. Well, most of me did.' He tapped his wooden leg. 'I still think about the ones left behind.'

'What will we do if Howard doesn't come home?'

'Remember him as he was, and live our lives to the full for him.' Harry put his hand on Peter's shoulder. 'It's what he would want you to do. But don't go down that road till you have to. There's always hope until we know different.'

Peter nodded. He knew all about hoping. He did it every day, hoping and praying his parents were alive and he'd see them again. He would do the same for Howard and all the crew of the Peggy Sue. Perhaps, if he hoped hard enough, it would work.

'Oh, Bessie! I can't stop thinking about Howard.'

Bessie sat on the bed and put her arms around Marigold and gently rocked her.

'I know, my girl.' Bessie stroked Marigold's back. 'He's in our thoughts tonight. And all those other young men who were with him in the Peggy Sue.'

Gradually Bessie felt Marigold begin to calm and relax into her shoulder, but then she turned to look at her.

'Bessie, do you think he's died, like my daddy?'

What should she say? Bessie looked at Marigold's tear-stained face. She'd already suffered enough from the war, but it was no use lying to her.

'I don't know. I hope not.'

Marigold sighed and leaned back against Bessie's shoulder again.

'Daddy said he'd come home again, but he didn't.'

Bessie's throat tightened and she swallowed hard.

'I'm sure that's what he wanted to do more than anything. He would have, if he could.'

Marigold turned her head and smiled at Bessie. 'That's what Mrs Fox told me, too. She liked my daddy. He used to help her with jobs around the house.'

'What was he like?'

'That's his picture over there.'

Marigold pointed to the framed photograph she'd brought with her from London.

'He was funny and used to make me laugh. He was kind and always singing around the house.'

Bessie listened quietly as Marigold told her about her father, and their life in London before war split up her family for ever.

'What about your father's family? Where did they live?' Bessie asked.

'He didn't have any. He was an orphan and brought up in a children's home. He always said me and Mummy were all the family he ever hoped for.'

From the way Marigold talked about her father, Bessie felt it was a shame she'd never had the chance to meet him. Marigold said nothing about her mother's family, and Bessie couldn't help herself from asking.

'What about your mummy's family, Marigold? Do you ever see them?'

Marigold shook her head as she stroked the ears of Blue, her toy rabbit.

'No. My mummy's mother died when she was three years old, and her father died just before she went to London. She hasn't got anyone else.'

Bessie didn't trust herself to speak. She nodded and hugged Marigold tightly. Grace had completely cut herself off from the life she'd had in Norfolk before she'd gone to London, and she had passed none of it on to her daughter. Marigold was completely unaware there was a huge gap in her family, because that was how Grace wanted it to be.

All Bessie could do was hope that one day Grace might see fit to change all that. Until then, she had to keep to her promise, no matter how hard it was to keep quiet and not tell Marigold all the things she'd like to say.

## Letters Galore

Bessie slipped out of the front door and made her way across the lawn towards the large cedar tree which spread its branches wide casting a cool shade. On such a warm day, it was the perfect place to take her break and to read her letter, which had come in the post that morning.

She touched the outside of her pocket, through the material of her blue VAD dress feeling the letter's firm shape inside. She smiled. A letter from Harry was like having a part of him with her and helped ease the ache of missing him. He'd been true to his word and written to her every few days, keeping her up to date with his progress at St Mary's hospital in Roehampton.

Sitting down on the bench, Bessie took out the envelope and slit it open. She paused for a moment before unfolding the sheet of paper, enjoying the feeling of anticipation. Unable to wait any longer she started to read.

*My dearest Bess,*

*I hope this finds you well and happy. I've some good news! I walked 10 yards on my own today, just with my two walking sticks ready to catch me if I stumbled. But I didn't – I kept going! It feels wonderful to be walking upright again. Standing, seeing the world from where I used to. I wish you could have been here to see me, Bess.*

*The fitters here have done a grand job adjusting the*

*leg bucket. They marked the bit giving me trouble and cut the wood away and now it fits like a glove. No more blisters. It made all the difference. I've got to keep on practising so I can go further and further. One day soon, I hope, I'll be able to walk up the drive of Marston Hall to you. Then perhaps we can go for a walk to the beck, and watch the water swirl under the bridge like we used to.*

Bessie stopped reading and looked across the lawn to where some patients were sitting in the sunshine playing dominoes or cards at the tables they'd set up for the men. Harry used to enjoy being outside in the gardens when he was a patient here. That, and going for walks with Bessie pushing him in the bathchair, which almost always led them to the beck. She hadn't been back there since he left. Whenever she took a patient out she always went to other spots. Never to her and Harry's special place, where they'd talked and laughed so much. The next time she went there, she had vowed, it would be with Harry.

She started to read again.

*This afternoon we're going to see another football match at Chelsea. All the men, myself included, enjoy these trips. I'll still be going in my wheelchair for now, but before long I'd like to go on my new leg. That will be a grand day.*

*I miss you, Bess, and I keep telling myself that every day brings me one day closer seeing you again. For now I have to keep working hard at learning to walk again, and when I've got that right I can start the rest of my life. I'm still working on my plans and I've nearly got it all sorted out. We spend a lot of time here talking about our futures. No-one's sad. This is the most cheerful bunch of men I've ever known. We've all been through a lot, with our lost limbs and all, but we're enjoying life. Anyway, talking to the other men has given me more ideas. I can't tell you any more yet.*

*Take care of yourself, Bess. I know you work so hard looking after the men.*

*With my fondest love,*

*Harry.*

Bessie leaned back against the back of the bench and smiled to herself. She was glad Harry was happy and starting to walk better now. He'd suffered with problems from blisters on his stump, and had had to wait until they had healed before he could start to walk again.

But it sounded as if he was making real progress. Bessie wished she could visit him, but she knew it was out of the question. For now, she had to content herself with Harry's letters. She had quite a pile of them tied in a ribbon in her room, and the bluebell he'd given her, which she'd pressed in her diary and often took it out to smell. Its faint perfume instantly transported her back to the day in the bluebell wood. It was a day she'd remember for the rest of her life.

Bessie knew she had to be patient and wait. Harry would come back. The day he walked up the drive to Marston Hall would be one for celebration.

She had no doubt he would do it. And she would be waiting for him.

'Post for you, Mrs Rushbrook.'

Bessie put down the basket of wood she was carrying as the postboy brought his too-large

187

bicycle to a halt in front of her.

'Hello, Thomas. What have we got today?'

'Just the one, Mrs Rushbrook.' He rummaged through the bag slung across his shoulder and handed her an envelope.

'Thank you.'

Thomas smiled and nodded as he turned his bike around. 'Cheerio, then.'

He launched himself off, with one foot on the lowest pedal and the other scooting him along until he'd picked up enough speed to throw his leg over the bike and perch on the saddle, pedalling fast to keep upright.

'Mind how you go!' Bessie called after him as she watched him sail out of the yard and turn towards the village. He was a nice lad, Bessie thought, but he had one of the worst jobs in the village, as he also delivered the telegrams. Those unexpected and unwelcome messages which often brought bad news about the fate of loved ones far away, fighting for their country.

A lot of people dreaded the sight of him coming to their door. It wasn't fair on the lad. You shouldn't blame the messenger.

Bessie turned the envelope over to see who it was for. Every time Thomas came she hoped for a letter from Robert. But today's wasn't from him. It was addressed to her and Harry in writing that she recognised – Grace's. It was unusual for Grace to write to them specifically. Normally she included a brief note for them in Marigold's letters. Why was she writing now? Was something wrong?

Bessie tucked the envelope safely in her coat pocket, picked up the basket of wood and hurried across the yard towards the house. She longed to know what was in the letter. Did Grace want her daughter to go back to London? Surely not, with all those terrible V2 rockets falling! Bessie's stomach twisted itself into a knot at the thought of sending Marigold back while there was still so much danger. It would be foolish, and if that was what Grace wanted she, Bessie, would fight her all the way if necessary.

Once she'd stoked up the fire, Bessie perched on the edge of an armchair, opened the envelope and took out the single sheet of paper.

*Dear Bessie and Harry,*

*I'm writing to you separately as I have something special I want to ask you. Please think carefully about it and don't feel under any obligation to say yes, if you don't want to. I will understand and make other arrangements.*

*There's no easy way to say this, so I'll just jump straight in. If anything should happen to me, would you please take care of Marigold for me? I know it's a lot to ask, and that why I want you to think about it carefully.*

*I hope it will never be necessary, but I also know that nothing is certain these days, and with the V2 rockets landing on London you never know if one is going to have your name on it. If one does, I'll go happier if I know Marigold's future is secure.*

*With my love,*

*Grace.*

Bessie's hands were shaking by the time she'd finished. She'd never expected this. Only moments ago she'd been thinking she'd fight Grace to keep Marigold safe, when in fact it was Grace herself who should be kept safe! She should leave London, escape all the killing and destruction.

Bessie read the letter again, looking for more clues between the lines, but the message stayed the same. Grace was in fear for her life, and wanted to be sure her daughter would be cared for if those fears came true.

She was still staring at the letter when Harry came in, blowing on his hands as he headed straight over to the fire to warm them.

'Whatever's the matter, Bess?' he said.

'Read this,' she whispered, handing him the letter.

Harry's face turned pale as he read the words.

'That's a bolt from the blue.' He dropped down into the armchair opposite her. 'Things are bad in London to make her think like that.'

'She must believe it really could happen.' Bessie's voice came out in a croak.

'Well, Grace is living in it every day, and seeing the results in the hospital. It's bound to make her think the worst.'

'What shall we tell her? Yes?'

'Of course. There's no question we wouldn't give the girl a home. We've done it before.'

Bessie nodded.

'I'll write to her tonight and ask her again to come here. She ought to get out of London. There's plenty of nursing she could do in hospitals around here.'

'You can ask,' Harry said. 'But whether she'll do it is another matter. You know Grace as well as I do. Her stubbornness might get the better of her.'

'I could ask her to do it for Marigold's sake.

190

The child's lost a father – she shouldn't have to lose a mother as well before this war is done. Grace might do it for her daughter.'

Harry reached over and took hold of Bessie's hands in his.

'Don't get your hopes up. It will be up to Grace to decide, and all we can do is hope that, if she stays in London, none of those damn rockets has her name on it.'

Bessie squeezed his hands.

'We mustn't tell Marigold anything about this. If she had any idea her mother thought she was in real danger it would unsettle her. I know she worries about her as it is. I'll put the letter away in a safe place and hope we never have to tell her about it.'

'The war can't go on much longer. The Allies are breaking through.'

'Hitler's got a lot to answer for,' Bessie said bitterly. 'If the wives and mothers of people caught up in this could get their hands on him...'

'You'd wring his blithering neck,' Harry finished.

'There'd be a very long queue!' Bessie shook her head. 'Women don't start wars, but they have to cope with the mess war makes of lives.'

Harry got to his feet and, hauling Bessie up out of her chair, wrapped his arms around her.

'You were my antidote to war, Bessie Carter-as-was. If they could bottle you up and sprinkle you over the Nazis it would be over in a trice!'

Bessie kissed his cheek.

'You say the nicest things, Harry Rushbrook. I suppose I should take that as a compliment, should I?'

'Of course.' Harry looked at her more, seriously for a moment. 'We'll get through this together, Bess. I promise you.'

'Prune! Slow down!' Dottie yelled as her end of the bow saw rapidly sliced through the air towards her. 'I can't keep up with you at this pace. If you carry on like this, someone's going to get hurt.'

Prune let go of her end of the saw and it juddered to a halt in Dottie's hand.

'That's it. We're taking a break.'

She looked at her friend's pale face which had dark smudges under her eyes. Dottie was aware of how little sleep Prune was getting, because whenever she woke up in the night, Prune was always awake, too, usually sitting up in bed, with the corner of the blackout curtain lifted, staring out at the night. She hadn't slept properly since Clem brought them the news about Howard, two weeks ago.

'Come on?' Dottie stood up and held out her gloved hand to Prune. 'Let's have a brew-up.'

Prune shook her head.

'I'm not thirsty, Dottie. You go ahead.'

'I'm not asking. I'm telling you,' Dottie said, one hand on her hip. 'You can't go on like this, it's not good for you.'

'I know, but...' Prune shrugged her shoulders. Dottie saw her eyes were glistening with unshed tears.

'Let's get some tea in us first. It'll help.' Dottie grabbed Prune's hand and pulled her up.

'It's only an hour since we stopped for dinner!' Prune protested.

'What of it?'

Dottie led the way over to the fire they kept going just outside the little bivouac shelter where they ate their sandwiches. The fire provided a welcome warmth when they stopped work and a means of making tea in the billy of water hanging over it.

'There's no-one here to tell us what to do, and we always get our work done. We need to have some tea and talk – for your sake and the safety of my fingers!'

'OK.'

'Right, sit yourself down and I'll make the tea.'

Dottie busied herself adding some tea leaves to the billy can plus a small piece of wood, as she'd learned at her training camp. It helped to absorb smoke and improve the flavour, so she'd been told, and it always seemed to work.

A few minutes later Dottie sat down next to Prune, who was sitting hunched up under the bivouac, her long legs pulled up and her elbows resting on her knees.

'Don't let your tea go cold.' Dottie blew on her own cup of tea, her breath sending the floating tea leaves skidding across to the far side of the cup.

'I won't. Thanks, Dottie.'

'My pleasure.' She took a tiny sip of tea. 'Do you want to tell me what's wrong today?'

'Do I have to spell it out to you?'

'I don't just mean Howard.' Dottie threw her arm around Prune's shoulders. 'There's something else today. Is it that letter?'

'What letter?'

'Come on, Prune. I know you whisked it away

before I could see it, but Bessie told me a letter had come for you. Was it from your mother?'

Prune took a gulp of scalding hot tea and then spluttered as the hot liquid burnt her mouth.

Dottie slapped her on the back.

'It's hot, remember?'

Prune put the tea to the side and ran her hands through her hair.

'The truth is,' she said, looking into the glowing fire, 'I don't know what it says because I haven't opened it yet.'

'Are you going to?'

'I don't want to. It's my mother's reply to my last letter asking for her permission to marry Howard. I'm sure what she's got to say about it will be nearly enough to burn a hole through the paper.'

'It's taken her a while to write back. I thought she'd do it by return of post.'

'She's been away over Christmas and the New Year and then visited relatives so she wasn't due to go home until last week. She'd have found my letter waiting for her, and now...' Her voice faltered and she looked down at her mud-caked boots. 'It probably doesn't matter what she says now. She'll be happy about that.'

'Don't do that, Prune. You've got to keep hoping!'

'It didn't work out for you, did it?' Prune snapped.

Dottie drew in a sharp breath.

'No, it didn't, but there was no chance for my Jim. His plane blew up. No-one saw what happened to the Peggy Sue, Prune, so there's always a chance.'

Prune turned to look at Dottie.

'I'm sorry. I shouldn't have said that. I didn't mean it.'

'I know you didn't. But you mustn't give up hope.' Dottie took another sip of tea. 'So, are you going to open it, then?'

'I suppose I have to, some time.'

'I'll do it for you if you want.'

Prune shook her head.

'No. I'll do it.' She reached into the pocket of her cord breeches and pulled out the letter. 'Here goes.' She ripped it open and took out a single sheet of thick cream paper.

As Prune read the letter, her face developed a pink spot on each cheek.

'Did she say yes?'

Prune started to laugh.

'You're a crazy woman, Dottie!'

'It's good to hear you laugh.' Dottie squeezed her arm. 'Seriously, is it what you thought?'

'Take a look.' Prune passed the letter to Dottie.

Quickly reading the words written in bold handwriting, there was no doubting Prune's mother's reaction to hearing her daughter wanted to marry a GI, and not Jeremy. Her answer to Prune's request for permission was a definite no, and carried an unmotherly threat of consequences if her daughter choose to disobey her.

'No surprise there, then.' Dottie passed the letter back to Prune.

'None at all.'

Prune got up and threw the letter on the fire, and stood watching it burst into flames, curl and blacken into ash.

'So what now?'

'Wait and hope Howard comes back. If he does, I'll marry him without my mother's permission when I'm twenty-one.'

'What about her threat to disown and disinherit you if you marry him?'

Prune bit her lip.

'It's my life. I won't marry someone I don't love.' She swallowed hard. 'If she wants to disown me, that's her business. Her loss.'

'What about if ... if you never marry Howard?'

'I still won't marry Jeremy. Neither of us want to.' Prune took a deep breath. 'If Howard doesn't come back, then I'll choose another route for myself. *I'll* choose it, no-one else.'

'Will you tell her Howard is missing?'

'No. I couldn't bear the thought that she might be pleased to hear that.'

### The Patient Returns

As Bessie paced up and down outside the front door of Marston Hall, stopping every now and then to look down the drive, it took all her will-power not to go down to the station to meet Harry's train.

But she'd waited here because she knew how much he wanted to walk back up the drive of Marston Hall to see her. It would be so different from when he first arrived there in the back of an ambulance. That was a man who was withdrawn and quiet and in turmoil over his future, after having the one he'd planned snatched away from him by an enemy shell.

'Any sign of him yet?' Ethel's voice made Bessie jump. She turned to her friend, who'd poked her head around the front door.

'Not yet. Any time now.'

'I won't wait.' Ethel grinned. 'Don't want to spoil your reunion. Matron says to remind you about the tea later on. You'll bring him in, won't you?'

'Of course I will. He'll want to come and see everyone and show off his walking.'

'Enjoy yourself with your beau.' Ethel winked at Bessie before withdrawing her head and closing the door.

Bessie smiled at her friend's parting words. After Harry had left she'd finally been able to talk about her relationship with him, and now all the staff at the hospital knew about Harry's return today.

Patients didn't often come back to see them again as most of them came from other parts of the country. So Harry's visit was a rare joy.

Turning around to look down the drive again, Bessie saw a figure walking up the tree-lined drive. She couldn't make out his face clearly under the dappled shade, from the trees, but there was no doubt it was Harry.

Bessie ran down the short flight of steps and took off along the drive, holding up her skirt so she could run quicker. If Matron could see her, she would tell her not to run, but she was outside and nothing was going to stop her from reaching

Harry as soon as she could.

The closer she got, the clearer his face became. He was smiling at her and as she neared him, he held his arms out to welcome her. Bessie slowed to a walk just before she reached him, for fear of knocking him off balance.

Then she went into his arms, and they hugged each other tightly under the cool shade of the beech trees whose branches intermingled above them over the drive.

'It's so good to see you.' Bessie stepped back and held Harry at arm's length, studying his face. 'You look wonderful! So tall and upright.'

Harry smiled, his blue eyes filled with happiness.

'Bess. I've missed you.' He gently kissed her.

Her cheeks grew warm.

'I missed you, too.' Tears suddenly stung her eyes and Bessie looked down at this new leg for a moment to give herself a chance to compose herself. 'How's the leg? Did it bear up, walking from the station?'

'It's fine. I still walk with a bit of a limp, but that's nothing.'

'I'm so happy for you,' Bessie said. 'Everyone's looking forward to seeing you again, and you're honoured with an invitation to have tea with Matron. She would like to see you.'

'I'd be delighted to see her and everyone again.' He stopped and gently stroked Bessie's cheek. 'But first I want to be with you. Will you come for a walk with me, to the beck?'

Bessie nodded, unable to speak.

Harry smiled warmly and took hold of her arm,

linked it through his, and then laced his fingers through hers as they walked down the drive together.

'It's a slightly different view looking at it from up here,' Harry said, standing on the wooden bridge over the beck. He turned and met Bessie's eyes. 'I've often thought about coming back here with you and what I'd say to you.'

'What are you going to say to me?' Bessie asked. 'Are you going to finally let me in on your plan, or is it still a secret?'

Harry smiled.

'If you really want to know...'

'Of course I do!' Bessie squeezed his hand. 'I've been waiting for you to tell me for months.'

Harry lifted Bessie's hand up and gently kissed it.

'I'm sorry I couldn't tell you before. I had to know if I could do it first. I didn't want to tell you and then find out it was impossible.'

He paused for a moment and glanced down at the water sliding under the bridge. Then he looked straight into Bessie's eyes again.

'Do you remember what you said to me that day in the hospital, when I was still in bed and you should have gone off duty?'

'Yes. I didn't like seeing you so quiet and withdrawn and knew there must be something upsetting you.'

'You were right. You told me I should think of another way to do what I wanted to.'

Bessie nodded.

'Well, I have. Farming's all I ever wanted to do.

Being a shopkeeper wasn't for me. So, if I can't farm in the fells, then I should farm somewhere else where it's easier for me to get around and in a way I can manage.'

'You're still going to farm?'

Harry smiled.

'I am, but much smaller than on the fells, and no sheep. Grow crops to sell, things like fruit and vegetables and keep poultry. All things I can manage.' He took both Bessie's hands in hers. 'And I've found the perfect place to do it. I had money put by from the sale of my father's shop and it was enough to buy a small farm. I found one, Bess, here in Norfolk, in Rackbridge.'

'Rackbridge? I know it! The train goes through it on the way home.'

'The farm's small, just twenty acres, including a wood with bluebells.' He smiled at her. 'There are good solid barns and sheds, an orchard and fields. The only thing missing is a house, because it was part of a bigger farm that was carved up and sold in two lots.'

'It sounds good, but where are you going to live?'

'I've already sorted that out. I've bought two old railway carriages and I'm turning them into a house. By the time I've finished it will be almost perfect.'

'Almost?'

'There's one more thing.' Harry hesitated. 'I'd like you to do me the honour of becoming my wife. I love you, Bess, and if you married me, then my life would be perfect.'

Bessie's heart was thumping hard inside her as

she looked into Harry's eyes which were shining with love for her. There was only one answer she could give.

'Yes.' Her voice was thick with emotion. 'Yes, Harry, I would be delighted to marry you.'

'Engaged to be married?' Matron looked at them, her blue eyes twinkling with amusement. 'Congratulations to you both.'

Bessie inwardly sighed with relief. She'd been worried about telling Matron and had wanted to keep their engagement secret for the time being, but Harry had been bursting with happiness, wanting to tell the whole world straight away.

Bessie hadn't the heart to stop him. Besides, as her fiancé, he'd be welcome to visit her at Marston Hall.

'Thank you, Matron,' Harry said, shaking her hand

'When are you planning on marrying?' Matron asked.

'In the New Year,' Bessie replied.

'I need to finish the house first,' Harry explained.

'I hope the war will be over by then,' Bessie added.

'It can't go on much longer.' Matron smiled. 'In the meantime, we've some tea waiting for you. Mrs Taylor's baked a cake and everyone wants to take a look at you walking, Sergeant Rushbrook. To see what a good job we've done on you. Come along, then.'

Matron turned and strode off down the hall, expecting them to follow along behind.

Bessie squeezed Harry's hand and smiled up at him.

'Come on, we don't want to miss out on Mrs Taylor's cake!'

### Reunion

Bessie loved this part of the day, when everyone was home from school or work. There was a sense of shutting out the cold darkness and settling down for the evening, snug inside the house. She took the lid off the large pan of stew and dumplings, gently stirring it around. The rich aroma of rabbit and vegetables rose up and filled the air.

'Is it ready?' Marigold peered into the pan at the gently bubbling mixture.

'It smells lovely!' Peter came out of his bedroom.

'We can have it as soon as everyone's ready,' Bessie said. 'Not much longer to wait.'

Dottie and Prune were home from the woods and in their room, changing out of their dirty work clothes. When they'd had a wash, Bessie would send Peter out to tell Harry to come in.

Bessie had just put the lid back on the pan when there was a loud knock at the door. They weren't expecting anyone. Wiping her hands on her apron, she went out into the porch and opened the door.

It was Thomas.

Bessie's stomach instantly twisted into a knot. He'd already delivered the post today, so coming to Orchard Farm now could only mean one thing.

Bessie's eyes were drawn to the buff-coloured envelope he held in his hand. A telegram.

'For you and Mr Rushbrook.' Thomas held it out to her.

Bessie forced herself to speak.

'Thank you.'

Thomas nodded, his eyes full of understanding at what his appearance at their door could mean, and quickly retreated down the stairs and slipped away into the darkness.

Closing the door behind her, Bessie stood still in the porch and stared down at the telegram in her shaking hands. Was it Robert? What had happened to him?

'Bessie?' Peter opened the inner door and looked at her. 'Bessie, are you all right?'

She opened her mouth to speak, but couldn't seem to get the words out. Swallowing hard, she tried again.

'Could you go out and fetch Harry?' Her voice came out in little more than a whisper.

'Of course. What shall I tell him?'

'Just say ... a telegram's come.'

Peter nodded.

'I won't be long.' He grabbed his coat off the hook and went outside.

Alone in the porch, Bessie suddenly felt very cold. A foreboding chill was creeping through her body and she needed to be by the stove. Opening the door she went inside, thankful Dottie and Prune were still in their room.

She laid the telegram on the table set ready for their meal, and went to stand in front of the stove, her hands outstretched over the top to get some heat back into them.

'Is that a telegram?' Marigold asked from where she was sitting in an armchair drawing in her diary.

Bessie nodded unable to speak.

'I don't like telegrams.' She came to stand beside Bessie. 'Mummy got one of them telling her Daddy had been killed.'

Bessie slipped her arm around Marigold's shoulders and hugged the girl to her. She wished Harry would hurry and come, but at the same time she wanted to keep this moment for as long as possible.

Was it better not to know what might be in the telegram, to be living in a time when everything was fine? Living in a world where she knew her son was alive. Not here, perhaps, but alive, and doing his bit to serve his country.

Once the telegram was opened, who knew what news it would bring, or how it would change things. During wartime telegrams were usually the harbingers of bad news and no-one wanted to receive one, just in case.

How long it was before Harry and Peter came in, Bessie didn't know. It seemed like for ever and yet it was too soon that they came in, red-cheeked from the cold outside.

Harry's eyes locked with Bessie's and she knew he expected the worst, as she did. The door to Dottie and Prune's room opened and the two young women came out laughing.

'Bessie, you'll never guess...!' Dottie began, but stopped and looked round at everyone gathered there. 'What's going on?'

'We've had…' Bessie began.

'A telegram,' Harry finished.

Dottie put her hand to her mouth. She knew all about telegrams and how the news they brought changed people's lives for ever.

Prune stepped forward.

'Marigold, come into our room for a bit. Peter, can you bring a book to read to us?'

Peter nodded and with a quick look at Bessie and Harry, dashed into his room, reappearing moments later with a book.

He understood, Bessie thought. He'd told her about boys at his school receiving bad news about their fathers in telegrams. Peter knew very well what this one might mean.

'Come on, Marigold,' Peter said. 'I've got a good adventure story to read.'

Marigold looked up at Bessie.

'Go on, you go with the others for a few minutes.'

'Are you going to open the telegram?'

Bessie nodded.

'This way, Marigold.' Dottie took hold of her hand and led her into her and Prune's bedroom. She turned and gave Bessie and Harry a sympathetic smile, then quietly closed the door behind her.

The air in the room suddenly seemed charged, and the ticking from the clock on the mantelpiece became more pronounced. It was like the change in atmosphere just before a storm breaks. Bessie sank down in to an armchair and nodded towards where the telegram lay on the table.

'Can you open it, Harry? I don't think…'

Without saying anything, Harry picked it up and checked the address on the front as if to confirm it was for them. Then with one swift movement he slit it open and pulled out the single sheet.

Bessie closed her eyes as he unfolded it. She couldn't bear to watch his face as he read it. She concentrated on her breathing, trying to steady her heart which was pounding so hard inside her she could feel her blood pulsing in her temples. Then she suddenly felt Harry's hands on her arms as he quickly pulled her on to her feet and into his arms. He hugged her tightly to his chest. Bessie hugged him back hard, her throat aching with the effort of holding back tears.

Harry was laughing. His body was shaking with laughter! Bessie pulled back and stared at him.

'Harry?'

'It's all right, Bessie!' he managed to say. 'It's not what you thought.'

Pushing herself out of his arms, Bessie rushed across to the table and picked up the telegram.

*COMING TO RACKBRIDGE TONIGHT ON 9PM TRAIN STOP GRACE*

A wave of relief surged through Bessie. It wasn't about Robert! He was safe. Their son was still alive.

Harry shook his head and ran a hand through his hair.

'I can't tell you what a relief that is, Bess. I thought…'

'The worst.' She shuddered to shake off the shadow of fear that had descended on her. 'Grace is coming here, tonight! She never said so in her last letter to Marigold.'

206

'Perhaps she got some leave at short notice.' Harry took hold of Bessie's hand. 'It is good news. Grace is finally coming back. Think how happy Marigold will be.'

'She certainly will. But it'll be strange to see her again after all this time.'

Harry squeezed her hand.

'It'll be all right, Bess.'

Bessie's mind started to race through all the things they'd need to do.

'We must sort out where Grace is going to sleep.'

'The first thing to do is tell Marigold.'

Harry nodded towards the window of Dottie and Prune's room, where they could see four faces peering through the gap in the curtain at them, waiting for news.


'Is it time to go?'

Bessie looked up from the sock she was darning. 'No. Another hour yet.'

Marigold sighed.

'How about a game of draughts?' Dottie suggested. 'I've got to get you back from the last time you beat me.'

'All right.'

'Thank you,' Bessie mouthed silently to Dottie as Marigold looked out the board and box of pieces. Dottie soon had Marigold engrossed in the game, both laughing when they took each other's pieces.

Bessie understood how Marigold felt – she wanted to go herself. But there was no point in going too early. The train wasn't due until nine o'clock, and they'd done everything they needed

207

to, making up a makeshift camp-bed for Marigold to sleep in while Grace had her bed.

Darning socks gave Bessie something to do, keep her fingers busy while her mind drifted. Only a few hours ago she'd been looking forward to a normal evening, but it had turned into one of see-sawing emotions. First the shock of the telegram, when fear had turned her blood cold, followed by the relief and surprise of Grace's visit.

Now, they waited. Prune was sitting in the opposite armchair reading a book and the draughts game was in full swing while Harry and Peter plotted the Allies' latest movements on the map.

Only Bessie and Harry knew the significance of Grace's visit. To Marigold, it would be joy at seeing her mother again, something she'd been desperate to happen for so long. The others – Peter, Dottie and Prune – were happy for Marigold and eager to meet her mother, about whom they'd heard so much.

But for Bessie and Harry, Grace's visit was a homecoming. What would Grace be like after all this time? Would she tell Marigold about her past? Tell her who Bessie and Harry really were? Would she pretend she'd never been to Orchard Farm before? All Bessie could do was wait and see. But it was hard.

Her mind drifted back to the last time Grace had been at Orchard Farm. She'd been so angry, desperate to get away. She had refused to listen to Bessie and Harry's pleas to wait. Grace had been determined to go, and go she had.

'Shall I make some cocoa, Bessie?'

Prune's voice dragged Bessie's thoughts back to the present.

'Yes. Will I help?'

'You stay there,' Prune said. 'I can manage.'

Bessie glanced at the clock. Three quarters of an hour until they needed to leave. Time was dragging.

Prune was watching over a pan of milk on the stove when there was a loud knock at the door. Everyone stopped what they were doing and looked at each other. It came again, louder and more insistent. Who could it be? Had Grace caught an earlier train?

'I'll go,' Prune said.

Bessie waited, straining to hear. Prune had closed the inner door because of the blackout. Bessie was about to go to the door when Dottie cried out.

'The milk, Bessie!'

Bessie turned to the milk pan. A froth of bubbles were about to tip over the sides. She snatched it off the heat.

'Great reflexes, Bessie.'

Bessie turned round. It was Clem. His arm was around Prune, who was laughing and crying at the same time.

'Prune! What's going on?' Bessie asked.

Dottie rushed over and grabbed hold of Prune's hand.

'It's OK,' Clem said. 'She's had a shock. A good one.'

'Well, tell us what's going on!' Dottie snapped.

'He's alive!' Prune said through her sobs. 'Howard's alive!'

'Is it true? Is he back at Rackbridge?' Harry asked. The noise had brought him and Peter back into the living-room.

'It's true. We just got word, and I had to come and tell you,' Clem explained.

Dottie led Prune to one of the armchairs and pushed her friend down into it.

'Right, tell us everything,' she insisted, sitting on the arm of the chair with her arm around Prune's shoulders.

'When the Peggy Sue got hit, she did go down, as we thought,' Clem said. 'But everyone managed to get out and parachuted down behind Allied lines.'

'Why has it taken so long to hear about them?'

'Some were injured and it took time to get back.'

'Has the crew come back to base?' Peter asked.

'Some. Walt's back and some of the gunners. Howard broke his arm coming down. He had to get it fixed in a hospital. At least we know he's OK, and he'll be back soon.'

'Great news, Clem!' Bessie could hardly believe they'd been so lucky. All the crew was safe.

Bessie looked at Prune who, despite her puffy red eyes, looked happier than she had for weeks. She'd borne Howard's missing-in-action fate bravely, but it had taken a toll on her, giving her face a sadness which never left her, even when she'd smiled. But now, she could let that all go; her faith that Howard hadn't been killed had come through.

'Why did the Peggy Sue go down?' Peter asked.

'She was hit by flak and had three engines out,

no hydraulics or electrics. She couldn't keep flying.'

'Lucky they made it back behind the Allies' lines,' Harry said.

'Yes, sir.' Clem nodded. 'Could have been a whole different story otherwise.'

'We don't want to think about that,' Dottie said. 'It's been a night of good surprises.'

Prune stood up and looked round at everyone. Her eyes were still red, but her face was glowing with happiness.

'Who wants a cup of cocoa to celebrate?'

## Where Is Grace?

'What's the time, Bessie?' Marigold asked. She was desperate not to be late because she had to be there when her mother's train pulled in at the station.

'We've plenty of time, don't worry,' Bessie said. 'There's a good chance the train will be late, anyway. But we'll definitely be there at nine o'clock, especially if you keep going as fast as you are!'

Marigold laughed, her breath coming out in puffs in the frosty air. She'd skipped all the way from Orchard Farm. Sometimes she went ahead of Bessie, then turned and came back again. Her whole body felt like it was tingling with energy. Normally she'd have been in bed and asleep by now. But not tonight. Bessie had let Marigold stay up late for once. She couldn't have slept, anyway, if she'd stayed behind at Orchard Farm.

'I'm glad the moon's so bright tonight.' Marigold pointed to the big, cream-coloured full moon which was casting a milky light down on them. A bombers' moon, they called it, but she hoped there would be no bombers here tonight, just the wonderful, marvellous joy of seeing her mother again.

Marigold had hardly been able to believe it when Bessie had told her the news. She'd wanted her mother to come ever since she arrived in Norfolk. But she hadn't been able to come, not until now.

'Do you remember when you met me at the station?' Marigold asked.

'Yes, I do. I was nervous about meeting you.'

'Were you?' Marigold stopped skipping and slipped her gloved hand into Bessie's. 'I was really scared of coming here. I didn't want to come, but Mummy said I had to.'

'I think she was right. London's a dangerous place with all those rockets falling on it.'

'That's what she said. But I'm glad I did come, Bessie, because I love living with you and Harry. And Peter, Dottie and Prune.'

Bessie squeezed Marigold's hand.

'We love having you with us.'

Everyone at Orchard Farm had become part of Marigold's family. Though her mother wasn't there, they were the best people to be with if she couldn't be with her. Marigold's life in London seemed a long way away now.

'Do you think Mummy will like it here?' Marigold asked.

'I hope so. Though it will be a big change from London for her.'

Marigold nodded.

'A lot quieter and less busy. I can't wait to show her around! She can help me collect the eggs and feed the chickens. Do you think Harry will let her milk Beauty and Buttercup?'

'I'm sure he will, if she'd like to.'

Nine o'clock came and went, and there was still no sign of the train as they stood on the platform. Marigold's insides felt like they were squirming with excitement. She stared down the line, straining her ears for the sound of an approaching train, but there was nothing. Just the night-time sound of a tawny owl calling in the trees.

Marigold felt Bessie's hand on her shoulders.

'Don't worry, she'll be here soon. There aren't many trains running on time these days. Do you want to go and wait in the waiting-room for a while?'

'No.' Marigold shook her head.

Bessie smiled at her.

'Don't get cold, then. Keep moving around. Why don't you do some more skipping?'

'Can I do it on the platform?'

'There's only you and me here, so I think it will be fine. Just keep an eye out for anyone else.'

Marigold felt her blood surge through her as she skipped the whole length of the platform. All her excited energy was being put to use, powering her arms and legs along. It was if she was flying, her breaths bellowing out into the cold air, like the smoke out of an engine. Up and down the platform she went. Away from Bessie and back again.

She'd just reached the far end of the platform and stood for a moment catching her breath, when she heard it. A train. It was coming. Hushing and steaming its way through the night towards them, bringing her mother to her.

Marigold stilled the rope, turned and ran full pelt along the length of the platform.

'It's coming. It's coming!' she called to Bessie. She skidded to a halt beside Bessie and grabbed hold of her hand. 'The train's coming!'

Bessie smiled and squeezed her hand.

'Are you all right? Excited?'

Marigold suddenly couldn't speak. She just nodded and squeezed Bessie's hand back. For some strange reason, now the moment was almost there, she felt shy. But that was silly, she was going to see her mother again!

'I'm a bit nervous,' she whispered.

'Me, too,' Bessie said.

Marigold looked up at Bessie.

'Why are you nervous? You knew her before she went to London. And she trusts you. That's why she sent me here.'

'I know, but it's been a long time since I saw her.'

'When did you last see her?'

Bessie didn't answer because, with a hissing and squealing of brakes, the train they'd waited for pulled into the station.

Marigold's heart was jumping around inside her. Which carriage would her mother be in? Doors flew open and a few passengers stepped out. There were some Americans like Clem and

Howard and a few local people, but no sign of her mother.

'Where's Mummy?' Marigold tugged at Bessie's hand. 'Come on, we have to look.'

'Perhaps she fell asleep,' Bessie said.

They started to walk the length of the train, peering into carriages looking for a sleeping Grace. But Marigold's mother wasn't in any of them.

'She's not there!' Her voice came out in a squeak as panic started to rise inside her. 'Where is she, Bessie?'

Bessie patted her shoulder.

'Don't worry. I'll ask the guard to help me look again.'

Marigold stood on the platform while both Bessie and the guard rechecked the whole length of the train – compartments, corridors, guard van, everywhere. But they didn't find her. There was no sign of Grace anywhere on the train.

'I'm sorry, but she's not there.' Bessie put her arm around Marigold. 'She probably just missed the train from London and she'll be here tomorrow instead.'

Marigold's throat ached and her eyes stung with tears. She could hardly believe it. She'd been so excited and desperate to see her mother. She'd said in her telegram she'd be there on the nine o'clock train. But she wasn't. A surge of disappointment flooded through Marigold, quenching her excitement like water on a fire.

'She might be on the next train,' she whispered.

Bessie shook her head.

'This is the last train for today.' She pulled

Marigold to her. 'I know you're disappointed, but she probably just got delayed. It happens a lot with the war on.'

Marigold couldn't hold back the tears any longer. They slid hotly down her cheeks. She buried her face in Bessie's coat and sobbed, as the guard blew his whistle and moments later the train chuffed out of the station.

'Come on, we'd better go home.' Bessie held Marigold at arm's length and looked at her. 'She'll be here as soon as she can, perhaps on the first train tomorrow. Just you wait and see.'

Marigold nodded and tried to smile, but her face couldn't quite do it. She didn't feel happy and couldn't pretend. Instead, she took Bessie's hand, glad she was here with her.

As Bessie led them out of the station, Marigold turned her head to check the platform one last time, just in case her mother was there, and somehow they'd missed her. But she wasn't.

'Are you asleep?' Bessie whispered.

Harry turned over and faced her.

'No. Can't you sleep, Bess?'

Bessie sighed.

'I keep going over tonight in my mind. It doesn't make sense, Grace sending the telegram and not coming.'

'There's probably a good reason for it. You said yourself she might have missed the train.'

'I know, I know.' Bessie paused. 'But I've got a bad feeling about this, Harry. It seems odd she should telegram out of the blue, then not turn up.'

Harry took hold of Bessie's hand.

'She'll probably turn up tomorrow.'

'Do you think she changed her mind about coming here at the last minute? Decided she couldn't come back, after all?'

'No. Grace would not let her daughter think she was coming and then change her mind. She'd have known how much Marigold was looking forward to seeing her.'

'She was so disappointed, Harry. Poor little mite. I could see it in her face.'

'You know what trains are like these days. We'll probably get another telegram in the morning saying she's coming tomorrow afternoon.'

'I hope so, Harry. I really do. When she didn't turn up it made me realise how much I want to see her again. I've wanted that for a long time, ever since she left. But tonight, when it looked like she was finally coming back, I was nervous.' Bessie swallowed hard. 'Then, when she wasn't on the train, I wanted to cry along with Marigold.'

'You've never stopped caring for her, have you?'

Bessie shook her head.

'Of course not. Have you?'

'No. But I think it runs far deeper with you.'

'I made that promise about Grace a long time ago, Harry, and I meant it. Nothing's changed about that, even after what happened. It never will.'

Harry put his arms around Bessie and hugged her.

'You're a fine woman, Bessie Rushbrook. When you give your word, you stick to it through thick and thin.'

Bessie hugged Harry back fiercely. Whenever

she made a promise, it was, as far as she was concerned, for ever. She didn't take it lightly. It was what she'd been taught to do as a child. She'd given her word to Grace, and to Peter's parents, that she'd care for their children. She'd made her promises to Harry when she'd become his wife. Her promise regarding Grace still stood strong.

But there was one other promise she'd made, one forced upon her, which still grieved her. She'd followed it through, and kept to her word. But it haunted her, and she wish she'd never had to make it. Until her last breath it was her secret, one she had to bear on her own. She couldn't even share it with Harry.

## Spanish Flu

Bessie took a bite of toast and jam and closed her eyes as the flavour burst on her tongue. Creamy butter and strawberry jam on Mrs Taylor's freshly baked bread. It was the best thing she'd ever tasted.

'How's that?' Ethel asked.

Opening her eyes, Bessie nodded as she finished her mouthful.

'Wonderful. You wouldn't believe how good this tastes!' She took another bite and again the flavours and textures of the simple food entranced her. She hadn't eaten anything for the past two days while she'd been so ill. All she'd managed was sips of water which had soothed her burning

218

throat for an instant before it had started to throb again, matching the ache in her head and her limbs.

'I'm pleased to see you eating again.' Ethel perched on the chair beside Bessie's bed. 'We were all worried about you. You even had Matron sitting with you during the night.'

'Matron?'

Ethel nodded.

'You don't remember?'

'I vaguely remember someone like Matron being here when I woke up once. I thought I'd dreamed it.'

'I'm not surprised, with the high fever you had. Still, you're on the mend now.' Ethel patted Bessie's arm. 'We've got to build you up again and get some strength back into you. This Spanish flu is a real bad one. It's had people dropping like flies.'

'How many more have it?'

'There's you, and Agnes in the kitchen and four of the men. No-one has...' Ethel hesitated. 'Everyone's on the mend now.'

Bessie knew what Ethel was going to say. No-one had died, thank goodness. They had all escaped, because this influenza could be a killer. Bessie knew she'd been lucky, she'd survived it. Now she had to concentrate on getting stronger. She had a lot to live for, because she was going to marry Harry in the New Year.

'Eat up,' Ethel said. 'Then I'll help you wash and change, because there's someone wants to see you.'

'Who?'

'Harry.'

'I was going to see him...' Bessie remembered she'd been getting ready to go out when she'd been taken ill. It had come on so quickly, she hadn't even been able to send him word she couldn't meet him.

Ethel nodded.

'You had him worried when you didn't turn up. He came looking for you. He's been coming in every day since you've been ill, wanting to know how you are. Matron even let him come and sit with you for a few minutes while you were asleep.'

Bessie stared at Ethel.

'Matron allowed him to come up here, into my room?'

'Just for a few minutes, while she stood guard over you. She could see how worried he was, and took pity on him.'

'I didn't know he'd been here.' The thought of Harry sitting by her bedside made Bessie's heart swell with love for him.

'So come on, eat up so we can get you smartened up for your visitor. You're still too weak to get up, so Matron's letting him come up here again to see you for a few minutes. I'm to be your chaperone.' Ethel raised her eyebrows. 'Matron's orders.'

In a very short while Bessie lay, propped up on a pile of pillows, waiting. Washing, changing her nightgown, brushing and replaiting her long hair made her feel so much fresher and better. She was ready to see Harry. Dear sweet Harry.

A light tapping on the door made Bessie jump, and before she could call out Ethel opened the door and stuck her head in.

'Are you ready?' Ethel beamed at Bessie. 'I've brought your visitor.'

Bessie smoothed down the sheet, then nodded, her heartbeat quickening. Ethel opened the door wide and stepped aside to reveal Harry standing in the doorway, his cap in his hand.

'Hello, Harry,' Bessie said softly.

'Bess.' Harry's clear blue eyes met hers and he stood still looking at her.

'In you go,' Ethel told him. 'You've only five minutes, so don't waste it. I'll wait here, just outside the door.'

'Thank you.' Harry limped forward into the room and sat down on the chair beside Bessie's bed. He took hold of her hand. 'You look so much better.'

'I heard you came to see me. I had no idea you'd been.' She gently touched his cheek. 'I'm so very glad you're here.'

'Just for five minutes. Matron's orders. But she's been good to me, letting me see you.'

'I'm sorry I didn't meet you that day.'

'It doesn't matter. The important thing is you're getting better.' He smiled at her. 'Though I did worry if you'd suddenly had second thoughts about marrying me!'

Bessie grabbed hold of Harry's other hand.

'Listen to me, Harry Rushbrook. I'm going to marry you, like we planned. Nothing, or no-one, is going to stop me from being your wife and spending the rest of my life with you!'

Harry laughed.

'I love you, Bess.' His voice was soft and gentle.

221

'Marrying you will make me the happiest man alive.'

Wrapped up warmly in her greatcoat, scarf, gloves and hat, Bessie strolled around the garden. Having time like this to wander at will was alien to her. She was itching to get back on the ward and be useful.

She'd been up and out of bed for over a week now, but Matron still wouldn't pronounce her fit to work, not even for the easiest of jobs. A day or two more of rest, good food and fresh air, Matron had said that morning, then Bessie could start work again. The war might be over now, but they still had men to care for, so she would carry on nursing until she and Harry married in the New Year.

Bessie decided to walk down to drive to the gate and back before going indoors. She'd just turned onto the drive when she saw the telegram boy come pedalling back from the hall. Had he brought news of another convoy on its way, Bessie wondered. Perhaps she should make her way back up to the Hall. If more patients were expected, then Matron would be glad of any help, even hers.

Walking back in through the front door Bessie ran into Ethel, who was hurrying back to the ward.

'Matron's looking for you, Bessie,' Ethel told her.

'For me? Does she need more help with the convoy, do you think?'

'What convoy? We're not expecting one.'

'Oh. I saw the telegram boy and assumed that's what he was bringing news of.'

222

Ethel shrugged.

'If there's one coming, I don't know where we're going to put new patients. All the beds are full!'

'I'll go and find Matron. Perhaps she's changed her mind about me starting work!'

Bessie was excited at the thought of getting back to work when she tapped quietly on Matron's office door a few minutes later, after taking off her outdoor clothes.

'Come in.'

Bessie opened the door and stepped inside.

'I heard you wanted to see me, Matron.'

'Nurse Carter. Please sit down.' She waited until Bessie was seated on the chair opposite her desk. 'A telegram has come for you, my dear.'

The bubbles of happiness which had filled Bessie instantly popped as her stomach clenched tight. Telegrams usually brought bad news.

'Would you like me to open it for you?' Matron asked.

Bessie shook her head. Whatever it was, she had to see it for herself. She took the offered telegram and with shaking hands tore it open and took out the folded sheet of paper.

*MOTHER ILL STOP COME HOME AT ONCE STOP*

Her mother ill? She was as strong as an ox! Bessie could never recall her being ill before. What could be wrong with her?

'Nurse Carter?' Matron's voice was kind. 'Is it bad news?'

Bessie looked at Matron and nodded. She handed her the telegram to read for herself.

Matron sighed.

'You're not quite fit yourself yet, but you must go home.'

The walk home from the station seemed to be longer than ever before. Bessie was worried. For her father to send a telegram and want her home at once, something must be seriously wrong. She still was not fully fit after her own illness, but there was no question that she wouldn't go home and help to look after her mother.

Opening the front door of the house, it was unnaturally quiet. There was no sign of anyone, her parents, or of little Grace.

Putting down her bag, Bessie called out.

'Father? Mother?'

There was movement upstairs and Bessie heard the sound of someone coming down the stairs. The stair door opened and her father stepped down into the kitchen.

'Bessie.' He smiled wanly at her. 'You've come.'

'What's happened? What's wrong with Mother?'

'Influenza.' Her father sighed. 'She's got it bad, Bessie. The doctor's not hopeful.'

The doctor? Her father had had the doctor into their mother! Bessie had never known the family call in the doctor before, so her mother must be bad. Quickly shrugging off her coat and hat, Bessie made her way up the stairs, her heart thumping hard. At the top of the stairs Bessie crept quietly into the room and up to the tall double bed where her mother lay, breathing noisily.

Martha Carter's face had a pale sickly hue. Her skin seemed stretched over her skull and her eyes had sunken in and were ringed with dark smudges. Bessie had to stop herself from gasping.

'Bessie.' Her mother's voice was little more than a whisper and the effort of saying one word had her coughing.

'I'm here, Mother.' Bessie grasped hold of her mother's hand, which to her surprise felt icy cold. She cradled it in both of hers, trying to warm it.

'Promise me.' Her mother halted to catch her breath. She took several gasps, each one making her chest rise and fall sharply as she tried to suck in enough air. 'Promise me you'll look after Grace.' It took an effort for her mother to speak.

'Of course I will. I'll stay here until you're well and strong again.'

Martha's blue eyes bored into Bessie's and she shook her head slowly.

'When I'm gone. Promise me.' She gasped to catch her breath and then started coughing again.

'But you're going to get better, Mother. It's a bad flu, I know. But you will get better. I know you will!'

Her mother shook her head and with a great effort levered herself up on to her elbows and looked at Bessie.

'Promise ... me.' Then she collapsed back against her pillow.

Bessie looked up at her father who'd come to stand silently by his wife's side, his hand resting gently on her shoulder. He didn't say anything, but he gave her one brief nod. A rising panic welled up in Bessie's chest and she had to struggle hard to calm it. How could her mother be talking of dying? She was a strong woman. She couldn't die! She mustn't!

'Bessie?' Her father spoke just her name, but there was no need to say more.

'Yes, I'll look after Grace.'

If it would help her mother, she would tell her what she wanted to hear. She meant it, too. She would look after Grace, of course, if anything happened to her mother.

But it wasn't going to. She would get better, just as Bessie had done herself. It might take her mother a while to get back her full strength, but she would survive this.

'Thank you.' Her mother's voice was hoarse and she struggled to catch her breath as it rattled in her chest.

'Where is Grace, Father?' Bessie asked.

He turned to look at her briefly.

'She's with Mrs Williams, next door.'

Then he returned his gaze to his wife's face. He looked scared, Bessie realised, and this sent an icy trickle sliding down her spine. Her father was a man who seldom showed emotion, but from the look on his face it was if he had already given up and believed his wife was going to die.

A flame of anger flickered into life inside Bessie. She wasn't going to give up without a fight! She'd do everything she could to help her mother fight the influenza, using every ounce of her nursing knowledge.

Bessie laid her hand on her mother's brow. It was burning up. She needed to cool her down.

'I'm going to get a cloth and some water. I won't be long, Mother. I promise I'll be right back.'

Her mother looked at her and smiled at her.

'Thank you.'

Bessie smiled back.

'I've got plenty of nursing practice now, Mother. I'll look after you.'

'And Grace,' her mother whispered and then gasped for breath.

'And Grace. I promise.' Bessie left the room, climbing quickly down the curved stairs leading to the kitchen.

She found a cloth and filled a bowl with tepid water, and within a few minutes went back upstairs to her parent's room. But as soon as she entered it she knew something was wrong. Her father was sitting hunched forward in the chair beside the bed, his hands clasping her mother's, who from the look of her had fallen into a deep peaceful sleep. She was no longer labouring to breathe, gasping for each breath. The room was quiet.

Bile rose in Bessie's throat and she thought she was going to be sick. Swallowing hard, she rushed across to the bed, put the bowl and cloth down on bedside chest and reached for her mother's hand to check her pulse. But there was nothing. Her mother had gone. She was sleeping, the sleep from which no-one awoke.

Bessie held on tight to her mother's hand, struggling to keep a hold on the surge of emotion rushing through her. She could not believe it. Her mother was dead. She had known she was going to die and had accepted it, while Bessie had denied it and tried to fight against it. But there had been no chance. The influenza had claimed another victim.

'Father?'

He raised his head slowly and the sight of tears

rolling down his cheeks stunned Bessie. She had never seen her father cry before, not even when Robert was killed. He had always had a quiet strength about him, but it had crumbled, and Bessie knew she had to be strong now. She must not give in to her emotions, not now. She must keep strong for her father and for Grace, to get them through this.

'I'll see to her,' Bessie said, laying a hand on her father's shoulder. 'When you're ready.'

He nodded and bowed his head again. Bessie squeezed his shoulder and went out of the bedroom closing the door quietly behind her.

She gave her father time alone with his wife, and when he was ready Bessie took care of her mother, washing her, and laying her out. Usually people in the village called Mrs Neal to do that for them, but Bessie didn't want that. From helping Sister at Marston Hall when a patient had died, she knew what to do.

Bessie gently brushed her mother's hair, then plaited it into a long, honey-blonde rope, laying it across her shoulder and down her chest. Martha was ready. Washed, changed and looking at peace, as if she were just asleep.

Her work done, Bessie dropped down on to the chair beside the bed, her eyes stinging with tears and her throat thickened with emotion. Her mother was too young to die, only forty-two years old. She should have had years of life ahead of her, not been cut off so cruelly by influenza. Bessie had survived it, so why hadn't her mother? It wasn't fair! Bessie shuddered. It was no use thinking like that. Spanish flu hadn't taken the old and infirm, as any normal influenza would. This one had been worse, killing men who had survived the trenches and had deserved to come home and live in peace.

There was going to be a huge hole in the family without her mother, who had been the sun around which the rest of them had orbited. The centre of their universe. Her mother had known that, Bessie realised, and in her last minutes of life had sought to fill her shoes. She'd asked Bessie to promise, and she had. Bessie would take over from her mother and look after Grace and her father. It was her duty, her responsibility. She would move back home, and never return to Marston Hall to nurse the soldiers.

A sob rose up in her throat. Fulfilling her promise meant not only the end of her VAD work, but also the end of her future with Harry. She couldn't marry him now. Her duty to her family must come first. The future she'd planned, the one she'd been so happy about, was over.

Bessie's hands were shaking hard as she pulled out her handkerchief and dabbed away the tears coursing down her cheeks.

## Off To London

'I don't want to go to school today, Bessie. Please let me stay at home.'

'You have to go, Marigold. You don't want to miss your lessons, and it'll help the time pass.' Bessie put her arm around the girl's shoulders.

'Your Mummy wouldn't want you miss school.'

'But what if she comes and I'm not here?' Marigold's bottom lip wobbled.

'Then perhaps she'll come and meet you from school. But we don't even know if she'll come today.'

'I hope she does.'

'So do I, but we'll have to wait and see.' Bessie picked up Marigold's coat from where she'd been warming it in front of the stove. 'Come on, coat on, or you'll be late.'

When Marigold had finally left for school, Bessie poured herself a cup of tea and sat down in the armchair to drink it. The house was quiet and she was glad to be on her own. She'd nearly let Marigold stay at home – she'd looked pale this morning and had dark smudges under her eyes from too little sleep.

But keeping her off school wouldn't have helped. It was best for Marigold to carry on as normal and keep busy and hopefully, Grace would arrive some time today and they'd be reunited.

Bessie took a sip of tea and relaxed back into the chair. All she wanted to do was sleep, to forget all that had happened and escape from the worrying feeling gnawing away inside her. Harry had reasoned it all out with her last night, and she knew what he said made sense. But she couldn't shake off the feeling there was something else, some other reason, why Grace hadn't been on that train.

It wasn't like Bessie to be like this. She'd have said she was a down-to-earth sort of person, not one who tended to have strange feelings of foreboding. This worried her, but there was nothing she could do but wait. Perhaps Grace would arrive today, or at least send word.

Bessie focused her thoughts on the happy news from yesterday. Howard was alive, and he'd be coming back! It had been lovely to witness the change in Prune. All the sadness which had weighed her down over the past few weeks had lifted. Now they could start looking forward to a wedding, once Howard was back and well again.

It was something good to come out of the war, Bessie thought. She drained the last of her tea. She couldn't sit there thinking all day. There was plenty of work to do.

It was late morning. Bessie had just got the last of the loaves out of the oven, and the air was filled with the comforting smell of freshly baked bread when Harry came bursting into the house.

'Look what's come, Bess.' He waved a buff-coloured envelope in the air. Another telegram. 'I told you Grace would probably send one today. Young Thomas saw me in the yard.'

Bessie's heart started thumping loudly. The telegram might have brought good news, but the sight of it still sent a chill finger down her spine.

'Do you want to open it, Bess?' Harry offered her the telegram.

Bessie shook her head.

'You do it.'

'She'll probably be here this afternoon.' Harry slit the envelope open.

Bessie watched as Harry took out the sheet, unfolded it and read it. The look on Harry's face said it all. The telegram hadn't brought the news they'd hoped for.

A rising tide of panic welled up through Bessie. What did it say? Not, Robert. Please, not Robert. She snatched the telegram from Harry before he could say anything and read it for herself.

GRACE INJURED STOP IN ST THOMAS'S HOSPITAL STOP MRS FOX STOP

Bessie stared at the telegram, not quite believing what she'd read. Grace hadn't come last night because she'd been injured! How? When? How bad? Bad enough to be in hospital, and bad enough for someone else to send word, instead of Grace herself.

'I've got to go to her,' Bessie said.

'Hold on, Bess.' Harry took hold of her arm. 'Slow down. We don't know what's happened.'

'Injured and in hospital!' Bessie's voice was thick with emotion. 'I knew something was wrong. I could feel it in here.' She put her hand to her chest. 'But I just thought I was being...' She shook her head and took in a deep, steadying breath. 'I've got to go and see her.'

'You've never been to London before. How will you know where to go? Where will you stay?'

'I've got a tongue in my head! I can ask the way. London's full of strangers these days, and they get around fine. I can do it, too.'

'Do you want me to come with you?' Harry's voice was gentle.

Bessie shook her head and took hold of his hand.

'Thank you. But they'll need you here.'

'What will we tell Marigold?'

'Nothing. Not until we know what's happened. There's no point upsetting her.'

'Grace's letter, the one asking us to look after

Marigold if anything happened to her...' Harry squeezed her hand. 'I pray we don't need it.'

Bessie shuddered.

'So do I, but if Grace is injured I need to go to her.'

'What shall I tell everyone? They'll want to know where you've gone.'

'You'll think of something, Harry.' Bessie undid her apron and flung it on a chair. 'I need to get ready.'

Inside their bedroom, with the door closed behind her, Bessie leaned against the wooden bedstead for a few moments. Her heart was thudding hard inside her, and she felt on the verge of breaking down and weeping.

But she couldn't. She had to be strong and keep a grasp of her emotions. Grace was injured and she had to go to her. How bad her injuries were and what had caused them, they didn't know. There was no clue in the telegram.

Bessie swallowed hard against the raw ache in her throat. The feeling she'd had was right. She'd sensed something was wrong. Her instinct, her— Bessie took in a sharp breath. Don't even think about it, she ordered herself. It couldn't and wouldn't do any good. She had to be sensible and practical about this if she was going to get to London and to Grace.

Bessie took the small leather suitcase down from on top of the wardrobe and started to pack. How long she'd be away she didn't know, but she couldn't take much, a change of underwear and a clean nightgown, a dress, her brush, washing things.

The case was almost full, when Bessie's eyes were drawn to her old diary on the chest of drawers beside the bed. For some reason she had a strong urge to take it with her. Without stopping to think why she put it in the case with the rest of her things and shut the lid.

'Are you sure about this, Bess?' Harry asked as they waited on the train platform.

'I am. I've got to go, Harry, I just feel it.' Bessie held his hand tightly.

Harry nodded.

'I hope it's nothing more than a broken ankle. But at least, if you go, then you'll know.'

'I'll send word as soon as I know what's happened. I'm sure Dottie and Prune will help out until I get back.'

'What about those rockets, Bess?' Harry's eyes held hers. 'I'm worried about you going there.'

Bessie took hold of both his hands in hers.

'I'll be all right, Harry. You told me not so long ago that sometimes you have to take risks in life.'

Harry grinned at her.

'I did.'

'I'll be careful, Harry. I have every intention of coming back.'

When the train arrived late into the station, Harry hugged Bessie tightly.

'Take care, Bess.'

Bessie had to swallow back tears as she climbed into a compartment and looked out at Harry standing on the platform, his face strained with concern for her. This war had a lot to answer for, she thought.

# The Whole Truth

'Is she here?' Marigold burst into the house, her cheeks glowing pink. 'I ran all the way home from school!'

'No, she isn't.' Harry said, who'd been waiting indoors with Prune and Dottie for Marigold to come home.

After Bessie had left on the train that morning, he'd sent a telegram to London, then driven the pony and trap over to the wood where the two timberjills were working to ask for their help. He wasn't sure how to handle this on his own.

'We haven't heard from her.' Harry was being truthful; they hadn't actually heard from Grace herself.

Marigold's shoulders drooped. She looked at Harry and he could see tears glistening in her eyes.

'I've been thinking about her all day.'

Dottie put an arm around Marigold and hugged her.

'I know you're disappointed, my lovely. Come on, let's get your coat off and make you some bread and jam and warm milk.'

Marigold nodded.

'Put some milk on to warm, please, Prune,' Dottie said, helping Marigold off with her coat.

'I'll hang that up for you,' Harry said.

He was glad to escape out into the porch for a moment. Dottie and Prune being there had made it much easier. He was grateful to the two young women. When he'd told them what had happened they'd immediately offered to help, coming home early to be there when Marigold returned.

He was just about to go back into the room when he heard Marigold ask the question he'd been dreading.

'Where's Bessie?'

It wasn't fair to let Dottie and Prune answer.

'Bessie's not here, Marigold.' Harry walked back into the living-room. 'She's had to visit someone who's not well.'

He was telling the truth. Not the whole truth, but enough of it to be true.

'Who has she gone to see?' Marigold asked.

'Someone she used to know. She'll be back in a day or two.'

'So we're cooking the tea tonight,' Prune said. 'You haven't tasted our cooking before, have you?'

'You're in for a treat.' Dottie handed her a plate of bread and jam. 'Do you want to help us when you've finished this?'

'Can I?' Marigold looked pleased.

'Of course, you can, my lovely,' Dottie said. 'You'll be a big help to us.' She ruffled Marigold's hair and cast a look over to Harry.

He felt relieved. Marigold seemed happy and with Dottie and Prune's help they'd get through this without upsetting her. They would just wait until they heard from Bessie, hopefully with news that Grace had a broken ankle, and then they'd be able to tell Marigold the truth about why her mother hadn't arrived.

'I'll go and get on with the milking, then, unless

you want me to help cook the tea, too?' he joked.

Marigold giggled.

'I've never seen you cook, Harry.'

'Can you cook?' Dottie demanded.

'Well, I can make toast, boil an egg, bake potatoes and cook porridge.'

'We'll manage fine between us,' Prune decided.

He was in the wood shed, filling up the baskets of wood for the fire, when Prune came into the shed.

'Tea's ready, Harry. We're ready to eat as soon as Peter's home. He shouldn't be long now.'

He threw the last piece of wood into a basket and brushed the sawdust off his work-roughened hands.

'Thanks, Prune. I don't know what I'd have done without yours and Dottie's help.'

Prune smiled, her features shadowed in the low light of the tilley lamp.

'We're glad to help, and we'll do it for as long as you need us. Did Bessie know how long she'd be away?'

'No. It depends on what she finds when she gets there. If Grace is badly injured, she'll probably want to stay longer.'

Harry spotted movement as the shed door was pulled open and Peter stepped forward into the dim light.

'I thought I heard someone in here.' He was dressed in his school uniform, with his satchel slung over one shoulder and Hana sitting on the other, nibbling at his school cap. 'What's happened? Has Marigold's mother arrived?'

Harry and Prune looked at each other.

'No, she's not here,' Prune said quickly.

'Why didn't she come? Have you heard from her?'

'No,' Harry said. 'We haven't actually heard from her, but...'

'What is it?' Peter's eyes searched his face. 'What's wrong?'

Harry looked at the boy who so often seemed years older than his years. His circumstances had forced him to face up to some harsh things in his life, and it had moulded him into an intelligent and thoughtful young man. He didn't want to mislead the boy.

'Peter...' Harry hesitated, wondering if it was the right thing to do. He didn't want to lie to the lad. 'We heard this morning that Marigold's mother has been injured and is in hospital. That's why she didn't come. We don't know how badly hurt she is. Bessie has gone to London to see her.'

'What about Marigold? Has she gone, too?'

'No. Marigold's still here. She doesn't know about her mother. All she knows is that Bessie has gone to see a friend who is ill.'

A look of anger passed over Peter's face.

'But that's not the whole truth, Harry!'

Prune laid her hand on Peter's arm.

'It's part of it, Peter. We don't want to worry Marigold until we know exactly what's happened.'

'What we've told her isn't a lie, Peter.' Harry sighed. 'I don't want to lie to her. But you're right, we haven't told her the whole truth.'

'You must! You must tell her!' Peter's face was blotched with red. 'If her mother is injured she should be told. If it was me, I'd want to know straight away, with nothing held back!'

'But you're older than her.'

'I know, but she's tougher than you think. Look what's already happened in her life. She's survived the Blitz, her father's been killed and then she was sent to live with strangers and she coped with it.' Peter drew in breath. 'Holding back the truth might make it worse when you do tell her. Everyone else would have known, but not her!'

Harry shrugged his shoulders.

'I honestly don't know what's the best thing to do. Whatever we do has to be what's best for her.'

'Then tell her.'

'I think if Marigold knew about her mother she'd be terribly upset and worried, Peter,' Prune said. 'We only want to protect her.'

'It's hard enough being away from your parents and home, without things being kept from you,' Peter repeated. 'If I was her, I'd want to know the truth, even if it hurt.'

Harry rubbed the back of his neck.

'I'll have to think about it, Peter. I understand what you're saying, but I've got to be sure first. So please don't say anything to Marigold about it, will you?'

Peter shook his head.

'I won't. But believe me when I say children don't want to be kept in the dark about things, especially when it's about their parents. I'd better go and get changed.'

'Tell the others I'll be in soon,' Prune said. 'Then we can eat. I'll help Harry bring the wood inside.'

When Peter had gone, Harry looked at Prune.

'What do you think?'

Prune shrugged.

'I can see his point. Children have suffered a lot in this war, as much as anyone else. Perhaps more, in some cases, through losing their parents and being sent to live with strangers far from home. Marigold's been through a lot already, and that makes us want to protect her more.'

She bit her bottom lip.

'But I can't help wondering how I'd feel if I was her. She's only got her mother left now, and you know how much she thinks of her.'

'I know. I keep tossing it round and round in my head.' Harry said. 'Bessie's not here to talk it through with. She always knows what to do for the best.'

'Did she tell you what you should do?'

Harry shook his head.

'No. She was in a hurry to get away and her mind was on Grace. She said I'd think of something.'

'I've not seen Peter like that before. He didn't like the idea of anything being held back about parents, did he?'

'It's especially hard for him, not knowing where his own parents are, or if they're still alive. Us holding the whole truth back from Marigold clearly struck a nerve in him.'

Harry bent down and picked up a basket of wood.

'It makes me feel we ought to be completely honest with Marigold. I'll talk to her after tea.'

'Are you sure?' Prune asked, taking hold of the other basket.

He grimaced.

'No. But I'll go along with Peter on this one and hope it's the right thing to do.'

Marigold saw Harry blurry through the tears in her eyes. She couldn't believe what he'd told her. The reason her mother hadn't come was because she'd been injured and was in hospital! That was who Bessie had gone to see.

'We don't know how your mother's injured. That's why Bessie's gone to her. Hopefully she's just got a broken ankle and will soon be able to visit you here.'

Marigold swallowed.

'I want to go and see her.'

Dottie sat down beside her and put her arm around Marigold's shoulders.

'We know you do, my lovely. But we have to wait until we hear from Bessie.'

'How did it happen?' Marigold asked.

'We don't know that, either,' Harry said. 'She might have fallen over, or...'

Different ways her mother could have been injured started to file through Marigold's mind. She could have just tripped and fallen on the stairs going down the Tube, but there were worse ways to get hurt in London these days. Marigold shivered. The fear of Hitler's horrible rockets had made her mother send her away. Those landing now, the V2s, were even worse, coming with no warning. If her mother had been caught in one of those, she might die. That was her worst nightmare, the thing Marigold worried most about when she lay in bed at night trying to sleep.

The tears she'd held back spilled over and trickled down her cheeks.

'What if she dies?' Marigold said. 'I'll be an orphan like my daddy was, and have to go and live in an orphanage.'

'No, you won't,' Harry said immediately. 'Whatever happens, you will always have a home here with me and Bessie. But don't think about it now.'

Dottie pulled Marigold into her arms, and hugged her tightly.

'Your mother will be fine, my lovely. She'll come and see you just as soon as she can.'

Marigold closed her eyes and wished with all her might that her mother would be all right. Bessie had gone to see her, and she would make sure her mother got well. Good, kind Bessie would look after her mother, just like Grace had said Bessie would look after Marigold when she came to Norfolk. If Marigold couldn't go to her mother, then Bessie was the next best thing.

### Sound Asleep

As Bessie stood outside St Thomas's and stared up at the hospital there was enough moonlight to show that even a hospital wasn't immune from the German bombs. There had been no mercy shown for the sick and wounded. They had been just as much a target as the rest of London.

Seeing the damage the Luftwaffe had inflicted on London was a shock. Bessie had heard about

242

it on the radio, read about it in the paper, but she hadn't been prepared for the reality of it. For gaps where buildings once stood, empty now like missing teeth. For piles of rubble, wooden beams splintered like matchsticks. Yet life went on all around as Londoners went about their business, battered but undefeated.

Somewhere inside this hospital, Grace was lying injured. How, and in what way, Bessie had no idea. Her mind had run through hundreds of scenarios on the long journey to London – from Grace already back home with just a few scratches and bruises, to her lying fatally injured.

Bessie shuddered. She wouldn't think about that. There was only one way to find out how Grace was. She picked up her case, took a deep breath and marched into the hospital. As she went through the doors the familiar smell of carbolic hit her, clean and comforting. If Grace was hurt, this was the best place to be. The doctors and nurses could heal her physical wounds, and while she was here, perhaps Bessie and Grace could heal the deep wound between them.

The nurse had warned her, but the sight of Grace was still a shock. Bessie's throat tightened with emotion as she stared down at Grace lying in the bed. Her hair and face were grey with dust and she was still wearing her own clothes which were torn and filthy.

'It looks bad,' the nurse whispered to Bessie. 'But it's for the best. It helps to minimise the shock.'

Bessie nodded, unable to tear her eyes away from Grace laying so still, the grey dusty pallor of her face and hair giving her the appearance of a statue.

The nurse had explained that Grace had been buried under a fallen building and had been brought in unconscious, with two broken legs. Her legs had been seen to, cleaned and plastered, and were now hidden in the bed under a cage. The rest of her would be cleaned up later, when she'd recovered from the shock of what had happened to her.

'Can I stay with her?' Bessie's voice sounded hoarse.

The nurse nodded.

'Just for a few minutes.'

'Thank you.' Bessie swallowed hard against the tears building up in her eyes.

Standing beside Grace, Bessie was glad of the screens around the bed giving them some privacy. She couldn't stop a tear from escaping and running down her face. She'd never expected her next meeting with Grace to be like this. It should have been in Norfolk, with Grace arriving on the train, and she should now be enjoying her stay at Orchard Farm. Not lying in a bed after being pulled out from a ruined building brought down by a German rocket.

Damn the war, Bessie thought. How many more lives was it going to hurt before the end?

She reached down and gently took one of Grace's hands. It felt cool beneath the layer of powdery dust. Bessie had held that hand so many times before, right from the day Grace had been born.

'Grace,' Bessie whispered. 'It's me, Bessie. I've

come to see you.'

She knew Grace probably couldn't hear her in her sleep, but she had to tell her she was here, just in case somewhere deep inside her brain it might register.

'I'll come back again tomorrow. I promise.'

She squeezed Grace's hand gently, and laid it carefully on top of the bedclothes. With a final glance at Grace she parted the screens and walked towards the door.

'Mrs Rushbrook?'

Bessie looked at the woman who'd stepped forward as she left the ward.

The woman smiled at her.

'I'm Ada Fox. Grace's landlady, and her friend.' She held out her hand.

Bessie stared at her, not quite registering at first.

'Mrs Fox? You sent us the telegram!' She shook the woman's hand. 'Thank you for that. We couldn't understand why Grace hadn't come.'

'I thought you'd be worried. How is she?'

'Sleeping now. I only stayed a few minutes.'

'Sleep's the best thing for her. After what she's been through, she needs it.' Mrs Fox sighed. 'Grace was so excited about seeing Marigold again. She'd only left the house ten minutes before, on her way to the station, when the rocket hit. I ran out to see what was going on, see if I could help. I didn't know she'd been caught at first. I thought she'd escaped it!'

Her eyes filled with tears. She took a deep breath and gathered herself together.

'When they started digging out where the shops

had come down, there she was. She'd been saving her sweet ration for Marigold and must have gone in to the shop to buy some sweets.'

The older woman patted Bessie's hand and smiled.

'I'm glad you came to see her. Where will you be staying tonight?'

'I hadn't thought about it. I just wanted to see Grace. I suppose a hotel.'

Mrs Fox held up her hand.

'Come home and stay with me. Grace would want that.'

Bessie frowned.

'It's very kind of you, but...'

'I'd be glad of your company at a time like this. You'd be helping me out.'

'Perhaps I should stay here at the hospital, to be near Grace.' Bessie waved her hand helplessly. 'I'd be here when she wakes up.'

'You won't get much sleep sitting on a chair in a corridor, and you'll be no good to Grace tomorrow if you're tired. My house isn't far away, so it won't take you long to get back here in the morning.'

Bessie did feel tired, so very tired. The horror of the telegram, the long journey, seeing Grace like this, it had taken it out of her. She felt weary to the bone.

'You're right, Mrs Fox, I know. It's just...'

'Call me Ada. Grace does.' She linked her arm through Bessie's. 'I understand how you feel, honestly I do, but Grace is in the best place and they'll take good care of her.'

Bessie glanced back towards the ward where

246

Grace lay and then back at Mrs Fox.

'Thank you. I'll be glad to come and stay with you.'

'I don't know about you, Bessie, but I could do with a nice hot cuppa,' Ada said, shrugging off her coat and hanging it on a hook in the hallway.

Bessie smiled.

'Yes, please.'

'Leave your case here for now, and let me take your coat, then I'll put the kettle on.'

Bessie took off her coat and handed it to Ada who hung it up, then led the way down the hall to the door at the far end. Bessie followed, her eyes drinking in the house which was Grace and Marigold's home. A place she'd never heard of until last summer. And now she was here, seeing it all for herself.

'I live in the downstairs half of the house,' Ada explained, putting a kettle on the stove. 'Grace lives upstairs. Marigold and poor John lived there, too, of course, before...' She shook her head and sighed. 'After Marigold went to live with you, Grace and I started having our meals together. Made sense to combine our rations and I like someone to cook for. Are you hungry?'

'I had some sandwiches on the train.'

'That was hours ago. How about some toast?'

'Thanks, but I'm not hungry, Ada. A cup of tea is all I need.'

Ada looked at her for a few moments.

'Well, if you're sure. Tea will do you good, anyway.'

A few minutes later they were settled at the

kitchen table warming their hands on their cups.

'Time to spill the beans, Bessie.'

'What do you mean?'

'I was at the hospital tonight expecting you. Your Harry sent me a telegram, telling me you were coming and asking me to look out for you.'

Tears welled up in Bessie's eyes.

'Bless him. He was worried about me coming here on my own. I've not been to London before.' She smiled. 'He was worried what I might find when I got here because we didn't know how badly Grace was injured.'

'He's a caring man.' Ada took a sip of tea. 'I was glad to do it. I'd been at the hospital earlier and it gave me a good reason to go back, me not being next of kin or anything.'

'Harry wanted to come with me, but he had to stay at home and look after everything.'

'Does Marigold know her mother's been hurt?'

Bessie shook her head.

'No. At least, she didn't when I left. She was upset when Grace didn't arrive on the train last night. We hoped Grace would arrive today, or at least send word.' She sighed. 'Marigold was at school when your telegram arrived. I left it to Harry to decide what to tell her, though I imagine he'd wait until he heard from me. There's no point in upsetting her unless we have to.'

'You can let them know how she is tomorrow.'

Bessie nodded.

'I'll wait until I've been to see Grace first. Then send a telegram.'

Bessie lay awake. She was tired, but she couldn't

248

stop herself from worrying. Images of Grace lying in the hospital bed kept playing through her mind. Then there were thoughts of what was happening back at Orchard Farm? How was Harry managing? Was Marigold all right?

She turned on to her side and tried to get comfortable in the unfamiliar bed in Marigold's old room. Bessie wasn't used to sleeping without Harry. His presence beside her was always reassuring and comfortable, and now, when she could have done with some of that, he wasn't here.

He would have come, if she'd asked, of course. But he had to stay at home to take care of everything. Coming to see Grace was something she had to do on her own.

It was no good, sleep wasn't going to come. Bessie flung back the covers, swung her feet down on to the floor and padded over to her suitcase. She took out her diary, and climbed back into bed. If she couldn't sleep, she'd read.

## *The Best Of Men*

It was still dark outside when Bessie made her way downstairs. Glancing up at the clock on the mantelpiece she saw it just past five o'clock, still too early for her father and Grace to be stirring. She banked up the embers of the fire and soon had a warm blaze going which threw out a welcome heat.

Bessie was wide awake and had been for a

while. She'd tried hard to get back to sleep, but there was too much going on in her mind.

*Harry's coming tomorrow. I'm meeting him at the station and will talk to him there. Then he can go straight back on the next train. It will end, there and then.*

She'd decided to get up. Pass the time and take her mind off what she was going to have to do today.

Crouching on the rag rug in front of the range, Bessie held out her hands to warm. She wished she could warm up her heart as easily. Since her life had suddenly changed, she felt as if her heart had been frozen, like a fallen leaf encased in an icy puddle on a winter's morning.

Bessie shuddered. She had to forget the life she'd planned because events had shunted her down another path. Bessie accepted it, but it wasn't easy. The hardest thing would be telling Harry everything had changed and that had to be done today.

She could have written to him and told him, but it wouldn't have been fair to the man she loved. She owed it to Harry to tell him face to face.

So she had waited until after her mother's funeral, then had written to him, telling him what had happened and asking him to come and see her.

He'd be expecting to come to the house and see her father and Grace, but Bessie had decided to tell him at the station, making the split short and swift. It would be better for him in the long run, she had reasoned. Then he could go away, and she would return to her new life caring for her father and Grace. That was the plan she'd spent hours agonising over, but carrying it out would be harder than just thinking about it. In the meantime, she had jobs to do. Standing up, Bessie smoothed her long skirt down and pushed the kettle on to the hot plate. It would be coming up to the boil by the time her father came down and wanted a cup of tea.

Some hours later she watched the train chuff into the station, her stomach clenched into a tight knot. She wanted to be here and yet a hundred miles away at the same time. How she was going to tell him he had to make a life without her, she didn't know. But she must. She had no choice. The promise she'd made had changed her life.

The train halted and Bessie glanced up and down the train looking for Harry. There he was, stepping carefully down from a compartment near the far end of the train. He waved at her, then limped along the platform towards her as fast as he could, a warm smile on his face.

Her bottom lip suddenly started to tremble and she tried to stop the tears from spilling down her cheeks, but she couldn't. She fumbled in her bag for a handkerchief, but before she could wipe away her tears, Harry was beside her.

'Bess!'

He took the handkerchief from her hands and dabbed away her tears. Then he bent down and kissed her cheek.

'Harry.' Bessie's voice sounded hoarse from her tight throat.

'Come on.' Harry linked one arm through hers and drew her towards the station exit. 'Let's get you home.'

Bessie allowed him to lead her out through the station yard. It was such a relief to be with him again. It felt right to walk alongside him, his arm linked through hers, the familiar sensation of his arm pressing against her. But it must stop. Bessie had to stop him. Tell him now before it went any further.

'Harry. Stop!'

He stopped and looked at her, his eyes full of concern.

'I need to talk to you, Harry.'

'We can talk at your father's.'

'No! Not there.'

Bessie's mind rapidly worked out where they could go. Not back to the station now, not before she'd had a chance to tell him. They needed a quiet place where they wouldn't be disturbed. The church! They could sit in the porch. She would tell him there.

'This way.'

'Where are you taking me?' Harry asked.

'Somewhere quiet, to talk.'

Bessie led Harry to the church and in through the lychgate under which her mother's coffin had been carried just a few days before. Glancing over to the right, she could see the brown earth piled on top of her mother's grave.

Pushing all thoughts of that aside for now, Bessie walked into the church porch and sat down on one of the benches running along the sides. She motioned for Harry to do the same.

'What's wrong, Bess?' Harry sat beside her and took hold of her hand. 'I can see from your face something's the matter.'

Bessie hesitated. Now the time had come, she didn't want to say words she didn't really mean.

But you must, a voice said in her head. You have to.

'Harry.' Bessie's voice came out in a squeak. She cleared her throat, looked him straight in the eye and started again. 'I'm so sorry to tell you this, but I can't marry you any more.'

There, she'd done it. And she felt like howling.

Harry stared at her.

'Why not? Don't you love me?'

Bessie shook her head.

'I do love you.'

'Then why? I don't understand.'

'It's because I can't marry you.'

'What's changed, Bess? The last time I saw you, you were talking about us getting married in the New Year.'

Bessie looked down at her hands, tightly wringing her handkerchief which she'd fished out of her pocket. 'I do want to marry you, but I can't.'

Harry stood up and started pacing around the small porch.

'Let me get this straight. You say you can't marry me. But it's not that you don't want to, so why?' He frowned. 'What's happening here, Bess? Tell me!'

Tears stung Bessie's eyes again, but she was determined not to cry. She had to be strong about this.

She swallowed hard and began.

'Just before my mother died, she asked me to promise to take care of Grace if she died. I promised her, gave her my word.' She hesitated for a moment. 'So you see, Harry my life has changed. I've got to take over from my mother, and that means I'm not free to marry you.'

'The reason you can't marry me is because you promised your mother you'd look after Grace?'

Bessie nodded and looked up at Harry. His blue eyes held hers and then he began to smile. He sat back on the bench beside her.

'Looking after Grace shouldn't stop you marrying me. You can be my wife and look after Grace, too. She can come and live with us at the farm!'

Bessie stared at Harry for a moment as his words sank in.

'You'd be happy to have my sister living with us if we married?'

It hadn't occurred to Bessie she could do both – be Harry's wife and look after Grace. Most young men wouldn't want their wives to come with responsibilities and more mouths to feed. But Harry wasn't like that. He was Harry. Lovely, caring, sweet-natured, kind-hearted Harry, whom she loved with all her heart.

Relief flooded through her. She could marry him!

'Thank you.' Bessie smiled happily at Harry through blurry eyes.

'Your father could come, too, if he wanted.'

Bessie's heart sank. Her father! Would he allow Grace to go and live with her and Harry? If he didn't, then she still could not marry, since she must be wherever Grace was.

'He might not want to, or even let Grace live

with us.' Bessie's voice was hoarse with emotion. 'If he won't let her leave, then I can't.'

Harry put his arm around Bessie.

'One step at a time, Bess. We need to ask him what he thinks. There are lots of ifs and we can't plan until we know how he feels.' He pulled back and looked deep into her eyes. 'Remember this, Bess Carter. I love you and you love me. Right?'

Bessie nodded.

'So, one way or another, we're getting married. And you can keep your promise to look after Grace. We'll sort it out, together.'

Grace was slowly drifting off to sleep, lying snuggled in Bessie's arms. Bessie could feel the weight of the little girl growing heavier against her chest as sleep took hold of her and her body relaxed. She kept the gentle momentum of the rocking-chair going, to and fro, back and forth. Bessie found the rhythm soothing, like the pulse from a heartbeat, while she waited to find out in which direction her future lay. Out in the forge her future was being discussed as Harry talked to her father. Bessie would have gone with him, but he'd insisted he should do it alone. Man to man.

Grace stirred slightly in her sleep and snuggled in closer. Feeling the warm little soul cuddled against her stirred something in Bessie's chest. She plopped a kiss on Grace's blonde head and closed her eyes, trying hard to relax with the gentle rocking. But her mind wouldn't be still.

She wanted to marry Harry, but would only do so if Grace went with her. Harry was happy for Grace to live with them. All that was agreed on, but depended on one thing – her father's permission. He must agree to Grace leaving the forge and moving to the farm, if Bessie and Harry married.

'Bess?'

She struggled to surface from the foggy depths of sleep. She must have dropped off, her lack of sleep from the night before finally catching up on her.

'Bess!' Harry's voice came again.

She forced her eyes open and looked at Harry, who was standing in front of her. Her heart started to pound inside her chest.

'What did he say?' She sat forward in the rocking-chair, her arms tight around the sleeping Grace.

'Your father said yes. He said yes!' Harry's face broke into a wide smile. 'Grace can come and live with us after we're married.'

Bessie could hardly believe it.

'Really?'

'Really and truly.' He reached out and gently stroked Bessie's cheek. 'We'll be married in the New Year and Grace will come and live with us. Your father thinks it's a good idea, as long as he sees her often.'

Relief and happiness flooded through Bessie. She was going to marry Harry and they were going to spend the rest of their lives together. Tears blurred her eyes as she smiled up at him.

That evening, Bessie came downstairs and looked across the room at her father sitting quietly by the fire. He was staring into the open door of the range, where the flames flickered brightly.

Her heart hurt at the thought of him being left

here on his own when she and Grace left. Would he be all right? She needed to talk to him, check he really was happy they were doing the right thing.

'She's asleep.' Bessie said, sitting down opposite her father. 'Drifted off as soon as her head hit the pillow.'

Her father looked at her and nodded.

'She's a busy little thing. It's no wonder she tires herself out.'

'Father? I need to ask you something.'

'Go on.'

'Are you sure about Grace coming to live with Harry and me?' She hesitated. 'I'm worried about you being left on your own. How are you going to manage the house as well as the forge?'

Her father leaned back in his chair, elbows on the arm rests and his work-hardened hands clasped in front of him like the roof of a church, and smiled at Bessie.

'I'm certain it's the right thing to do. For you, Bessie, because Harry's a fine man, and will be a good husband to you. And the best thing for Grace, too, because she needs you to look after her. I'm sure your mother would approve.'

'But what about you?'

'I'll be all right, don't you worry. I'll miss Grace, of course I will. So that's why I'll still want to see her often. You'll make sure it happens, won't you?'

Bessie nodded.

'Of course. You could come and live with us, too. Harry did ask you, didn't he?'

'He did. But my life is here, my work is here.' He waved one hand around. 'This is where I belong. It's my home and I don't want to go anywhere else.'

'What about the house? Your meals?'

'I've been thinking about that. I can cook a little, Bessie. Not the way your mother or you can, but I'm not completely useless. I thought I might get Mrs Williams from next door to come in and look after the place, for me. Do a bit of housekeeping and cooking for me.'

Bessie's heart lifted.

'I would have been happy to stay and look after you.'

'I know you would, Bessie. And I thank you for it. But you are doing what your mother asked you to, looking after Grace.' He leaned forward and added another bit of wood on the fire. 'It shouldn't stop you from following your own wishes and marrying Harry. Your mother wouldn't have wanted that to happen. She was as pleased as punch about you marrying him.'

Bessie's eyes stung with tears.

'I'm lucky Harry is happy to have Grace with us.'

Her father nodded.

'He's a good man.'

True, Bessie thought. Harry Rushbrook was the best of men. Just that morning she'd believed her future with him was over. But Harry hadn't wanted to let her go and had made it possible for them to be together, him and her father. The two most important men in her life.

## A Promise Kept

The tinging, plinging sound of jets of milk hitting the bottom of the pail, usually made Harry feel contented and happy. No matter how many times he'd heard it before, he still loved hearing it. But not Saturday morning. Nothing felt right. Bessie wasn't there and the whole house felt wrong. The worry about what was going on in London had kept him awake. Then there was Marigold to think about.

Buttercup raised a back leg and took a well-aimed kick at the bucket. It went skittering across the floor and a puddle of warm milk spread over the stones.

'Whoa, girl.' Harry stood up from the milking stool and righted the rolling pail, then went around to Buttercup's head, where she was tethered to the wall while she ate from the trough. 'You can feel it, too, can't you?' He rubbed under her chin which she loved. Buttercup stuck out her head, exposing more of her chin for Harry to rub.

There was nothing he could do but wait until they'd heard something from Bessie. Worrying wasn't going to get them anywhere. All it did was upset the milk. He just had to get on with it.

Giving Buttercup's chin a final rub, he sat back down on the milking stool and started to milk again. This time he hummed gently which helped to keep his thoughts concentrated on the job in hand. Buttercup seemed to approve, letting her milk flow free, and the pail quickly filled with creamy milk that frothed and foamed.

When Harry had finished milking, he led the cows out to the orchard and stood leaning on the gate looking at them for a few moments, thinking about the day ahead. The best thing to do was to keep everything going as normal. There was plenty of work to be done, and with Dottie and Prune doing the cooking, they would manage while they waited to hear about Grace.

Bessie's heart was fluttering in her chest as she stood outside the screen around Grace's bed. Grace was awake, the nurse had told her, and waiting to see her.

Pull yourself together, Bessie told herself. How many times had she wanted to see Grace since she'd left? It wasn't happening the way she'd have wanted, but it was what it was.

She took a few slow, deep breaths, plastered a smile on her face, then pulled the screen aside and stepped through.

'Bessie.' Grace smiled from her bed, where she lay propped up on some pillows. She held out her hand.

'Hello, Grace.' She smiled at the young woman who looked so different from when she'd seen her last night. The dust and dirt was gone, and she was dressed in a hospital gown. Grace's face was still pale, with bruises and scratches, but the real Grace was there to see, from her wavy blonde hair to her blue eyes.

'They told me you came last night.'

Bessie nodded.

'You were asleep, but they let me stay for a few minutes. Then Ada came and took me home.'

'That was kind of her. She's like that.' Grace looked Bessie straight in the eye. 'I had a dream about you. You were saying you'd come back. You promised.'

Bessie's breath caught in her throat.

'That's what I said to you before I left. Perhaps you heard me.'

Grace smiled.

'Perhaps I did.'

They fell into silence for a few moments.

'How are you feeling?' Bessie asked. 'You look much better than last night.'

'Much cleaner, you mean. It was lovely to have a wash and get rid of the dust.' She shuddered. 'I'm lucky to be here, Bessie. If I'd gone any further down the road I'd have been a goner. I stopped to buy Marigold some sweets. Then there was this almighty bang and a roar, and it all fell in around us.'

Bessie gently squeezed Grace's hand.

'They had to dig you out.'

'I don't remember.' A look of horror passed over Grace's face and she looked older than her years for a moment. 'I'm not the first it's happened to. I've seen plenty of other cases come in here.'

'Ada sent us a telegram to say you'd been injured. I came straight away.'

Grace's eyes sparkled and she smiled a wobbly smile.

'I'm glad you came.'

'I had to. I wanted to.' Bessie swallowed hard

against the tightness of her throat.

'Where's Marigold?'

'At home. She was at school when Ada's telegram came. We thought it best I come alone. We didn't know what to expect and I didn't want to risk bringing her to London with these rockets falling.'

'I want to see her so much.' Grace's voice wavered. 'But I'd rather she was safe.'

'She wants to see you, too.'

'They're moving me this afternoon, Bessie. Out of London. They need to get the beds empty for the next wave of casualties.'

'Where are they taking you?'

'I'm not sure yet, but it should be safer than here. I'll come and see Marigold as soon as I can.' She nodded towards the cage than surrounded her broken legs. 'When I can walk again.' Grace bit her bottom lip, then went on. 'I need to talk to you before I go, Bessie. I…'

A nurse popped her head around the side of a screen.

'Everything all right in here?' It was Helen MacDonald, who had brought Marigold to Norfolk last year.

'Bessie! It's good to see you again. How's Marigold?'

'Hello,' Bessie said. 'Marigold's fine, thank you.'

'Good. Grace has cleaned up nicely, don't you think? What a difference a wash and brush up makes.' Helen winked at Grace. 'Shall I bring you a chair, Bessie? Be more comfy for you.'

'Yes, thank you,' Bessie said. 'I'll come and get it.'

'No need. I'll be back in two ticks.'

Helen's head disappeared and Bessie and Grace looked at each other and smiled.

'I never thought I'd end up a patient on Helen's ward,' Grace said.

'I didn't see her here last night.'

'She wasn't on duty then.'

'Is this the ward you work on?'

Grace shook her head.

'No. Mine is the next floor up.'

The screen parted and Helen came in with a chair.

'There you go.'

'That's kind of you, thank you.'

'My pleasure. Right, I'll leave you two to talk.' Helen turned to go and then twirled back again. 'I nearly forgot. We've had word that you'll be leaving earlier than expected, Grace. We're just waiting for the ambulances to be organised and then you'll be off. It shouldn't be too long.'

She disappeared behind the screens again.

'Please sit down, Bessie,' Grace said. 'We haven't got much time.'

She waited until Bessie had settled herself down on the chair and then looked her straight in the eye.

'I've got to tell you I'm sorry for what I did. I was wrong.' She swallowed hard and continued. 'I should have listened to you and Harry, but I didn't. I thought I knew better, but when I got to London, it was a complete sham. The address he'd given me didn't exist. I never saw him again.'

Bessie grasped hold of Grace's hand and squeezed it gently.

'We all make mistakes, Grace. When we're young we want to make our own way.' She paused. 'But why didn't you come home again?'

Grace shrugged.

'I was too ashamed. Too stubborn. I was scared you might not want me back after what I did, and I suppose I didn't want to risk that. So I stayed, and started to make a life for myself here.'

'We would have welcomed you home, Grace.' Bessie's voice was thick with emotion.

Grace nodded and plucked at the sheet with her free hand.

'I missed you both so much.' Her eyes welled up with tears. 'I wanted to come home many, many times. But I thought cutting myself off completely would make it easier. I had to get on with life in London, and forget about my home with you and Harry.'

'We missed you, Grace.' Bessie's throat was hurting and her voice came out hoarse. 'There hasn't been a day gone by when I haven't thought of you, wondered where you were and what you were doing. I only hoped that wherever you were, you were happy.' She took a deep breath. 'We were so pleased when you wrote to us again, trusting us to have Marigold.'

Grace nodded.

'If she couldn't be with me, then you and Harry were the two people I'd trust her with. You both cared for me. Took me in when I was small and looked after me. You've been the best sister to me, Bessie.' Grace halted as tears started to run down her cheeks. 'I let you down.'

'No. No, you didn't.' Bessie stroked Grace's

264

hand. 'We were happy to look after you, Grace. We both loved having you with us.'

'You promised our mother, didn't you? Promised her you'd look after me. You kept that promise.'

Bessie nodded.

'I did. But believe me when I say, it was a promise I was glad to make and keep.'

Bessie's heart was hammering inside her, and her hands shook. Now was the time to do what she had wanted to do for years. She closed her eyes and breathed out slowly. Opening her eyes again, she looked at Grace.

'I was brought up to believe when you give your word, make a promise, you keep it. For good. Mother was very strict about that. No matter whether big or small, your word was your word. But she once made me make a promise that I didn't want to.' She swallowed hard. 'Every ounce of me screamed and raged against it, but I had to do it.' She shook her head. 'I've stuck to it since you were born, Grace. I've kept to my word.'

'I don't understand. Mother didn't die till I was three, and that's when she asked you to look after me.'

'The promise I'm talking about came before. On the day you were born. She made me promise I would never tell you who I really was.' Bessie took a deep breath and stared up at the ceiling for a few moments. 'I had to give her my word I would never tell you that I'm your mother, Grace. Not your sister.'

Grace's blue eyes stared back at her.

'My mother?'

265

'I'm your mother. Not your sister.'

'But how?'

'I was engaged to William, your father. We'd planned to marry on his next leave from the Front. Only, he was killed before he could come home and marry me. I found out I was expecting you after he was killed. He never knew.'

She frowned.

'Mother arranged I should leave my work as a VAD for a while and come home, supposedly to look after her because she was ill. I was kept out of the way once it was clear I was expecting a child, and Mother pretended she was having one. The plan was to pass my baby off as hers, and I'd go back to working as a VAD again. My baby would be brought up as my brother or sister.'

'Is that what you wanted?'

'No.' Bessie shook her head. 'But what choice did I have? She threatened to disown me. I would have been an unmarried mother, with no support and all the shame such a position brought, and would probably have ended up in the workhouse with my baby. With you.'

Grace frowned.

'What about our father – I mean, your father?'

'He went along with it. My mother was the strong-minded one, and Father went along with what she said for a quiet life. He probably thought it was the best choice. At least my baby would be cared for in a family.' Tears started to roll down Bessie's cheeks. 'I really didn't have a choice, Grace. If I wanted my baby to have any chance in life, I had to go along with it. So I gave Mother my word, and I've stuck to it all these

266

years. But when I saw you lying here in bed last night, I knew I couldn't do it anymore. You are my daughter, and I had to tell you the truth.'

'I'm glad you did.' Grace's voice caught as she swallowed down a sob. 'You've always been like a mother to me anyway, Bessie. Looked after me like a mother. It makes sense that you really are my mother.' She beamed. 'That makes Robert my real brother, too! I like that. We were more like brother and sister than aunt and nephew.'

Bessie sniffed and nodded.

'I think Robert will like it, too.'

'What about Harry? I bet he wasn't happy about your mother making you do that?'

Bessie's stomach clenched.

'Harry doesn't know about it. As far as he's concerned, you are my sister.'

Grace's eyes widened with shock.

'Even your husband doesn't know?'

Bessie clenched her free hand into a fist, making her knuckles white.

'I'm going to tell him, Grace. I've had enough of secrets. I don't know how he'll take it – he's always said I'm the most honest, straightforward person he knows. But all along I've been hiding the truth.'

Grace grabbed hold of both of Bessie's hands in hers. 'You don't have to tell him, Bessie. This can stay between me and you. No-one else has to know.'

Bessie sighed.

'Thank you for that.' She squeezed Grace's hands. 'But I can't not tell him, not now I've broken my word to my mother. I owe it to Harry to be truthful to him. When he married me he didn't just become responsible for me, but for you, too. And he was happy to do that, Grace. Harry has always loved you like a daughter. It's only fair I tell him. But I don't know what he'll say, or if he'll ever trust me again.'

'Harry loves you, Bessie. He's a good man.'

'I know. I wanted to tell him so many times, Grace, but I couldn't.' Bessie fished in her handbag, brought out a white handkerchief and dabbed at her face. 'I hope he'll forgive me for what I've done.'

## Debriefing

'Do you think Marigold's mother will be all right?' Peter asked, pulling on his end of the bow saw and sending another shower of sawdust spurting on to the dark ground, peppering it like snow.

'I hope so.' Harry glanced at Peter, who didn't look his normal self. 'Are you feeling ill? You look a bit pale.'

Peter shook his head.

'No. I'm fine.' He didn't look at Harry, keeping his eyes focused on the saw.

Harry didn't believe him. Something was wrong with the boy, but he clearly didn't want to say. He'd talk when he was ready.

Peter was a good lad, Harry thought, and a pleasure to spend time with when they worked together on the farm. Peter's natural way, with animals had given him an advantage, turning a city boy from Vienna into one completely at home in the countryside.

'What if Marigold's mother doesn't make it?' Peter suddenly said. 'What if she dies? What will happen to Marigold then?'

Marigold had asked Harry the same question last night, and his answer to her had been simple.

'She'd stay here with Bessie and me. This would be her home, Peter,' Harry said.

It would be what her mother wanted, what she asked for. Still, it had been a request Harry hoped they'd never have to carry out.

Peter nodded.

'She's lucky. I really hope her mother will be fine. But if she doesn't make it, then at least Marigold will have you and Bessie.'

'Don't put ideas into Marigold's head about her mother, will you? We don't know how badly she's hurt. I don't want Marigold worrying.'

'Of course I won't,' Peter said. 'I don't want to upset her.'

They carried on sawing in silence, with just the rough sound of the saw blade biting its way through the wood. Harry stole a few glances at Peter and could tell from his face there was something else bothering him.

'Harry?'

Harry looked up and saw Prune heading their way.

'Peter, stop sawing. Is everything all right, Prune?'

'Yes, fine. Dottie and I are going to take Marigold out for a walk. Keep her busy.'

269

Harry nodded.

'Good idea. Perhaps we'll have heard something from Bessie by the time you get back.'

'Do you want to come with us, Peter?' Prune asked.

'No, thanks. I'll stay here and help Harry. We want to get this wood finished.'

He gestured towards the pile of branches still waiting to be sawn up, where Hana was prodding her beak inside bits of loose bark looking for insects.

'We'll see you both later, then.'

Prune headed off towards the gate where Dottie and Marigold were waiting for her.

'I can manage on my own, Peter, if you want to go with them,' Harry offered, taking hold of his end of the saw again.

Peter shook his head.

'No. I want to stay.'

He pulled on his end of saw and they fell into an easy rhythm, back and forth, as the metal blade bit into the wood. Down and down it went until just a thin sliver connected the two pieces of wood, and then the heavy weight of the unsupported piece broke the last remaining wood and it tumbled on to the pile of logs they'd already cut.

Harry moved the branch along the saw horse and made the first few cuts to form a groove, and then they were ready to start again.

But Peter didn't take hold of his side of the saw. He was staring down at his feet.

'Peter?'

He jerked his head up and looked at Harry. For a split second, Harry would have sworn the boy's

270

eyes were glittering with tears. Then Peter blinked and they were gone.

'Are you ready? Or do you want to take a breather for five minutes?'

'No. I'm ready.' He took hold of the saw and once more they fell into the rhythm, back and forth, working in silence, adding to the pile of logs, piece by piece.

They were on the very last branch when Peter suddenly spoke.

'Harry, do you think my parents are still alive?'

Harry stopped sawing. Of course! That was what he'd been thinking about – his parents.

What should he say, Harry wondered. The truth. That's all he could do.

'I hope they are, Peter. I really do.'

'But do you think they are?' Peter's face wore a pinched, haunted look which Harry had never seen on him before.

Harry sighed.

'I really don't know, Peter. These are difficult times. All I can say is, I hope they are. I know that's not what you want to hear, but I know you'd want me to say the truth.'

What had happened to Peter's parents, or where they were now, Harry had no idea. When Peter had first come to Orchard Farm they had written to him regularly.

But then the letters stopped coming. Why, Harry didn't know. He had ideas, but all of them were ones he'd rather not have.

The fact remained that, knowing the danger Jewish people were in from the Nazis, it was likely Peter's parents had stopped writing

271

because they couldn't anymore. Not because they didn't want to.

'If…' Peter began, and then halted. He took a deep breath and tried again. 'If they've died, what will happen to me when the war's over? Where will I go?'

'Nowhere, not if you don't want to.' Harry leaned across the saw horse and laid a hand on Peter's shoulder. 'Whatever happens, Peter, you will always have a home here with Bessie and me. I hope you will be reunited with your parents again. But if that can't happen, then you know you can stay here.'

Peter looked at Harry and nodded quickly.

'Thank you.'

Harry patted Peter's shoulder and swallowed hard against his thickened throat.

'This business with Marigold's mother has made you think of what might happen, then?'

Peter nodded.

'War is a nasty business, and the terrible thing is it doesn't just affect adults. Children get caught up in it, too. But you're not to worry about not having a home, Peter.' Harry took hold of the saw. 'Come on, let's get this last one finished and we can go in and have a hot cup of tea.'

'Marigold's quiet today,' Prune said, watching her skipping along in front of them.

'Not surprising.' Dottie sighed. 'Her father killed, and now her mother injured by this blasted war.'

'It could be just a broken ankle, or…'

'Or worse. We don't know anything for sure until

we hear from Bessie.' Prune touched Dottie's arm. 'Come on, let's catch her up, cheer her along a bit. Race you!'

She started to run, her long legs eating up the road. Dottie took off behind her friend, her shorter legs and a later start keeping her behind Prune.

'Watch out, Marigold!' Prune shouted, waving her arms. 'We're coming.'

Marigold turned round and smiled.

'Are you two having a race?'

Prune reached Marigold first and stood, hands on hips, laughing as Dottie came in close behind.

'Unfair start – you went off before me!' Dottie's breath steamed in the cold air.

'You could have another race,' Marigold suggested.

Dottie shook her head.

'Let's do something together, help to keep us warm.'

She linked her arm through Marigold's and nodded for Prune to do the same on the other side.

'Have you seen the "Wizard Of Oz" film at the pictures, Marigold?'

Marigold nodded.

'Back in London. My daddy took me.'

'Well, do you remember when Dorothy, the Lion, the Scarecrow and the Tin Man went along the yellow brick road? They linked their arms like us, and they danced along.' Dottie demonstrated the movement 'Do you think we could do that?'

'Easy,' Marigold said.

Prune caught Dottie's eye over Marigold's head

and nodded her approval. Taking Marigold's mind off her worries was the best thing to do. Good old Dottie, coming up with something like this.

'So we skip to the right, and then to the left,' Dottie said, urging Marigold and Prune to match her movements. 'That's good. Now a bit quicker.'

The three of them started to progress along the road, almost spanning the width of it as they moved from side to side.

Marigold giggled.

'Can we sing, too, Dottie?'

'I don't see why not. Prune, are you up for a sing-song?'

'Count me in.'

'Ready, then!'

And off they went. Any words they didn't know they just hummed and then started all over again.

They had warmed up and had almost reached the turning leading down to Rackbridge base when a man on a bike rounded the bend and headed straight towards them. Dottie quickly pulled on Marigold's arm, dragging her and Prune out of the way as the man careered past them and came a screeching halt yards down the road.

It was Clem. He jumped off his bike and pushed it back to meet them.

'Was that me riding on the wrong side of the road again, or were you guys all over the place?' Clem shook his head. 'I know I've got it wrong in the past, but I was pretty sure I was riding on your British side!'

'We were going down the middle,' Dottie told him.

Prune started to laugh and Dottie and Marigold

274

joined in.

'I'm sorry if we scared you, Clem!' Dottie managed to say a few moments later.

'That's OK. I was on my way to see you. I've got some good news for you.' He smiled broadly. 'Howard's back!'

Prune's heart seemed to jump an extra beat. She stared at him as the news sank in.

Howard was back!

'Really?'

'Yes, ma'am. And he's desperate to see you.'

There wasn't anything she wanted more in the world than to see Howard again.

'I'll come straight away.'

'Sorry. It's not quite as simple as that. He's confined to base for a few days for debriefing, so he can't come out and you can't come in,' Clem explained. 'But there's no reason why you can't meet through the fence. Not if we're careful!'

Prune nodded.

'Anything. When? Where?'

'Eleven hundred hours. At the perimeter fence, where it meets the corner of the wood off Brights Lane. No-one should see us there. Do you know where that is?'

'I do!' Marigold said. 'Peter and I have been round there. I'll show you.'

Clem glanced at his watch.

'I've got to get back. Remember, eleven hundred hours.'

'I'll be there,' Prune said. 'Tell him I can't wait.'

'I will.' Clem climbed back on to his bike and pedalled off fast in the direction of the base's main gate.

'When's eleven hundred hours?' Marigold asked.

'Eleven o'clock.' Dottie said. She glanced at her watch. 'That's in half an hour!'

'We'd better get a move on, then. I don't want to be late,' Prune said. 'Marigold, are you sure you know the way?'

Marigold nodded.

'I know where he means. Don't worry, Prune, I'll get you there.' She held out her hand to Prune. 'Come on!'

Prune took Marigold's hand.

'Lead the way, then.'

'You take my other hand, Dottie,' Marigold said.

'I think it would be better if Prune went with you on her own. She hasn't seen Howard for a while and they've got a lot of catching up to do. I'm sure she doesn't want lots of people there, as well.'

'But I'll be there,' Marigold pointed out.

'I'm not going without you, Dottie,' Prune said. 'Howard's a friend to you, too.'

'Well...' She hesitated. 'All right, then, I can just say hello, and then Marigold and I can go off for a bit to leave you two to talk.'

'That sounds perfect.' Prune smiled at her friend. 'Thank you. Now, no more talking! I've got a date to keep!'

Prune stood waiting under a large oak tree at the edge of the wood, while Dottie kept Marigold occupied scuffing through fallen leaves further in. Prune's stomach was turning somersaults as the

276

seconds slowly ticked by. Glancing at her watch again, she saw it was almost five past eleven. They were late. Perhaps they weren't coming.

Her doubts disappeared with the sound of an approaching jeep coming towards them along the perimeter track. It was them! The sight of Howard sent her heart racing.

'Prune, they're coming!' Marigold shouted as she ran past her towards the fence.

'Marigold!' Dottie ran after her, stopping briefly by Prune. 'I'll let her have a quick hello, then take her off for a bit.'

'Thanks.' Prune stayed where she was, watching as Clem stopped the jeep not far from where Marigold was waiting.

As Howard climbed out, Prune could see his right arm was in a sling, but otherwise he looked well.

'Hello, Howard!' Marigold called. 'I'm glad you came back.'

'So am I, honey,' Howard replied.

'It's lovely to see you, Howard,' Dottie said, smiling. 'Welcome back.'

'Thanks, Dottie.'

'If you'll excuse us, Marigold and I have leaf-scuffing to finish.' Dottie put her arm around Marigold's shoulders and steered her back towards the wood.

'Sure.' Howard looked past them and his eyes locked with Prune's.

They stood staring at each other for a few seconds, before Prune launched herself across the few yards to the fence. The bones in her legs seemed to have turned into jelly, but somehow she managed to propel herself along and rushed headlong into the wire, bouncing into Howard who stood on the other side of the fence, as close to her as he could get.

'Hello, sweetheart.' Howard pushed the fingers of his left hand through the wire to reach out to her.

'Howard!' Prune entwined her fingers with his and savoured the sensation of his touch on her skin again, something she feared would never happen again. 'I…' she began, but Howard silenced her with a kiss. Their lips met in a gap in the wire.

'I've been thinking about doing that all the way home,' Howard said, drawing back and studying her face. 'I've missed you so much, Prune.'

Prune smiled.

'You can do it again, if you like.'

Howard raised his eyebrows.

'I do like.' He kissed her again.

A cough made them pull apart. Clem was standing just behind them holding a bulky parcel.

'Prune, Howard, I hate to break you up, but we've only got a couple of minutes here. We don't want to risk being caught.'

Howard smiled at Prune.

'We've got a lot of time to make up for. But not right this minute, I know.'

'I'll throw this over. You won't be able to do it with one arm. Here you go. Catch, Prune!' Clem sent the parcel flying up and over the fence and Prune just managed to catch it in both arms. 'Great catch! I'll be in the jeep, Howard. One minute, OK?'

Howard nodded. Clem smiled at them both

and returned to the jeep.

'What's this?' Prune asked.

'A present for you. It's my 'chute for you to make your wedding dress from. It saved my life, so I reckon it's kinda perfect to dress the woman I love in when she marries me.'

Prune's eyes filled with tears.

'Thank you.'

'Now I'm back, we'll get the wedding in motion. I want you to be my wife.'

'Come on, Howard,' Clem called. 'Time's up.'

'When will I see you again?' Prune asked.

'As soon as they'll let me out.' Howard leaned towards the fence again and kissed her again. 'I love you, Prune. I can't wait for you to be my wife.'

## Necessary Journey

'Mr Rushbrook!' Thomas the telegram boy strode across the yard from where he'd left his bike by the gate.

Harry quickly put down the pail of milk before he dropped it.

'Another telegram for you.' Thomas pulled one of the familiar envelopes out of his bag and held it out.

Harry's heart started beating faster. Just the sight of one of those telegrams had that affect on people these days. After the ones they'd had in the past few days, he didn't know what sort of

279

news it held. Good or bad.

He smiled at the young lad who had the hard job of delivering them.

'Thank you, Thomas.'

The lad nodded his head and quickly turned on his heel heading straight back for his bike. He didn't wait around to see what was inside.

Harry looked down at the envelope. It was just addressed to him. Was it from Bessie? There was only one way to find out. He quickly tore it open, and unfolded the single sheet of paper.

*GRACE BROKEN LEGS STOP MOVED OUT OF LONDON STOP HOME TONIGHT STOP*

'Thank God,' Harry breathed.

Broken legs would mend. And better still, Grace had been moved out of London. It was good news to tell Marigold.

Best of all, Bessie was coming home tonight. He'd be there to meet her. He didn't know which train she'd be on, so he'd meet each one until she arrived.

Harry smiled in relief. He couldn't wait to see Bessie again. She'd only been gone since yesterday, but it had felt like for ever. He wanted his wife home beside him, where she belonged.

*Is your journey really necessary?*

The words on the poster caught Bessie's eye as she made her way across the crowded Liverpool Street Station forecourt. Yes, it was, she thought to herself as she headed towards Platform 10 and the Norwich train. She'd always minded the messages on the posters, and did her bit for the war effort, but this trip to London had been necessary. Very necessary. Probably the most important one she'd ever made! And now she had to get back home again.

There was no sign of the train. The tracks stood empty, dirty and dusty. It was likely to be delayed, like they all were these days. All Bessie could do was wait, like the other people lining the platform. Many were in uniform, armed with kitbags and on their way to who knew where.

Picking her way along the platform, Bessie received and returned many smiles from the waiting passengers. There was a feeling of camaraderie, that they were all in this together. That was one good thing about the war, Bessie thought, the way it had brought out a sense of togetherness in the country. Hitler hadn't broken that!

Bessie found a space against a wall and put her small suitcase down, standing it upright so she could use it as a seat until the train arrived. Perched on top of her case Bessie sat and watched people coming and going for a while. She felt restless, too worried about what was to come and she needed some distraction. She rummaged inside her handbag and took out her diary. Opening it where she'd marked her place with ribbon, Bessie looked down at the date of her final entry in the diary. January 2, 1919.

*Our Wedding day! Harry and I are getting married this afternoon at two o'clock. I shall become Bessie Rushbrook instead of Bessie Carter. How strange that sounds! But I like it. I'm so happy and I'm not nervous, not a bit. I know it's the right thing for me to do. It's what I want. To be married to Harry for the rest of my life.*

That hadn't changed, Bessie thought. And it never would, as far as she was concerned. But that might all change on Harry's part. How he would take what she had to tell him, she didn't dare consider. What was certain was she had to tell him the truth, and accept the consequences.

She closed the diary and ran a finger over its soft cloth cover before putting it away in her bag. After she got home she would put it back in the drawer where it had lain for years. She'd finished looking into the past, it was the future that counted now. Perhaps, one day, she would look at it again.

As the miles passed, Bessie sat in the corner of the compartment with her eyes closed, shutting out the other passengers. She didn't want to talk. The journey had taken hours and she was tired. She'd been lucky to catch the last train from Norwich. Every clickety-clack of the wheels was taking her closer to home where everything was familiar, where there was green outside the door instead of the dull greyness she'd seen in London.

Home was where Bessie longed to be, but the tight knot wrapped around her stomach reminded her yet again that the truth might blow it apart. What she had to tell Harry had the potential to crumble her life to dust.

She was scared. How would Harry react? Telling him the truth would make everything he'd known about her false. Worse was the fact she'd lied to him. But her secret had haunted her for years, and it wasn't going to any more. She'd had enough, and wanted to be free to acknowledge her daughter. Nearly losing her in the rocket blast had made everything crystal clear to Bessie. Promises were for keeping if you meant them, and they came from your own free will. But not those promises pressed upon you by others. She owed it to herself, and to Grace, her daughter, to be true.

The train started to slow. Rackbridge was the next stop. Bessie opened her eyes and gathered her things together. She stood up and pulled her case down from the overhead rack, then sat back down.

'Your stop next?' an elderly lady in the opposite corner asked.

Bessie nodded.

'It's been a long journey. I'll be glad to get home.'

'No place like it,' the woman said. 'That and your family are what's important in life. Especially these days.'

'I've just been to see my daughter.' The words spilled out before Bessie had time to think about them.

Then she smiled. Calling Grace her daughter felt right.

The train slowed and came to a halt alongside the platform.

'Good night, then,' the woman said.

Bessie smiled at her.

'Goodnight to you,' She turned the handle on the door and climbed down the steps on Rackbridge station.

The cool, clean air hit her like a shower of water on a hot summer's day. Bessie felt like her senses had woken up. She breathed in deeply, taking in the familiar scent of the countryside.

'Bess!'

She spun around and saw Harry limping towards her, the smile on his face clear in the moon light. Her heart flipped over at the sight of him. She rushed towards him, throwing her arms around him, and nearly knocking him off balance.

'Harry!' Bessie spoke into his chest as he tightly hugged her to him.

He pulled back and looked at her.

'I missed you, Bess.' He kissed her tenderly.

Bessie's eyes filled with tears.

'I missed you, too. I'm so glad to be back.'

'Let's get you home.'

'I didn't expect you to meet me,' Bessie said as Harry helped her up into the trap. 'How did you know which train I'd be on?'

'I didn't.' Harry climbed into the trap and took up the reins. 'I've already been to meet the earlier one. You weren't on it, so I came back.'

'Oh, Harry.' She leaned across and squeezed his hand. 'I'm glad you were here.'

He smiled at her.

'I wanted to see you again as soon as I could. And I thought you'd be tired.'

'I am.'

'So how's Grace?'

'She'll be all right now. Both her legs are broken and they've sent her out of London to convalesce. She's going to write and let us know where she is.'

'Broken legs aren't so bad. It could have been a lot worse. How did it happen?'

'She was caught in a V2 blast.' Bessie's voice caught in her throat. 'She was buried under a fallen building. They had to dig her out.'

Harry blew out his breath hard.

'Buried alive!' He shuddered. 'It used to scare men at the Front. Buried underneath things. How is she?'

'She was unconscious when they dug her out. But she was scared by it – she looked like an old woman when she talked about it.' Bessie sighed. 'She's seen a lot of buried survivors in the hospital. I think that helped her.'

They fell into silence for a few moments with just the sound of Jenny's hooves clip-clopping on the road.

'I don't think we should tell Marigold about Grace being buried,' Harry said. 'It would be best coming from Grace, when she sees her again. If she wants to tell her. Broken legs are enough for Marigold to know about.'

Bessie nodded.

'I agree. How is she?'

'She's fine now she knows her mother's going to be all right. She wanted to go and see her in hospital, but I told her we'd have to wait and see when you came home.'

'We'll see. I'll do what I can, but it depends on where Grace is. She said she'll come here as soon as she can.'

'It'll be good to see her again. It's been far too long.' He paused. 'How was it with Grace, Bess? Was she ... did she say anything?'

'She told me what happened to her in London. She said she was sorry for what she did.' Bessie squeezed Harry's hand. 'We straightened it out and got everything in the open. I'll tell you about it properly tomorrow. I'm too tired now.'

'That's good.' Harry leaned over and kissed her

cheek. 'The family's back together again.'

An icy hand gripped Bessie's heart. Would Harry still think so when she told him about the lie she'd lived all these years? She had to tell him, but not now, not when she was so tired. She'd have just one last night as the wife Harry thought he knew.

She'd tell him tomorrow.

### Be True

Bessie sat on the bed and stared down at the words written for her so long ago.

*Whatever you are, be that.*
*Whatever you say, be true.*
*Straightforwardly act,*
*Be honest in fact,*
*Be nobody else but you.*
*All that is best for thee,*
*That best I wish for thee.*

Would Sergeant Harmer have written this if he'd known what secret Bessie carried?

*Whatever you are, be that.*

But she hadn't, at least not in name. From the time Grace had come to live with her and Harry, she'd treated her like a daughter and loved her like a daughter. But never had she openly acknowledged her as her daughter.

Bessie closed her diary. Reading it again had taken her back to her life in the last war, when she'd worked hard looking after the men. It had been tough, but there had been many moments of joy and laughter. Best of all had been Harry's arrival at Marston Hall. Dear, sweet, loving Harry.

She pulled open a drawer, laid the diary inside and then quickly shut it away. The past was the past, it was the future she had to focus on now.

The farm was quiet. Prune and Dottie had taken Peter and Marigold out on a bike ride with a picnic and the promise of a campfire. Harry was still indoors after their meal, enjoying a quiet read of the paper by the fire. It was the perfect time to tell him, when no-one else was around to disturb them.

Bessie stood up. It was time to tell Harry.

'All unpacked?' Harry asked, looking over the top of the paper as Bessie settled down in the chair opposite him.

'Yes. There wasn't much.' Bessie tried to smile but her face didn't want to.

'Are you all right, Bess?'

Bessie's mouth felt dry and her heart was pounding. This was it.

'Harry, I need to talk to you about Grace.' She hesitated. She had to do it quick, before she lost her nerve. 'You see, I've not been honest with you about who she really is. Grace isn't really my sister. She's my daughter.'

It was out. She'd said it. Bessie looked at Harry's face. He'd put down the paper and was looking at her with an unfathomable look on his face. Was he angry? She willed him to say something but he didn't. He just nodded at her encouraging her to go on.

'I'm sorry.' Her voice caught in her throat and

she had to stop for a moment to gather herself together. 'I'm sorry I lied to you, Harry. I didn't want to. But I had to if I was going to keep my promise.'

She paused again waiting for Harry to say something, but he didn't. His face was calm and betrayed no hint of what he was thinking or feeling.

'Aren't you going to say something?'

'Finish your story first, Bess. Then I will.'

She closed her eyes. She hadn't expected him to be so calm. Whenever she'd imagined herself telling him, she'd seen him upset, angry; at least showing some emotion. This calmness was unnerving. Swallowing hard, she opened her eyes again and fixed them on Harry's face.

'I'd better start at the beginning. I was engaged to William, as you know...' Bessie told him what she'd told Grace the day before, and all the time Harry listened quietly. 'I wanted to tell you about Grace, to be honest with you. But I couldn't! Please understand I had no choice in the matter.'

She stopped and took several steadying breaths.

'When Grace came to live with us after we were married, it was as if I had been given a chance to be her mother. To care for her like a mother. Only I could never let her know. But I could live with that. I had to.' Bessie looked down at her hands tightly clenched in her lap. 'I hated deceiving you.' She looked up at him again and her eyes filled with tears. 'I'm so sorry, Harry. I haven't been the person you thought I was.'

She hung her head and closed her eyes waiting. The room was quiet except for the ticking clock. Then she felt Harry take hold of her hands in his

288

and she raised her head to look at him.

'I've always known what sort of person you are. Good, kind and caring, and the one who I wanted to be my wife. Will always want.' He squeezed her hands in his. 'You haven't told me anything I didn't already know.'

Bessie stared at him.

'What?'

'I've known for a long time that Grace is your daughter.'

Bessie's stomach lurched.

'How?'

Harry's clear blue eyes held hers.

'Your father told me. After your mother died, and we decided Grace would come and live with us. He thought I should know the truth. He wanted me to know he was unhappy that your mother forced you make that promise when Grace was born. But he had feared she would disown you, and you'd both end up in the workhouse, if he didn't go along with it.'

All this was hard to take in. Harry had known all these years?

'Why didn't you tell me you knew?'

'It wasn't my secret to tell, Bess. I thought you'd tell me one day.' He smiled. 'And you have.'

'But ... what must you think of me for lying to you?'

'I don't think of it as a lie. More keeping to your promise. I admire you for sticking to your word, even though it must have hurt you.'

'But aren't you angry I deceived you over such an important thing?'

Harry shook his head.

'No. Not at all. I saw things in France which made me know how lucky I was to come through it. Your fiancé didn't. There, but for the Grace of God, go I. I was lucky to meet you, and even luckier that you wanted to take up with me. So I wasn't one to judge you for something forced upon you. A choice which only love for your child made you make, and hold to.' He touched her cheek gently. 'I don't judge you on it, Bess. I never have.'

Bessie nodded, unable to speak.

'You were a good mother to Grace, and it saddened me she didn't know who you really were, mind.'

'She does now.' Bessie's voice sounded hoarse. 'I told her yesterday. I hadn't planned to, not when I left here, but when I saw her lying in that hospital bed, I knew I had to tell her, promise or not. I broke it.'

'It should have ended when your mother died. You could have taken Grace as your own daughter then. She was young enough to have accepted it.'

'Easier said than done. You didn't know my mother. She'd probably have come back and haunted me.' Bessie smiled weakly.

'From what you've said, and your father, I've a good idea what sort of woman she was.' He looked at Bessie and smiled. 'You're free now.'

Bessie sighed.

'But it's not finished yet. There's Marigold.'

'Your granddaughter! And you a grandmother! When are you going to tell her?'

'I'm not. Grace wants to be the one to tell her. It will have to wait until she sees her. We have to wait. What Marigold will say when she finds out,

I don't know.'

'My guess is she'll be pleased. She loves you, Bessie. She was lost when you weren't here and has been following you around like a lost sheep since you got home. She'd be right beside you now, if Dottie hadn't taken her out.'

'I hope she doesn't think badly of me for lying to Grace all these years.'

Harry pulled Bessie up to standing and drew her into his arms and hugged her tightly.

'You've nothing to worry about, Bess. Nothing at all.'

### Wedding Dresses

'Do you think she'll change her mind?' Howard stopped walking and wrapped his good arm around Prune and hugged her tightly.

Prune shook her head.

'No. I wrote and told her that you're back and we're still going to get married. But she won't give in. I'm sorry.'

'Hey, it's not your fault. We'll just have to wait until you're twenty-one. That's in only a few weeks now.'

'I know. It's just...'

Prune shrugged. Even after all they'd been through with Howard being missing, her mother's attitude hadn't softened. Not one inch. Her refusal to give permission for the wedding saddened Prune. Since they wouldn't need it soon, wouldn't

291

it have been so much easier, kinder and loving to have given her blessing to something which was going to happen anyway?

'Maybe she'll come round when she realises we're going to get married whether she likes it or not.'

'I doubt it.'

Howard took hold of Prune's hand and they started walking towards Orchard Farm again.

'I'll get the paperwork sorted out. As soon as you're twenty-one you can sign it yourself and we're on our way to being married. By my reckoning we'll be able to marry around the twelfth of May. How would that suit you?'

'Wonderful.' Prune smiled at him. 'Bessie's going to make my dress, and one for Marigold and Dottie, too. There's enough parachute silk to do all of them and still have plenty to spare.'

'You can relax about me going on any more raids for a while, too. The doc says this arm is going to take a while to heal and get back to working again properly. Because it's my right hand, it needs to be fully functional again before I can fly. I'm on ground-based duties till then.'

'Good. I hated you going up.'

'I know, honey, but it had to be done. At least the Peggy Sue didn't let us down. Even when she was done for, we all got out.'

When they reached the farm gate, Prune stopped.

'I should warn you that Peter wants to hear what happened. He's desperate to know about the Peggy Sue.'

'It's OK. He flew in her, too, so it's only natural.

Don't worry, Prune. I'm happy to talk about it. No-one died.'

'Thank goodness.'

'Hey, I told you I'd always come back. And I did.'

Prune kissed him gently.

'I'm so happy you did.'

'The flak knocked out two engines. We had no hydraulics or electrical systems. No controls. The Peggy Sue wasn't going to make it back, so Walt ordered us to bail out.'

Prune watched as Howard told his tale. Everyone at Orchard Farm was gathered in the house to hear him – Harry, Bessie, Dottie, Peter and Marigold. All delighted he was back and wanting to know what had happened to him. As he spoke about failed engines, no controls and the order to bail out, an icy finger trailed down Prune's spine. It could have turned out so differently, with the whole crew going down with the plane. They were lucky they had all had time to get out. She and Howard had been given another chance at a life together, and she wasn't going to miss out on that for anyone. Not even her mother.

'What happened to the Peggy Sue?' Peter was asking.

'She went down in the sea, just off the coast of Belgium.' Howard paused. 'You know, I kinda like the thought of her being buried at sea, not all smashed and burned up on the ground. She was a good plane, and deserved a good resting place.'

'You make her sound like she was a person,' Marigold said.

'She was as important as a person to the crew! She carried us safely there and back on all our missions, except the last one. We were fond of her.'

Peter leaned forward in his chair.

'What happened when you baled out?'

'The 'chute opened, thankfully. I could see some of the other guys coming down. It was windy and we were blown about a bit. I had a bumpy landing and ended up with this.' He held up his arm. 'Luckily, we were behind Allied lines, so it was safe.'

'Why did you save your parachute?' Dottie asked.

'I thought would make a good wedding dress for Prune. It would have been a waste to leave it there, with material in short supply.'

Bessie laughed.

'There's enough for several wedding dresses!'

'I'm only planning on getting married once.' Howard smiled at Prune.

'What happened next?' Peter asked.

'I gathered up my parachute as best I could with one arm and started walking for the nearest farmhouse. They gave me tea and food, then took me to a United States Army post. From there I was sent to an Army hospital for an operation on my arm. That's why it took longer to get back than the others. I'm sure glad to be here again.'

'It's good to have you back. We were worried about you,' Harry said. 'Will you have to fly again?'

'No, sir. Not for a while, till I'm properly healed.'

'Thank goodness for that,' Bessie said.

'Will Walt and the crew fly again?' Peter asked.

'Yep. They're being given another plane. Walt

told me he's gonna name her the Peggy Sue Two.'

'I like that,' Peter said.

April, 1945.

'Ow!' Marigold yelped. 'You pricked me.'

Bessie sighed.

'I'm sorry, but you keep jiggling about. It's hard to pin the material when you're moving so much.'

'I'm excited, Bessie. I can't help it!' Marigold had never felt so excited in all her life. It was like all her Christmases and birthdays rolled into one. 'Is it time to go yet?'

Prune laughed.

'Marigold, that's the fourth time you've asked in the past half hour. Anyone would think something exciting's happening today from the way you're carrying on.'

'But it is!' Marigold looked hard at Prune and then started to giggle. 'You're teasing me.'

'Take no notice of her,' Dottie stood on tiptoe and planted a kiss on Marigold's cheek. 'It's only natural you're excited about seeing your mum again.'

'We need to get this pinning finished first, Marigold,' Bessie said firmly. 'I won't be going to the station until it's done.'

From her elevated viewpoint standing on the chair, Marigold looked at Bessie kneeling on the floor, with a no nonsense look on her face which she got when she meant business. Marigold knew Bessie meant every word. She didn't want to risk not being at the station when her mother's train arrived, so Marigold nodded meekly and stood as still as she could. She had to be patient and wait while Bessie pinned and tucked the material, turning her this way on the chair as she worked. But it was hard.

'That's better.' Bessie's voice was muffled as she spoke with her lips clenched around some pins. 'Good girl.'

'You're doing great,' Prune said. 'You'll soon be done. Then it'll be my turn.'

Marigold grinned at Prune who'd changed out of her usual clothes and, like her, was wearing a dress made from parachute silk, her wedding dress. It wasn't finished yet, but already it looked lovely. The material was smooth and hung in long drapes down to the floor, which swished about when Prune walked.

Marigold usually loved the dressmaking sessions with Bessie, Dottie and Prune. Ever since Howard had given Prune his parachute they'd spent hours working on the dresses at the weekends. Bessie was making all of them – Prune's wedding dress, her bridesmaid dress and Dottie's matron-of-honour dress. Working on the dresses had been fun as they'd joked and laughed, and told stories. It had made Marigold happy being part of it. It was only because her mother was coming, and she was desperate to see her again, that Marigold was so jumpy.

She'd watched Bessie and Prune work out the designs for the dresses. Then Bessie had cut out patterns from paper, pinned them on to the material and cut out the pieces. Next, she'd sewn the pieces together and gradually the dresses had come to life, growing from a drawing to real things they could wear.

Marigold loved the whole process. She'd never seen it happen before. Her mother bought all her clothes, she always said she couldn't sew. Marigold had asked Bessie to teach her to make clothes, and she'd said she would, but not yet, not till after the wedding, when she'd have more time.

'All done.'

Marigold stared at Bessie. She'd been so busy thinking she'd not taken notice of what had been going on.

'Really?'

Bessie nodded.

'All pinned and ready to hem. Dottie, can you help her take it off so she doesn't get pricked again?'

'Come on, then, Marigold,' Dottie said. 'Hold up your dress and step down gently.'

Wary of the sharp pins, Marigold held the bottom of the dress away from her bare legs and stepped down off the chair.

'Before you ask, we've got to leave here in half an hour,' Bessie said. 'Harry's getting Jenny and the trap ready. So after Dottie's helped you take your dress off, you can get dressed in your best clothes and do your hair, then we'll be ready to go.'

Marigold didn't need to be told twice.

'Thank you, Bessie!'

'You're welcome. Right, Prune, your turn, let's see if you can stand as still as Marigold did.'

Bessie winked at Marigold then turned her attention to the hem at the bottom of Prune's wedding dress.

Half an hour later, Peter walked back from the house to where Harry was waiting with Jenny, the pony, now harnessed up to the small trap and ready to go.

'Are they ready?' Harry called.

'Not quite.'

Harry took his watch out of his waistcoat pocket and checked the time.

'If they don't get going soon, they'll be late.'

'Bessie was finishing Prune's dress.' It was the first time Peter had seen it and it looked lovely.

'I reckon it'll be the best wedding dress for miles from the amount of time they've spent working on it.' Harry smiled. 'I bet Prune looks a treat in it.'

'Will she go and live in America with Howard after they're married?' Peter asked as he stroked Hana, who'd flown up on to the side of the trap near him.

'I think so. Though not till the war's over,' Harry said. 'Be strange for her, living in a foreign country. America sounds a fine place from what Howard and Clem have said. I expect she'll do fine there.'

'I've done well since I came to live in a new country.'

'You have, lad,' Harry agreed. 'The way you've settled in and become one of us, I often forget you weren't born here.'

'At least I can speak English now, not like when I arrived.'

Harry laughed.

'You soon learned. You knew more English than we did German! I only had a few words I'd learned in France, and they weren't much good.'

'Now I know English better than German. I've

forgotten a lot of German words.'

'Can you remember much about your home in Austria?'

Peter shook his head.

'Austria seems a long time ago. Another life. My memories of it have become all misty. I can't remember it all, just bits.' He closed his eyes to help him focus his memories. 'I can remember our home and the smell of Mamma's cooking. My friend, Wilhelm.' A picture of his friend's face grew in his mind. 'His parents tried to get him a place on the train I was on, but they couldn't.'

Wilhelm had been his best friend and he had no idea what had happened to him. Had he managed to get on a later train and come to live somewhere else in England? Peter's eyes opened and met Harry's.

'I remember some nasty things, too. Things we weren't allowed to do anymore. Like going to school.' He sighed. 'I never thought I would come to England on my own.'

'You were a brave lad,' Harry said gently.

Peter shrugged.

'I don't know that I was brave, because it felt like an adventure at first, with us children going off on our own on the train. I didn't really know what was happening until we got to England. Then it sunk in that I was on my own, until Bessie came to get me and brought me here.'

'Do you want to return to Austria when the war's over?'

'I don't know. It depends on where my parents are. I couldn't go back without them. I wouldn't want to. My home's here for now.'

'For as long as you want and need it to be.' Harry laid a hand on Peter's shoulder. 'I don't think the war will last much longer. They've almost reached Berlin. Then it's got to end.'

'What will happen after that?'

'Life will start to go back to normal. There'll be no more fighting and our soldiers will come back.'

'What about the Americans?'

'They'll go home, too. It'll be a lot quieter around here without them. We'll miss them.'

Peter nodded. It was hard to imagine life without the war. It had been happening for so long and they'd lived with it day after day. It would seem strange when it finally ended, even though it was what everyone wanted to happen. But after the war where would he be? Who with? He couldn't know where his future lay until he found out where his parents were, and what had happened to them. When the news came, would it be good? What if it wasn't? Peter shuddered. He wasn't going to think about it. Not until he had to.

'Here they come.' Harry nodded towards the house where Bessie and Marigold were hurrying down the steps.

### Family Matters

It still looked the same, Grace thought as she watched the Norfolk countryside pass by outside the train window. There were signs of wartime, the criss-crossed paper on windows, the sandbags piled up at stations, servicemen and women on the trains and platforms. But deep down it looked the same familiar country she'd known so well. That was comforting after all her years away.

Grace eased out her legs and stretched them as far as she could. Sitting still on the train was making them ache.

'Are you all right?' the WAAF servicewoman sitting opposite her across the compartment asked. 'Do you want me to move so you can stretch your legs out properly?'

'No, I'm fine, thank you. My legs aren't long, they're at full stretch now. I broke them both and they still ache a bit if I sit still for too long.'

'Both legs is hard,' the WAAF said, sympathetically. 'If it's one, at least you've the other one to take the strain. How'd it happen?'

'V2 rocket, in London. But I'm lucky, I survived. Two broken legs can mend and I'll soon be able to walk again without these.' Grace nodded to the two walking sticks she'd stood in the corner by the window. 'It's good to be out of hospital and on my way home.'

The WAAF smiled.

'It's the best place to be. No place like it.'

Grace smiled back and they fell into silence again, both of them looking out the window.

Home, Grace thought. She'd said she was going home. The word had slipped out without her thinking. Home for the last 13 years had been London, and now she was heading in the opposite direction. She hadn't been in London for months, not since they sent her to the convalescent hospital straight from St Thomas's. The thought of calling Orchard Farm home again after all this time gave her a warm feeling. It had been the only home she could remember. Where she lived before her mother died – no, her grandmother – was just a vague memory of the smell of hot metal and heat from the blacksmith's forge. It was Orchard Farm which was her proper home.

Things had changed so much in the past months for Grace. The foundations of her life had shifted after Bessie's revelation at the hospital. It was taking a while for her to think of the woman she'd thought of as her mother as her grandmother, and Bessie as her mother instead. Grace was gradually getting used to it. Bessie had been like a mother to her anyway, in everything but name.

Grace had had plenty of time to think while she'd been in the convalescent hospital. To decide what she was going to do, what she wanted for the future for her and Marigold. She'd made her decision, and was happy with it. She hoped Marigold would feel the same way when she told her, because it would completely change their lives.

The train started to slow, and from the sight of familiar landmarks, the square tower of St Andrew's church, the tall elms just outside the village, Grace knew where she was. They were coming into Rackbridge. A wave of excitement surged through her. She was going to see her daughter again.

As the train pulled in alongside the platform, Grace saw them waiting. Marigold and Bessie. She waved frantically, hoping they'd see her as her carriage slid past them and came to a halt.

Grace grabbed her sticks and got to her feet.

'Let me help you with your things,' the WAAF said. 'Is that your case?' She pointed to Grace's brown leather case in the overhead luggage rack above the seat.

'Yes, it's mine.' Grace leaned down to open the door, but she was beaten to it as it was opened from the outside. She looked down and there was Marigold beaming up at her with Bessie standing behind.

'Mummy!' Marigold shrieked.

Grace's throat tightened.

'Hello, darling. Hello, Bessie.'

'Hello, Grace.' Bessie smiled at her. 'Just step back a moment, Marigold. I need to help your mummy out. Then you can give her a cuddle.'

With the help of Bessie and the WAAF, Grace carefully lowered herself down the steps and onto the platform. Then Marigold gently and lovingly put her arms around her and hugged her tightly.

Leaning just on one stick, Grace wrapped her free arm around her daughter. She closed her eyes and kissed Marigold's hair, leaving her head resting on it while she breathed in the scent of her daughter.

'Thank you for your help,' Grace heard Bessie say. She opened her eyes and looked at the WAAF who was passing her case down to Bessie. She smiled at Grace and Marigold.

'That's some welcome home,' she said. 'Lucky you.'

Grace nodded.

'Yes, I am lucky.' Very lucky to survive and be back with her daughter again. 'Thank you.'

'My pleasure. Goodbye, then.' The WAAF pulled the door closed and with a wave settled back in her seat.

Grace looked over at Marigold's head and smiled at Bessie who nodded back, her face warm with love.

'It's good to see you.' Bessie leaned over and kissed Grace's cheek.

'We came in the trap so you wouldn't have to walk back,' Marigold said, loosening her hold around Grace's middle and holding out her hand for her mother to take.

'I'm sorry, I can't hold your hand with these.' Grace nodded at her sticks. 'Can you take my elbow instead?'

Marigold looked at Grace's walking sticks.

'Why do you need them? I thought your legs were better?'

'They are, but I still walk a little stiffly and they help me balance.' Grace smiled at her daughter. 'The doctor told me I won't need them for much longer.'

Marigold nodded and gently linked her arm through Grace's elbow.

'I'll show you the way to go. The exit's over here. When we get home, I'll show where everything is, too. Don't worry, you'll soon get to know your way around.'

Grace caught Bessie's eye and they smiled at each other, each thinking the same thing. Marigold had no idea that Grace didn't need to be shown where anything was.

'This is Orchard Farm!' Marigold proudly announced a short while later as the pony automatically turned into the gate.

Grace nodded, unable to speak. She'd dreamed about Orchard Farm so many times over the years. Now she was finally back.

It looked the same. The barn and sheds, the gate leading to the orchard, and the house. The lovely little house. Grace couldn't take her eyes off it. It was just as she remembered it, except for the paper strips criss-crossing the windows. It was still painted the same deep green.

Marigold noticed her staring.

'That's the house where I live. Remember I told you in a letter it's made from two railway carriages?'

Before Grace could reply she heard a familiar voice calling out.

'Grace!' It was Harry. 'Hello.'

The sight of him walking across the yard towards the trap jolted her. His thick hair was streaked with silver. The last time she'd seen him it had been a very dark brown. But that had been thirteen years past. She should have come back a long time ago. Not left it so long.

But what was past was past and she couldn't turn the clock back. It was what she did now and in the future which was important.

Grace smiled.

'Hello, Harry.'

Walking close behind Harry was a boy with a jackdaw perched on his shoulder. He must be Peter, going from the description Marigold had given her in one of her letters, Grace thought. He smiled shyly at her, and took hold of Jenny's bridle to steady her as Bessie halted her.

'Mummy walks with sticks, Harry,' Marigold informed him as he opened the trap's little door ready to help them out.

Grace saw Harry's eyes dart to the two sticks propped up in the end of the trap next to her case.

'Just like I used to have, Marigold, when I got my new leg. Sticks are helpful to get you going again,' he said, winking at Grace.

'The doctor says she won't need them for much longer,' Marigold added.

'I'm sure she won't.' He held out his hand and helped her out of the trap.

Marigold jumped down on to the ground, then turned back to Grace.

'Don't you jump out, Mummy!'

Grace laughed.

'I'm not going to, don't worry.'

Marigold nodded, her face serious.

'I'll go and help Peter hold Jenny steady while you get out. Harry, can you help Mummy climb out?' Without waiting for a reply, she rushed round to the front of the pony and starting talking to Peter, telling him about her mother's walking sticks.

Grace slid herself along the bench seat and gladly took hold of Harry's offered hand. She smiled at him, her eyes meeting his.

'It's good to see you.'

Harry nodded.

'You, too. It's been far too long.'

'I know,' Grace said. 'I should have done this a long time ago.'

'You're here now.' Harry took hold of her elbow with his other hand and carefully guided her down to the ground.

Bessie passed the walking sticks down to Grace, and Harry held on to her elbow until she had them in place to keep her balanced. Then Grace took her first steps back at Orchard Farm.

A warm rush of contentment radiated through her. She looked around her, wanting to go everywhere, see everything. She wanted to milk a cow again, collect the eggs. Take part in life on the farm again. But she couldn't do it all yet. There would be time, plenty of time and there was no need to rush any of it. She was going to enjoy being here with Marigold.

'That's enough story for tonight.' Grace closed the book, and put it on the chest of drawers beside Marigold's bed.

'Just a bit more, Mummy, please!' Marigold said.

'No.' Grace took hold of her daughter's hand. 'I'll read you some more tomorrow. I want to talk to you.'

'What about?'

'Something important.'

Grace hesitated. She'd been thinking about how she'd tell Marigold the truth for months. Planning what to say. Worrying over what Marigold would think. Now the moment had arrived she wondered if it was the right time to tell her. But if not now, when? Tomorrow? When was a good time to tell someone you hadn't been completely honest with them? What they'd been living with wasn't the whole story, just an edited version of it.

'Mummy?' Marigold said. 'What do you want

to tell me?'

Marigold's voice interrupted Grace's thoughts. She smiled at Marigold, and swallowed hard.

'Do you like living here?'

'Yes. I love it.'

'What do you like about it?'

'Everything, everybody. The people and the animals. I like milking and collecting eggs. I like the countryside.' Marigold looked at Grace, her blue eyes narrowing. 'Why are you asking me? I thought you wanted to tell me something important?'

'I do.' Grace said. 'I just wanted to check something first.' Her mouth had suddenly gone dry and her heart was bumping hard in her chest. Grace met Marigold's eyes. 'I'm glad you like it here, Marigold, because I did when I was a child.'

'Did you come and visit here?'

'Not exactly.' She paused. 'I grew up here.'

Marigold's eyes widened.

'I don't understand.'

'I haven't told you the whole story about my life, Marigold. Only bits of it. I hid important things from you and I'm sorry. I thought I was doing the right thing at the time, but now I think I shouldn't have. It wasn't right for you. Or me.'

'What are you talking about, Mummy? I don't understand.'

'It's a long story.' Grace stopped and stretched out her legs.

'Are your legs hurting?' Marigold's face was full of concern and pity.

'They're aching a bit. I'll stand up and stretch them out.' Grace grabbed her walking sticks and eased herself off the bed. She stood up and walked around the room, up and down between the two beds for a couple of minutes. Once the ache had faded she sat back down on Marigold's bed.

'Come and lie down beside me.' Marigold threw back her covers and motioned for Grace to come in. 'You can stretch your legs out and tell me your long story. You'll be comfortable and warm at the same time.'

'Good idea.' Grace carefully lowered herself down beside Marigold who threw the covers over them both.

'Comfy?' Marigold asked.

'Yes, thank you.' Grace looked at Marigold, who had turned to lay on her side facing her, her head supported by one arm. 'Right. My long story. Well, I suppose the best place to start is at the beginning.'

If she'd told Marigold the story a few months ago, before Bessie had broken her news to her, then it would have been a different tale. The one she was about to tell her daughter was the true one. True for her, her daughter and her mother. What had gone before didn't count anymore and would only be confusing. She might tell Marigold one day. Or she might not. The truth from the past and what affect it had on the future was what was important here.

'Mummy!' Marigold said.

'I'm sorry, I was just gathering my thoughts, getting everything straight in my mind. So from the beginning, then. I was born in a village about fifteen miles north of here in 1915. My father was a soldier and my mother was a VAD nurse.'

'Like Bessie.' Marigold interrupted. 'She was a VAD nurse, too.'

'Yes.' Grace's voice wavered. 'Marigold, Bessie is my mother.'

Grace watched the colour drain from Marigold's face. She stared back at Grace, not saying anything. Grace could see her mind was working furiously trying to make sense of what she'd just been told. Then to Grace's relief, a smile started to curve at the corners of Marigold's mouth.

'If Bessie's your mother, then she's my grandmother. And Harry's my grandfather!'

'You're half right. There's a lot more of my story,' Grace said. 'Harry isn't actually my real father. Though he brought me up as good as any father could, and I loved him like a father. My real father died at the Front, in the Great War. He and Bessie were going to be married on his next leave, but it never happened. Bessie found out she was expecting me.' Grace paused for a moment and then went on. 'For a woman to have a baby when she's not married, well, lots of people don't approve of it. They still don't. After Bessie had me, her mother, my grandmother and your great-grandmother looked after me. When I was a few weeks old, Bessie went back to work as a VAD, and she met Harry a few, years later.'

'And they got married,' Marigold said.

'Yes. Bessie and Harry got married after the war was over, and I came to live with them here at Orchard Farm when I was three years old. My grandmother had died in the Spanish flu epidemic just a few months before. This is where I grew up.'

Marigold nodded and looked at Grace, her blue eyes questioning.

'Why didn't you tell me who Bessie and Harry really were when I came here? You always told me your father and mother were dead.'

Grace bit her bottom lip. Marigold had asked the obvious question. She'd planned to say she'd meant her grandmother if Marigold queried what Grace had told her over the years. But how could you confuse your grandmother with your mother who had brought you up all the years. Loved you, cared for you. No, if she followed through with what she'd planned, it would only be adding more lies on to the fire. If she was going to tell Marigold the truth, it had to be the whole truth, every bit of it.

It would be hard to tell her, because it would show her daughter what a fool Grace had been. But if they were going to be free of all secrets, then Marigold had to know everything. The whole story. Grace could only hope Marigold would understand.

Grace turned so she was lying on her side, looking directly at Marigold's face.

'Because I thought my mother was dead, Marigold. I honestly did. But I found out a few months ago that who I thought was my mother, was actually my grandmother. I didn't know Bessie was my mother, Marigold. I'd always been told she was my sister.'

'Your sister? But why?'

'Remember how people think badly of unmarried mothers and their children? Well, my grandmother offered to raise me as her daughter.

311

She wanted to protect me and Bessie, and thought it was the best way to do it. Otherwise Bessie and I could have ended up in the workhouse. My grandmother insisted Bessie promise never to tell me who she really was. And she didn't. Not even after my grandmother died, and I came to live here with her and Harry. She hated not telling me. She kept her promise, even though it upset her.'

Marigold frowned.

'That's sad. So how do you know that Bessie's your mother?'

'She told me when she came to see me in hospital. I'm glad she told me. It was the right thing to do. Bessie had been forced to make the promise when she didn't want to. She kept it for too long.'

Marigold nodded and lay silently absorbing everything she'd been told. Grace was glad Marigold seemed to be taking the news calmly. She seemed happy Bessie was her grandmother, and Harry as good as any grandfather.

'Mummy, why didn't you tell me about Bessie and Harry and growing up here?' Marigold asked.

Grace swallowed hard.

'Because I was foolish.' She bit her bottom lip. 'I did something I wasn't proud of, and I was too stubborn to go back and say sorry. Instead, I decided to try and forget about my life here with Bessie and Harry, and stay in London. I never lied to you, Marigold. I just didn't tell you everything.'

'What did you do?'

'When I was eighteen, I met a young man from London while I was doing some work for Bessie's cousin who has a guest house in Sheringham, down on the coast. He was staying there and I thought myself in love with him, and he with me. He wanted me to move to London. He spun a yarn tempting me with tales of bright lights and fancy living. Bessie and Harry advised me not to go, not straight away. You see, I hardly knew him and yet I was prepared to leave everything I knew and move to London to be near him. I foolishly believed I might even marry him one day. I wouldn't listen to anyone's advice, certainly not Bessie's, or Harry's. I ran away to London on my own.'

Marigold gasped.

'What happened? Was that Daddy?'

Grace shook her head.

'No. Your daddy was a far better man than the one I ran away for. When I got to London, I found he'd given me a false address. I never saw him again. I'd made a big mistake.'

'What did you do?'

'I found a job in service for a while. Then I trained as a nurse, met your daddy and we got married, and eventually you came along.'

Marigold looked thoughtful.

'But why didn't you come back here?'

'Because I was young and foolish.' Grace sighed. 'Too stubborn for my own good. And I was afraid they wouldn't want me back after I'd run away.'

'Bessie and Harry wouldn't have turned you away.'

'I know that now. I wanted to come back so many times. The longer I left it, the harder it became.'

'Why didn't you tell me?' Marigold asked.

'Because it was simpler just to tell you the bare facts. It made it easier for me to try to forget.' She took a deep breath. 'But the war came, and...' Grace's voice wavered '...and your daddy was killed. Then the rockets started falling. I had to get you out of London. This was the best place to send you, where you'd be safe and well cared for, with people I could trust.' Grace couldn't stop her tears from spilling over.

'Don't cry, Mummy.' Marigold put her arms around Grace and hugged her. 'I think you did the right thing sending me here. I love it. I love Bessie and Harry, too.'

Grace looked at Marigold.

'Aren't you angry with me for not telling you the truth?'

Marigold shook her head.

'No. I think you were silly not to come back straight away. But I'm glad you sent me here. It feels like my home when I am not at home.'

'How would you feel if it was your home for good? If we didn't go back to live in London after the war?'

Marigold stared at Grace.

'You mean, not go back and live in Mrs Fox's house?'

Grace nodded.

'Live in Norfolk. Somewhere near here. Rent somewhere and I could get some nursing work again as soon as I'm fit. Would you like that?'

Marigold's face was beaming.

'I'd still see Bessie and Harry! Mrs Fox could come and stay with us.'

'You'd like it, then?'

'Yes, please, Mummy! I want to stay here. I don't want to go back to London anymore.'

Grace laughed and hugged her daughter tightly. What a lovely child Marigold had grown into. Taking the chance to send her to live away from her had been worth every minute of missing her. Marigold was safe, and at last knew where and who she came from. Just like Grace did.

'Mummy told me about your secret promise.'

Bessie stopped stirring the porridge and pushed the saucepan off the heat, her stomach suddenly lead heavy. She turned to face Marigold, who had settled herself in the armchair near the stove and was looking up at Bessie, her blue eyes wide with expectation. Bessie was glad it was just the two of them in the room. Harry and Peter were milking and everyone else still in bed. This was something she needed to talk with Marigold about on their own.

'What did she tell you?' Bessie kept her voice as level as she could, trying hard not to betray how she felt inside.

'That you're my grandmother!' Marigold smiled, jumped off the chair and flung her arms around Bessie. 'What shall I call you?'

Bessie's throat tightened as she hugged Marigold tightly. Was it going to be that simple, Bessie wondered, Marigold accepting the truth so well? But then, she wasn't a stranger being thrust upon the child and told that she was her grandmother. Marigold had come to know Bessie properly by living with her, day after day.

Marigold loosened her hold and stepped back

and looked up at Bessie.

'Should I call you Granny, then?'

'If you want to, my dear.' Bessie's voice caught in her throat. 'What do you think of me being your granny? And Grace being my daughter?'

'I think it's wonderful, Bessie. I mean Granny.' She beamed at Bessie. 'If I had to choose someone to be my granny, then I'd pick you.' Marigold looked thoughtful. 'But I think it's sad you weren't allowed to tell Mummy who you really were.'

'There were good reasons for it.' Bessie tucked a loose strand of Marigold's blonde hair back behind her ear. 'But at least Grace knows who I am now, and so do you.'

'Mummy said you and her could have ended up in the workhouse.'

Bessie nodded.

'Perhaps. It happened to some unmarried mothers and their babies. I was lucky my parents helped me.'

'Will Mummy call you Mother now, instead of Bessie?' Marigold asked.

'I don't know. She's called me Bessie all her life, so it might be hard to change. I don't mind if she doesn't. It's enough she knows who I am.'

'Can I call Harry Grandad?'

Bessie smiled.

'I think he'd like that, Marigold.' He would, she knew it. 'I'd better get on with the porridge or it won't be ready for breakfast.' Bessie moved back towards the stove and pulled the saucepan back on to the heat and started stirring again.

'Wait. I've got something else to tell you. Something important.' Marigold took a deep breath.

'We're not going to go back to London after the war. We're going to live here in Norfolk!'

Bessie dropped the wooden spoon back in the porridge and stared at Marigold, who had started hopping from foot to foot with excitement, a smile on her face.

'Are you sure?'

'It's true.' Grace stood in the door of her bedroom, leaning on her sticks. 'I had a lot of time to think over what I want to do while I was in hospital. I decided I want to come back and live in Norfolk. Rent somewhere and get a job nursing again. Be a district nurse. I've always fancied that.'

Bessie opened her mouth to speak, but no words came out. She swallowed and tried again.

'That's wonderful news, Grace. Wonderful!' She rushed over and threw her arms around her daughter and hugged her close.

'You're pleased?' Grace asked, her eyes sparkling when Bessie released her.

'Very.' Bessie put her hand on Grace's arm. 'You can live here with Harry and me for as long as you want, Grace. This is your home, if you want it to be.'

The smell of something burning reached Bessie's nose.

'The porridge!' She rushed across the room and grabbed the saucepan off the stove. Stirring the spoon round revealed a thick black layer sticking to the bottom of the pan.

Just then the door opened and Harry walked in.

'What's that smell?'

'Burned porridge,' Bessie said. 'It doesn't matter.' She pushed the saucepan to the back of the stove. 'We've got something much important to tell you.'

'Can I tell Grandad?' Marigold asked.

Bessie watched Harry's face as what Marigold called him sank in. The look on his face spoke a thousand words.

## Safe In France

Bessie glanced at the clock on the mantelpiece. One minute to three. Harry, who was standing behind her chair, laid a hand on her shoulder and gentle squeezed it. Bessie put her hand on his and kept it there, glad of his quiet support.

Everyone was waiting. Grace was sitting in the opposite armchair with Marigold on her lap. Dottie, Peter and Prune, standing in a row with their arms linked together. The room was silent, just the clock ticking, counting down the seconds and the hum from the radio.

The sound of Big Ben rang out. Bessie stiffened. One, two, three, she counted as the rich, resonating tone of the bell filled the room.

'This is London, the Prime Minister Winston Churchill...' The announcer declared.

Then Churchill's deep tones spoke out through the radio. Bessie closed her eyes and focused on Churchill's words announcing the Germans' surrender. The war in Europe was over.

Bessie sighed. They'd known it was coming, but she couldn't fully believe it until she heard it

318

from Churchill. Her throat tightened and tears smarted behind her eyelids. It finally was over.

'Have we won?' Marigold asked.

'Shh!' Grace said.

Bessie opened her eyes and smiled at her grand-daughter as she listened to Churchill's reminder that there was still work to be done. The war against Japan wasn't yet won. But it would be, Bessie thought. It was only a matter of time and then the world would be at peace again.

'It's over,' Dottie said as Harry turned off the radio at the end of Churchill's speech. 'It's really over.'

Prune and Dottie hugged Peter between them. Bessie stood up and walked into Harry's open arms. As she rested her head on his chest her mind drifted back to the last time she'd heard the war was over. Armistice Day, 1918. She never dreamed then that she'd ever be in the same position again. Once was enough. Twice was too much. She never wanted to go through a war again as long as she lived.

'Listen!' Peter said. 'They're ringing the church bells.'

Everyone stopped and listened as the sound of bells came floating in from St Andrew's down in the village.

'It's a shame they're all confined to base,' Prune said. 'I'd loved to have celebrated with Howard tonight.'

She and Dottie were sitting on the farm gate watching the light show over Rackbridge base. Bessie and Harry and the children had been out there with them enjoying the spectacle, but had gone inside as it was getting late.

'It's probably for their own good,' Dottie said. 'Going by what they're doing on the base tonight. Can you imagine if they'd been let loose in the village in such high spirits? The bobby would have had forty fits.'

Prune laughed.

'I suppose you're right.'

'You can't blame them, though. Think how they must be feeling now, not having to face flying over Germany anymore, never knowing if they'll come back. It's over for them and they'll be going home soon.'

Another burst of flares exploded upwards in arcs over the base, lighting up the sky with red and green glows like a beautiful firework display.

Dottie sighed.

'It's so good to see the sky lit up again at night. No more hiding away in the darkness. Life's going to get back to normal again, though it's been so long, I'm not sure I can remember what normal is now And you...' she nudged Prune '...will soon be married. Only three more days to go. Are you getting nervous?'

'No, not at all. I've never been so sure about anything in my life.'

'Do you think your mother will turn up?'

'I'm not expecting her.'

Prune shrugged. Her mother had maintained a deathly silence, not replying to Prune's last letter in which she'd told her, where and when her wedding would be and asking her mother to come.

'It's up to her. I've invited her. She knows the

time and place. I'm going to marry Howard, and if she chooses to cut me out of her life, then it's her loss. I'm not the one closing the door.'

Dottie linked her arm through Prune's.

'Perhaps she'll have a change of heart and turn upon the day. Surprise you. You're her only child and you'll be off to live in America soon, and it'll be a whole lot harder to come and see you there.'

Prune laughed.

'I know, you know and so would any sensible person. But I'm afraid my mother's stubborn, opinionated and ridiculous views hold her back.'

'You never know,' Dottie said, squeezing Prune's arm. 'She might come round.'

'I'm not going to let it spoil my wedding day.'

Whoosh! More flares zoomed skywards and exploded over the base in an arc of light.

'Look at that! It's so pretty,' Dottie said. 'Looking on the bright side, at least Howard's parents are happy about the wedding.'

Prune nodded.

'They've been so kind, writing to me and welcoming me into their family already. His mother's so warm and friendly. Not like mine.'

Bessie stepped back and surveyed the dress.

'Lovely. Fits you like a glove.' She smiled at Prune. 'You look beautiful. Howard's going to…'

'Hardly recognise you.' Dottie grabbed hold of Prune's hand and squeezed it tightly. 'Only kidding. Bessie's right. You do look beautiful. Scrubbed up well for a timberjill.'

'You've turned out nicely yourself.' Prune looked at Dottie in her parachute silk matron of

321

honour dress. 'Shame you're not walking out with some nice GI, too. Perhaps one of Howard's friends might take your fancy today?'

Dottie shook her head.

'You know I'm going to be a career girl.' Dottie grinned. 'I'm perfectly happy the way I am.'

'Shame. We could have had a double wedding,' Prune teased, her eyes sparkling and her cheeks slightly flushed.

'One bride-to-be is enough to cope with,' Bessie said. 'How long have we got, Dottie? Can you check the time for me?'

Dottie put her head around the bedroom door and looked at the clock on the mantelpiece.

'It's one o'clock.'

Bessie nodded.

'Half an hour until we need to go. I'll go and check how Grace is getting on with Marigold.' She started to walk out of the door and then looked back. 'Try to keep her calm, Dottie.'

Popping her head through the door of Marigold and Grace's room, Bessie saw everything was under control in there. Marigold was already wearing her bridesmaid dress and Grace was doing her hair, taking out the rags and carefully shaping the curls around her fingers.

'You look lovely, my girl,' Bessie said. 'The perfect bridesmaid. Can I do anything to help?'

Grace shook her head.

'Go and sit down for five minutes. You've been busy all morning.'

Bessie nodded. A sit down sounded just what she needed. A chance to rest and gather her thoughts before the wedding started.

Settling down in the armchair by the stove she stretched out her legs and pushed herself back into the chair and closed her eyes. Just five minutes, and then she'd have to get on.

'Bessie.' Harry's voice made her start. She opened her eyes and looked at him standing in front of her, smart in his suit. He didn't wear it very often, which was a pity because he looked so handsome in it.

'Bess?' Harry's face was drawn into a frown. 'This has come for Peter.'

He held out a white envelope bearing a French stamp. Peter's name and address were typed on the front.

Bessie's heart plummeted. Peter hadn't received a letter from anyone for ages. Not since his parents' last one. Who was it from?

She reached out and took it, examining it carefully. There was no indication who it was from, just an official-looking typed address on the front.

'Should we give it to him?' Harry asked.

'Does he know about it?'

Harry shook his head.

'No. I took it from the post boy.'

'I don't know.' Bessie sighed. 'Today, of all days, with Prune's wedding...' She looked up at Harry. 'It could be bad news.'

'That's what I thought.'

'If it is, then it would spoil the day for him and for everyone.' Bessie swallowed. 'I think we should give it to him tomorrow. One more day won't make a difference.'

'I don't know, Bess. It's addressed to the lad. I think he should have it. It's been long enough for

323

him not to know anything. He'd want to know.'

'How do you know what he wants?' Bessie said.

This was the last thing they needed on Prune's wedding day. She didn't want to risk the young woman's special day being blighted, not after all she'd been through with Howard being missing.

Harry laid a hand on Bessie's shoulder.

'Because he told me. When Grace was injured he was adamant Marigold should know. It upset him deeply that she was being kept in the dark. He said if it was him, he'd want to know. Straight away.'

'I don't know,' Bessie said.

'How would you feel if it was you?'

'I'd want to know, of course. But I'm an adult. He's a child.'

'Not such a child as some. I think we should give it to him. If it's bad news, then we'll have to deal with it.' Harry squeezed her shoulder. 'It might not be.'

'You decide, Harry.' She glanced at the clock. Ten past one. 'We need to leave for the church in twenty minutes.'

He nodded and stooped to kiss her cheek, then went outside without another word.

Bessie sighed. Of all the days for a letter to come, this had to be the worst. What they would do if it was bad news, she didn't know. They'd have to try and keep it from everyone.

She was about to get up, when Peter burst in through the front door, the white envelope in his hand. He rushed past her without saying a word and straight into his room, Bessie's old sewing-room, which he'd swapped with Marigold while Grace was here.

324

Once alone, Peter stared at the front of the envelope. His name was there in black type. *Peter Rosenfeld.* Then Orchard Farm's address, with the word *Angleterre* added at the bottom and a French stamp in the corner. From France. Who did he know in France? No-one. What was this about? Why were they writing to him? He never had any post, not since his parents stopped writing to him. There was no-one else who wrote to him here.

There was only one way to find out. Open it.

His hands were shaking so much, he could hardly open the envelope. He grabbed a pencil and thrust it into the top of the envelope and slit it open. Inside was a single sheet of paper. With his heart pumping fast he pulled it out, unfolded it and stared down at the words, which misted and twisted out of focus as his eyes filled with tears.

Peter wiped his eyes with the back of his hand and started to read the once-familiar writing. His father's.

*Dear Peter,*

*We are so happy to be able to write to you again. Both of us are alive and well. We have spent the last three years in hiding, in France. Hidden by a good woman who risked her life for us. We have been so very lucky to survive. All those years in hiding we thought of you every day and hoped you were well and happy. Not being able to tell you of our plan to go into hiding was difficult, but essential. We couldn't tell you for fear the letter would fall into the wrong hands and our secret be exposed. Now the war is over and we are free again, and will come and find you as soon as we can.*

*We send you our fondest love.*

*Papa and Mama*

They were alive. Alive! Great gulping sobs surged up making his body shake as he cried. All the worry he'd been carrying dissolved, replaced by a huge sense of relief. He'd been so scared that his parents had been taken to a concentration camp. Had become victims of the Nazis' wicked regime. But they had survived, hidden by some kind person. His family would come back together again.

Breathing steadier and feeling calmer, he lay back and stared at the letter again. Rereading it, word by word, he searched for every meaning, every ounce of information.

'Peter?' Bessie's voice called from the other side of the curtain. 'Can I come in?'

'Yes.' His voice sounded hoarse.

Bessie pulled the curtain aside and Peter saw the colour drain from her face as she looked at him.

'It's all right, Bessie,' Peter said. 'They're alive.' He held the letter up. 'My parents are alive!'

His voice broke and he couldn't stop more tears from rolling down his cheeks. He didn't sob this time, just cried silent tears.

Bessie swooped down and wrapped her arms around him, sitting on the bed beside him and cradling him in her arms.

'Thank God,' she said as she rocked him gently.

Peter closed his eyes and let Bessie's warm arms comfort him. His tears soon stopped and a sense of peace and contentment filled him.

When he heard someone else come quietly into the room, he opened his eyes. It was Harry.

He stood looking down at Peter, his face drawn with concern.

Peter smiled a watery smile at him.

'They're alive, Harry! My parents are alive!'

Harry let out a sigh and put his hand on Peter's shoulder.

'That's the best news. I'm so pleased for you, lad. Where are they now?'

'In France.' He looked at the address at the top of the letter. 'Near a place called Orange. They've been in hiding. Now they're free and are going to come and find me as soon as they can.'

'We'll welcome them here,' Bessie said. 'I look forward to meeting them.'

'Where is everyone?' Dottie's voice called from the main room. 'It's nearly time to go!'

Her words dried up when she stuck her head around the curtain and saw Peter, Bessie and Harry.

'Peter's had some good news, Dottie,' Bessie said.

'I've had a letter from my parents,' Peter said. 'They're in France.'

'That's wonderful, Peter. I'm so happy for you.' Dottie leaned down and kissed Peter's cheek. Straightening up she said, 'I know it's traditional for the bride to be late, but we don't want to get Howard too worried, do we?'

'The wedding!' Bessie said. 'I almost forgot. Come on then, everyone, we've got a wedding to go to!'

## Mother's Day

'Are they ready?' Bessie whispered to Dottie who had stuck her head round the church door to look.

Dottie nodded, stepping back.

'Howard's looking a bit nervous.'

'That's normal.' Bessie turned around to watch Harry, Prune and Marigold walk towards them. 'Though our bride is quite calm and serene.'

'You've done a marvellous job with our dresses, Bessie. You're a real dab hand with a needle.'

'It was my pleasure to make them. I–' Bessie stopped, her eyes drawn to a soldier who'd just walked in through the church gate and was striding up the path towards them. 'It can't be!' She started to walk towards him and then ran into his open arms. 'Robert!'

'Hello, Mum.' Robert picked her off her feet and hugged her tightly.

'What are you doing here?' Bessie asked when he put her back on the ground.

'I came over with some POWs on a transport plane. I've got a seventy-two hour pass, so I thought I'd come home. Hello, Dad.'

Bessie watched her husband and son embrace.

'Come on, you're just in time for the wedding.' Bessie linked her arm through Robert's and led him into the church. 'How did you know we'd be here?' she whispered as they took their places in the pew beside Grace, who'd thrown her arms around Robert as he sat down beside her.

Robert leaned over and whispered in Bessie's ear.

'Tom Bussey, our vigilant stationmaster, told me where you'd be.'

Bessie smiled. Good old Tom. He never missed a thing.

The first few notes of the organ began and Bessie rose to her feet along with the rest of the congregation, a mix of British and Americans. All of them there to see two young people marry, and wish them well for their future life together.

Bessie thought Orchard Farm had never looked more beautiful. The orchard was full of pale pink apple blossom, its gentle perfume filling the air and attracting a humming orchestra of bees. Arching high up above them was a perfect blue sky dotted with chattering swallows.

'Penny for them?'

Bessie smiled at Harry as he slipped his arm around her waist. She let out a contented sigh.

'I was just thinking how lovely everything looks.' She gestured with her arm. 'And how wonderful it is to have everyone here together.'

Harry nodded.

'And Robert home.'

'And Robert home.' Bessie nodded. 'That's an extra bonus.' She paused, trying to put her feelings into words. 'It's as if we've come out the other end of the tunnel, Harry. We made it through and have a lot to be thankful for. We can all get on with our lives again without the war hanging over us. We're free again.'

She looked round at everyone enjoying themselves, family and friends, all there to celebrate Prune and Howard's wedding.

Robert took another Norfolk shortcake from the spread of food and drink set up on a table beneath the boughs of an apple tree, and bit into it.

'Hey, that's the second one of them you've had in a couple of minutes.' Dottie said watching him eat it. 'Don't they feed you in the Army?'

'Not on food like this.' Robert waved the last piece of shortcake before popping it into his mouth. 'Ma's cooking is the best.'

'I agree with you,' Dottie said.

'How did you know it was my second one?' Robert teased, his blue eyes meeting Dottie's. 'Are you keeping an eye on me?'

Dottie's cheeks grew warm.

'I, er...'

What could she say? She was actually lost for words. She had been watching him, but she wasn't going to admit it.

'Bessie asked me to look after the food, to make sure everyone had something to eat. I just happened to notice you seemed to be fond of those shortcakes. That's all.'

Robert smiled at her.

'Would you like some?' He took another shortcake from the pile on the plate, and broke it in half. 'Share one with me?'

Dottie raised her eyebrows and looked into his eyes. They were a beautiful clear blue, full of light, like the sky arcing above them.

'All right, then.' She smiled at him. 'Thank you.'

'So your parents are in France?' Clem asked.

'They were hiding there all this time. I never knew!' Peter crumbled the crust from his Spam sandwich and dropped it on to the ground for Hana, who was hopping around searching for insects in the grass.

'I'm real happy for you.' Clem patted Peter's shoulder. 'You must have been worried about them.'

'I was.' Peter had done his best to get on with life in England, working hard at school, but all the time at the back of his mind, there had been the nagging worry about his parents. What was happening to them? And, lately, were they even alive?

He was lucky, his parents had come through it, and one day soon they'd come here to find him and they could start to rebuild their lives together.

'I'm looking forward to seeing them again. And you'll be going home soon, too, Clem.'

Clem took a sip of his ginger beer.

'Yep, we'll be shipping out as soon as we can. Everyone's eager to get back to their families again. It's a long time since I was there and I'm ready to go home.'

'You've liked England, though, haven't you?' Peter asked.

'I sure have. Meeting all you folks, who made us so welcome, and visiting the old buildings. I love the churches and castles. We don't have them like that back home.'

'How are you're feeling, Mrs Peterson?'

Prune smiled at her husband.

'Happy. Very happy.'

'I'm glad to hear it,' Howard said. 'You're sure you're not upset your mom didn't show up?'

'No, not really. I honestly didn't think she'd come. Even if, I suppose, deep down, part of me hoped she would.'

Howard pulled her into his arms.

'It's a shame. I'm sorry she feels that way. We could go and see her, if you like. She might change her mind if she saw us together.'

Prune shook her head.

'We might get there and she would refuse see us. I don't want that. It's better to wait for her to change her mind. If she ever does.' She sighed. 'Your parents are different. They've been so welcoming to me.'

'They're looking forward to meeting you. I've told them all about you.'

'Only the good things, I hope!'

Howard smiled at Prune, his eyes holding hers.

'There are only good things to say about you, Prune. I'm a lucky guy. I got through the war, and now I'm taking a fabulous wife home with me to keep.'

'Ready?' Grace asked.

Marigold nodded and picked up the basket with a white cloth draped over the top.

'Let's go, then. Nice and steady so we don't drop anything.' Grace followed her daughter out of the house, carrying the wedding cake which Bessie had made for Prune and Howard. It was a beautiful cake – no traditional white icing, because of rationing, but instead it was decorated with delicate violets and primroses dipped in precious sugar, which sparkled in the sunshine.

'Are you all right, Mummy?' Marigold asked, walking beside her across the farm yard towards the orchard where the reception was in full swing.

Grace smiled at her daughter, who looked lovely in her parachute-silk bridesmaid's dress.

'Yes, I'm fine.' Marigold had been like a mother hen, fussing over her since she'd arrived at Orchard Farm. She still kept a careful check on Grace, even though she was finally off her walking sticks. It was so good to be back with Marigold, and here at Orchard Farm with Bessie and Harry. Grace felt like she'd truly come home and back to her family again.

'Do you think Prune's going to like her surprise? We've done really well keeping the secret!'

'We have! I don't think she suspects a thing.'

Bessie watched Prune lift the white cloth off the basket. Her face went pale as she read the label tied onto the neck.

'Are you OK, honey?' Howard asked.

Prune nodded.

'It's from my mother.'

'Your mom?'

'It's the bottle my father put away for when I got married. She's been saving it for years.'

'She sent it here last week and asked us to give it to you today,' Bessie said. 'With strict instructions not to give it to you until after the wedding.'

'It was a surprise for you, Prune,' Marigold said. 'Do you like it?'

Prune nodded.

'I'd forgotten about it. But my mother remembered.' Her voice wavered. 'It was kind of her to send it.'

'We should go see your mom,' Howard said.

Prune nodded and smiled at her husband, unshed tears glittering in her eyes.

'Soon, before you get shipped back to America.'

'I'm sure she'll be pleased to see you,' Bessie said. 'It will give her a chance to get to know Howard and see what a lovely young man he is.'

'Whoa, Bessie, you'll have me blushing if you carry on!' Howard said.

'Let's open this, then.' Prune took the bottle of champagne out of the basket.

'No,' Bessie protested. 'Keep it for you and Howard to share on your honeymoon.'

'I'd like to share it with you all,' Prune insisted, looking round at everyone. 'You've all been like a family to me and I'd like you to have some.'

'Can I have some, too?' Marigold asked.

'If it's all right with your mother,' Prune replied.

'Go on, then, just a drop to taste,' Grace said.

Howard popped the cork from the bottle, and the champagne was shared around between everyone, poured into an assortment of glasses and cups.

Prune raised her own glass.

'To my lovely new husband and my very dear friends.'

'And to Prune's mother,' Howard added.

'To all mothers.' Grace raised her cup to Bessie.

Bessie looked back at her daughter and smiled.

'To all mothers, everywhere.'

The publishers hope that this book has given you enjoyable reading. Large Print Books are especially designed to be as easy to see and hold as possible. If you wish a complete list of our books please ask at your local library or write directly to:

**Magna Large Print Books**
Magna House, Long Preston,
Skipton, North Yorkshire.
BD23 4ND

This Large Print Book for the partially sighted, who cannot read normal print, is published under the auspices of

**THE ULVERSCROFT FOUNDATION**